THE WHITE HORSE AND THE EAGLE

ROGER RIMKAUDLIS

Written on WriteItNow ©Ravenshead Services Ltd
Cover Design by graphics_inn at fiverr.com
Map by jessidanielle at fiverr.com
Formatting by marissalete at fiverr.com
Published by Independent Publishing Network
ISBN **978-1-80352-053-7**
The author can be contacted at rogerrimkaudlis@aol.com

Hibernia

Brittania

White Horse Hill

the Henge

Belerion

Keresk

Ictis

Gaul

Daritorium
Corbilo

Liger R.

Gwilen R.

Legend
road
settlement
river

Duunna R.

Olt R.

Burdigala

Segodunum

Cadurcorum

via Domitia

Tarn R.

Torlosa

via Aquitania

Narbo

Brigantia

Garunna R.

Portus
Veneris

Hispania

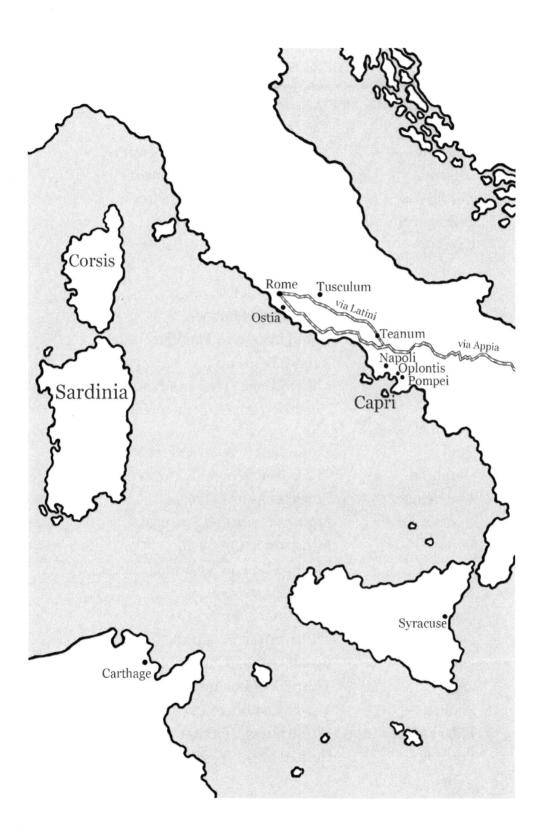

Corsis

Sardinia

Rome   Tusculum
            via Latini
Ostia
                    Teanum
                        via Appia
            Napoli
            Oplontis
            Pompei
        Capri

Syracuse

Carthage

INDEX OF PLACE NAMES

Portus Veneris	Port Vendre in France.
Rhodes	Island in eastern Mediterranean.
Rome	The capital of the Empire.
Salernum	Salerno in Italy.
Sardinia	Island south of Corsica.
Segodunum	Rodez in France.
Syracuse	Ortygia on south eastern coast of Sicily.
Tarn	The Tarn river in France.
Teanum	Teano in Italy.
Tolosa	Toulouse in France.
Tusculum	A Roman town near Frascati.
Tyre	City on coast of Lebanon.
White Horse Hill	The Uffington White Horse.
Via Appia	Route to Rome via the Pontine marshes.
Via Domitia	The road linking southern Gaul and Hispania.
Via Aquitania	The road between the Mediterranean and Atlantic coasts of Gaul.
Via Latina	A road to Rome from Campania.

'Knowing yourself is the beginning of all wisdom.'

Aristotle

CHAPTER ONE

I've had this dream for as long as I can remember. I am high up, with the wind in my face, held in the claws of an eagle. A long way from where I was born, yet returning to the place I am from. This dream keeps coming back, it won't stay away.

But I should start at the beginning. I am the boy with three names. I cannot choose, because I am all of them. Born in a villa north of Pompeii, on the Ides of March. A festival that both begins the year and is the anniversary of Caesar's murder. The fact I favoured my left hand was confirmation. I was ill omened. A symbol of betrayal.

Our estate has orchards, and goats graze on the southern slopes of Vesuvius. My father, Caecilius, is a merchant. I have his dark curls, but that is all. He has a roman wife Octavia, but no children. We live in the large villa he built as a refuge from work. Covered in red tiles, surrounded by vines and olives, near the foot of the mountain.

My mother, Orlagh, was a Celt, a slave taken from Gaul. She had red hair and her skin burns in the hot sun. But in some strange way, he must have loved her and me in turn. Even though she was a barbarian and beneath him.

I slept in a room with older male slaves, tolerant of my constant questions, which they ignored. I was the youngest, tucked in the corner beneath a table. It wasn't much, a rough mattress and a blanket. But I felt safe, squeezed in there. Just as well, because small spaces would be my salvation.

That place was my home. I was there until that fateful day, when everything changed. My twelfth birthday. But we will come to that.

My mother worked in the kitchen. She'd learned how to prepare food the Roman way, plucking geese and preserving pork. We made our own bread and goat's cheese. Fish and other goods came up from the port of Oplontis on a cart. Of course, the food she made was mostly for my father, Octavia, and her guests. We ate coarse bread and porridge, but there was always cheese, oil and vegetables from the garden.

I was curious about my mother's people. They were called the Atrebates, a barbarian tribe from the north. She was born somewhere a white horse was carved into a hill. It was always green, she said, and the summers were cool. She was the daughter of a chief and once wore a twisted torc around her neck. Now her only reminders were a swirling blue tattoo on her left shoulder and a little coin she kept in a thong about her neck.

I didn't look anything like the Roman coins I'd seen. It was marked on one side with a horse and on the other, an eagle. It was the only thing she managed to keep from before she was enslaved. My father had bought her at the market in Oplontis, a household servant for his wife Octavia. If he thought her red hair would bring luck, he was mistaken.

Now I wonder if that was her real purpose. She said Octavia shunned her. Perhaps she was too young and pretty. But when Octavia was away, he took her to their bedroom. He did not force himself, but she could not say no. A few months later, she could no longer conceal she was with child. It seems my father denied it at first, then he confessed. Octavia took a whip to my mother until he stopped her.

Then I was born, on that inauspicious anniversary, when Caesar was murdered with pointed knives. I'm told the blood ran freely as I screamed and bawled. My mother nearly bled to death, but somehow she survived. Octavia demanded we were both sold, but my father refused. So, he suffered the tyranny of an unhappy wife. Perhaps a cursed son was better than none at all.

I never liked my name, Quintus. It didn't fit me. It never felt right. My mother called me Caden, and I learned her language. We could speak of secret things that no one else could know. My father had a clever Greek called Simon. He had bought him as a slave, but freed him. He was old, but his mind was still sharp. Simon helped with accounting, reading, and translating contracts. My father liked discussing philosophy with him. He was to be a tutor for the son by Octavia, who never arrived.

When I was seven, I given the job of milking Simon's goats. He'd stroke and soothe them as I pulled the teats. I was an annoying little fool, pestering him with questions. He'd answer them, but I'd just ask more.

'You have a yearning to be Greek,' he told me.

I didn't know what that meant.

'The mind is the most powerful thing in the universe,' said Simon. 'Shall I show you how to use it to discover the truth?'

I nodded, with no clue about the path I'd embarked on. Apparently, wisdom begins with the knowledge of how little you know.

So, Simon got agreement from my father to tutor me. My father told Octavia he needed an educated slave to help his business. But told my mother that when I was old enough, he would recognise me as his son. The last emperor had passed a law, a slave had to be thirty before they could be freed. So, I am not sure which one he lied to. My father was a weak man, but he was kind.

It was just as well, because everything would change.

Simon was old. I'm not sure of his age, he never told me. He had a white beard, a conical cap, and a stick he used for walking. He had his own cottage high up on the estate, away from the main buildings, on the other side of the vines. It sat next to rough pasture that ran down the mountain. But the soil was fertile. He grew lettuce along with herbs, like fennel, rosemary, and basil. He tended his precious goats and had a hive for honey.

Simon told me long ago the mountain spat smoke and fire, but had been quiet for hundreds of years. The Romans believed the circling eagles contained the spirit of the mountain, sacred to Jupiter. On clear days, you could see across to an island called Capri. At a distance it looked like separate islands, but Simon said that was an illusion, because it had two hills. It was often covered in mist in winter, but in summer the white cliffs shone. I asked Simon if he had been there. He told me no one could visit, so to put it out of my mind. It was the Emperor's island, a forbidden place, his sanctuary from Rome.

When Simon first came, he had been a slave. But my father treated him as an equal and freed him. Not that his life changed, he lived as he had always done. Simon told me he liked his cottage because it was quiet. The goats and the mountain made him think he was in Greece. Even though he had once been a slave, he carried himself with dignity. It seemed Romans admired Greeks, but I was not sure if the feeling was mutual. I suspect Simon thought anyone who wasn't Greek, was a barbarian.

Simon had trained as a scholar in Alexandria in Egypt. A place he told me was founded by Alexander the Great. Alexandria had a lighthouse and a magnificent library, though much of it was destroyed just before he was born. The closest I had seen Simon to crying, was when he told me about that fire. When he was a younger, he was captured by pirates. But he wasn't wealthy enough for ransom. So, they sold him to a rich Roman on the island of Rhodes. He spent his life teaching their children about the greatness of Greece. Simon said it was a noble cause. Those who educate children are more honoured than those who produce them. He said it almost justified being a slave, as he would have chosen it, anyway. It was his Telos, or purpose in life. Once he mentioned our Emperor Tiberius had also lived on Rhodes, but would speak no more about him.

I asked him about the work he did for my father. Simon said he calculated how much his boats could carry and checked agreements in Greek and Latin. It was very important to get everything right. Too much cargo could sink a boat. Ships that might float at sea would perish in a river. One word in a contract made all the difference. A piece of papyrus could own you or set you free. If Simon remained living Alexandria, there's no telling what he would have done. Developed his own school or made new discoveries. I can't believe he would have spent his life reading dull contracts or tutoring the ignorant children of Romans.

I learned a lot from Simon. He believed it was foolish to resist the Empire. 'What is the use of all this fighting and death' he would say. 'If only we could resolve our arguments by reason. You must accept and make the best of your fate. Being a slave, you suffer many injustices. It is a hard burden to bear, but it will make you a better man.'

There wasn't much in his house, apart from what he needed to live. He had a bed, a table, and a large chest. This was his most treasured possession, because it was full of scrolls, a puzzle, and two stones. One was a crystal from Egypt for reading small letters, because he said his eyes were weak. You had to be careful. It was fragile and it could draw down the sun and start a fire. The other stone was golden, like honey. It contained tiny insects, and if you rubbed it on a piece of fur, it would attract a feather. Some thought it was because it had a soul, but Simon said no one could explain it. He also had a square puzzle made of wood. Fourteen pieces made of triangles and other strange shapes. Simon liked to watch me sit at the table and work out ways to put it back together. My introduction to something Greeks call geometry.

For the Romans, great men were one's like Caesar, who had conquered countries. But to Simon, it was those who discovered the truth. Truth, he said was the most important thing. But even conquers need tutors. Alexander had one called Aristotle. Caesar had another one, Sosigenes, design his calendar.

There were so many Greeks whose greatness came from learning. It was hard to remember them all. Posidonius, Pythagoras, Euclid, and the great Archimedes. Plato and Socrates we studied as well. Pythagoras believed the world was a sphere. Aristarchus said our world circled the sun. I learned astronomy, and that constellations moved around the pole star. How the earth turned to make day and night.

Not all these philosophers agreed with each other, and some seemed a bit crazy. Simon said patience was a virtue, and he had learned this from Zeno. But there was another Zeno who bit someone's ear off just before he died, so it couldn't have been him. There was Diogenes, who never had a bath, so he must have smelled terrible. Thales was so busy thinking, he fell down a well. Empedocles jumped into a volcano to prove he was a god. Socrates sounded like a troublemaker who liked asking questions. But not everyone wanted to hear them, so they made him drink poison.

Simon said truth could be acquired through reason. Reason was immortal and numbers ruled the universe. I learned Plato's four virtues; wisdom, courage, justice, and temperance. He said a good man must have self-discipline, be modest and endure pain without complaint. Plato believed that perfect things existed in the world beyond ours. But Simon said the only thing that made sense for was geometry. There was a perfect circle and a perfect line. Our eyes couldn't see them in the world outside, but they existed in our mind.

Of all knowledge, Simon said, geometry was the most important. So, after writing Greek and Latin, I learned geometry, lots of it. I studied Euclid's principles with my ruler and compass. A point has position, but no dimension. Circles form triangles and triangles form circles. A line is a length that could go endlessly into the universe. An angle in a semicircle is always a right angle. It was a world where you could prove things, beyond the possibility of doubt.

'No one can change them,' said Simon. 'Not Zeus, or Jupiter, or the Emperor of Rome. They are indisputable and forever true.'

I'd spend the whole afternoon with my stylus, carving my waxed tablet. Simon would correct my mistakes, then I would erase it all and start again. It was hard and sometimes I would want to give up.

'Patience is bitter,' said Simon, 'but its fruit is sweet. You cannot learn without pain.'

I still remember the day I learned how Eratosthenes calculated the size of the earth. At the summer solstice, the angle of a shadow in two Egyptian cities, Alexandria and Syene, differed by seven degrees, or one fiftieth of a circle. It meant the circumference of the earth must be fifty times the distance between those two places. So, the world was twenty-five thousand Roman miles around. I rushed back to tell my mother.

'I've discovered the world is so large, the Roman empire is just one small part.'

'I hope so,' she said. 'The whole world cannot be ruled by Rome.'

'But Empires can fall. Simon said Alexander's only lasted thirty years.'

My mother laughed. 'Rome's Empire is growing larger all the time. A small boy cannot wish it away.'

Simon knew Homer's stories and could remember many by heart. I loved hearing those tales, but he would only recite them after we finished our important work. Achilles was strong and handsome, but ruthless and cruel. I much preferred the wily Odysseus. He freed beautiful Briseis and tried to negotiate Helen's return. The wooden horse was his idea and helped them win the war. His journey home was long and arduous, but he found contentment in the end.

Simon warned me that poets were the harbingers of doom. Apparently, too much poetry and not enough geometry was the downfall of the Greeks and could be the end of the Romans too.

'These things,' he explained, 'are in balance. When poets have the greater esteem, it is a sign that civilisation will end.'

I was not sure how reciting poetry could lead to the downfall of Rome, but I was too young to argue. At the end of the day, we would have discussions. Simon would ask me questions about what I thought and why. The questions became harder until I had to admit I didn't know anything at all. I was ignorant, but happy.

It couldn't last forever.

There was a shady place at the back of the slave quarters. A place overhung by trees, where rain collected into a small pond. I used to sit there sometimes, when the weather was warm and Simon was busy helping my father. I'd take a few dried figs to eat and practice writing on my tablet. But there were lots of distractions. Like the dragonflies floating in the air, or little creatures swimming in the water. Beetles and other diving insects, Aristotle, said they were born from warm mud. I could sit and watch them for hours.

One day I spied a small frog, its eyes peering just above the surface. I put my hand under and lifted it out of the water. It wriggled on my fingers, then sat still. Its back was blotched with black spots. It had a pale underbelly and splayed toes. Simon had told me there was a Greek play about noisy frogs. But this one didn't make any noise at all. It sat happily in my hand as I watched it breathe, staring back at me with trusting eyes.

I was about to lower it back in when I sensed someone behind me. A sweet, exotic scent. I turned my head. Octavia, my father's wife, was standing there. She bent over.

'Ah Quintus, is that your little friend? I have someone who would like to meet it. Come with me.'

I closed my fingers gently around the frog. I could feel it squirm a little in my palm as I followed her into the villa. We reached the atrium, a room that was open to the sky. Beneath was a pale marble pool called an impluvium. It collected the rain and the overflow from a cistern that drained the roof. I had seen older slaves clean it from time to time.

'Put your little friend in there,' she said.

I put my hand in the water and released it, as I was told. The frog seemed to swim around quite happily, but I sensed something wasn't right.

'He needs a playmate', said Octavia. She turned around and took a basket that was sitting in the corner. Then opened the lid and emptied something into the water. It slid in, dark green with white behind its head. It was her house snake.

I took a deep breath as the frog began a frantic swim. The snake chased the doomed creature around the pool. I hoped it would leap out and escape. In the pond, there were places to hide. But not here. There was no purchase on those smooth white walls. Then the snake caught it by one leg. It stopped struggling and went still. That little frog stared at me, as if I was responsible for its betrayal. Then another gulp and it was gone.

Octavia reached in and put the dripping snake back in the basket. She had a strange smile. I did not know what it meant. Perhaps this was a lesson like Simon's, to help me understand the natural order. Some animals are predators, others prey. The world of people is no different. You had to know your place.

But I would see that smile again.

CHAPTER TWO

Simon loved his goats. They learned my call and would come down every morning for their treat. Some were easy, and happy to be relieved of their milk. But others were more difficult and tried to kick my buckets.

'You have to speak to them kindly and have soft hands,' said Simon. 'They are not so unlike us, you see.'

Simon taught me everything he knew about goats. Mischievous but inquisitive creatures, who could sense if you were happy or sad. They had a strange enquiring bleat. If they could speak, they would be forever asking questions. Fearless climbers on steep mountain ledges to graze. Simon told me to be careful and not to follow them.

'They will get to places you can't. If you tried,' he said, 'you'd fall. Far better to train them to come to your call.'

Though I was born into a Roman world, Simon told me his purpose was to bestow on me the mind of a Greek.

'Wisdom,' he said, 'comes from asking questions. The right question is often more important than the right answer. The Romans can build and fight, but they just copy just what the Greeks have learned before. The Greeks are the greatest thinkers the world has ever known.'

Part of me wanted to be Greek. I really did. I asked Simon if he could give me a Greek name, just for when he was tutoring me. He thought about it for a little while.

'Very well, I will call you Cadmus. It means the one who excels'.

I liked that name, much more than Quintus and perhaps even as much as Caden. So, I had the trappings of a Roman, the mind of a Greek, and the soul of a Celt. But can one person be three things at once? Caden, Cadmus, Quintus, the boy with three names. Caden and Cadmus were like playmates, happy in each other's company. Cadmus, the thinker who liked languages and solving puzzles. Caden, the dreamer, who loved listening to Homer and dreaming the impossible. Quintus, burdened with expectation, who sat in the corner despising himself. A strange Cerberus, the three-headed dog the Greeks say guards the underworld, with two heads desperate to be free of the third.

I asked Simon about my mother's people, the Celts. There was a book he'd read by Posidonius, who had met their priests, called druids. They were fierce and had once tried to capture a sacred place called the Oracle of Delphi. The druids never wrote anything down, it was all passed on by mouth. They burned people alive, in sacrifice to their gods. I didn't want to believe that. But if a Greek wrote it, I thought, it must be true.

My father had warehouses in nearby Oplontis, Neapolis, and at Ostia, the port in Rome. His business was oil, which he imported from Hispania and sent garum sauce and red wine called Lympa back the other way. My father didn't like Rome, 'a cesspit', I once heard him say. I promised myself I would never go there. But like most of my promises, I never kept them. All except one.

He had a sealing ring that he pressed in wax. It marked his letters and goods with the winged horse, Pegasus. There was something special about a flying horse. It could carry you over mountains and across the sea. That ring was a symbol of my freedom. The gift he could give me.

On the estate, my father barely acknowledged me. But sometimes he would take me down to the dock at Oplontis. I would ride there on a pony behind his horse. He would ask what Simon was teaching me and question me about what I'd learned. I told him Archimedes invented the machine that Romans used to measure the distance on the road. He seemed pleased that I was making progress.

I saw the ships that carried his trade from Hispania and Gaul and back again. My father would leave me with the crew while he followed his cargo to the warehouse. The sailors allowed me to crawl around the hold. They showed me the rigging and let me climb the mast. I learned how the ropes and sails worked. They had a pulley system to lift out the cargo on a crane. Simon told me it was another of Archimedes' inventions. Then my father would return and take me back. On those days, I had a glimpse that I was not a slave, but his son. Then when we returned to the estate and Octavia's glare, it all returned to normal again.

My father was busy and often away. He had told my mother he loved me. He had gone to the trouble to have Simon instruct me and resisted Octavia's pleas to sell us. So, he must be telling the truth. Yet I knew Simon far better than him. He helped me think and taught me almost everything I knew. But my dreams, they came from my mother.

In summer I would help harvest olives, grapes and figs. When we finished, we were hot and covered in sweat. There was a deep pond in a quarry, where I learned to swim. I loved to spend as long as I could, floating like a fish in that cool water. Always the first in and last out. I made little rafts of sticks. Then I asked Simon to help me build a toy ship, like the ones my father had. We would set it on the pond and watch the wind blow it to the other side. Like crossing the great Mediterranean, carrying goods like garum, oil and wine. One day, I thought I would sail on ships like that. I would be brave and wouldn't worry about the storms. The wine of the winged horse would be drunk from Gaul to Egypt and beyond.

There were some places Octavia had forbidden to me to go. Like the dining room with a huge mural on the wall. I would sneak in there to look at it when she was away. It showed Mercury, the god of trade, and Dionysis, the god of wine. Below that sat the Lares, sons of Mercury, holding drinking horns. At the bottom, painted serpents writhed in the grass. The floor was decorated with mosaics of animals I had never seen. Lions, striped horses, tall-necked and long-nosed creatures from far away.

We had a household shrine to Janus in the atrium, a room open to the sky. I never knew why my father chose him as our house god. Most merchants had Mercury. Janus was the god of beginnings and transitions. Cakes were placed on his altar, but we weren't allowed to touch them. His bronze statue had two heads facing opposite ways, holding a key and a staff. Two faces, one staring back at the past, the other forward into the future. Now I wonder whether one face was what you wanted the world to see, the other what you wanted to hide.

Janus governed doors and gates, the passage from one place to the next. The borders of empires, maybe even the threshold between the living and the dead. Janus decided when doors were open and shut. Chose who were free to pass and others not. Manumission was the transit from slave to freedom. I would go through that door when I was thirty. But before that I must make the passage from boy to man. Though

I was tall for my age, my face was still smooth skinned. Both those journeys still seemed a long way away.

My life until I was ten was mostly happy. I was fed and clothed and had a safe place to sleep. Somewhere in the back of my mind lay my father's promise. When I was older, I would be free. I was a third of the way there. But that depended on me being Quintus.

To be free, I had to be the one thing I didn't want to be.

CHAPTER THREE

Titus was Octavia's nephew, her sister's only son. He was more than ten years older than me. He fancied himself a man, but had trouble growing a beard. Titus visited the estate to beg money from his aunt. He liked to scare the slaves with the house snake Octavia kept. I could tell Caecilius didn't like him, but my father was always polite.

Simon told me Titus had never met his father. He had died in a forest in Germania. Part of an army, three legions that were lost there. A barbarian Armenius, with citizenship, turned traitor and led them to their deaths. To make matters worse, Titus' mother ran off with an auxiliary soldier from the Rhine.

So, Titus hated anyone who wasn't Roman. But a barbarian with a Roman name, that was the very worst. His personal hero was our Emperor Tiberius. Titus liked to tell me had avenged his father, because together with Germanicus, they defeated all the northern barbarians. I found out that wasn't true, because Simon said they hadn't caught Armenius.

His greatest wish was to serve in the Emperor's Praetorian guard. He tried to join the legions, but I heard he failed the training. I doubted he could ever be a soldier. During his visits, he did nothing for himself, or anyone else. He spent most of his day in bed, sleeping off wine from the night before. The rest of his time was spent in Rome, betting on the chariots. But whenever he visited the estate, he carried out his personal vendetta against barbarians, especially me.

Octavia did not discourage him. When my father was away, I endured his regular attention. Though I was tall for my age, he was far larger. I remember the first time I met him. He was shouting in the late afternoon and they sent me to see what he wanted. He sat up in bed. I think he was hungover.

'So, you're Quintus,' he slurred.

I nodded. He beckoned me closer.

'See this hand' he said, 'What's its job, Quintus?'

I shook my head and told him I didn't know. Then he punched me in the chest so hard it knocked me over.

I was still lying on the floor. He leaned over and held his fist in front of my face.

'It's for beating barbarians into the dust. Take a good look, so you don't forget. A Roman fist, the hardest and the best.'

He knew it was forbidden for a slave to strike back. I had to endure whatever treatment he meted out. During his stays, he insisted I bring him food from the kitchens in the evenings. He had a collection of weapons that he'd show me. A gladius, a sword that soldiers used. A pugio, a horrible short pointed knife, like the ones that killed Caesar. He would hold it against my face. 'Feel how sharp it is,' he said. 'It wouldn't take much to slice you up.'

He was contemptuous of Simon and Greece. Titus told me he would give me proper Roman lessons. He loved to regale me with stories of heroic Romans. The one eyed Horatius, who held a bridge alone, or another one who burned off his own hand. He said this proved Romans were the bravest of all people and they had a duty to conquer the world. His favourite trick was to ask me to bring him wine, then pour it on his feet and claim I'd spilt it. When I knelt down to clean it up, he would wade in the puddle of wine and command me to lick it off his toes. I hesitated the first time, but got a beating for my trouble.

'You are fortunate even to lick a Roman's feet,' he said. 'Why waste a good Roman name on a wretch like you? It's an insult.'

I bit my lip and was silent. I didn't want a Roman name, not least the one I had.

Octavia wanted my father to adopt Titus and name him as his heir. More than once, I overheard them arguing about it. Caecilius said he couldn't leave his estate to someone who would gamble away all he had worked for. I held out hope he hadn't lied to my mother. In the end, none of this mattered anyway.

But I wasn't to know that then.

I was ten. It was midwinter, and it snowed for the first time in my life. Everyone else grumbled about the cold and fretted it might damage the vines. Not much work could be done outside, so we stayed indoors. That day was the happiest I had ever seen my mother. I helped her in the kitchen, making brine for olives, peeling eggs and skinning a hare. She danced and sang and spun me around.

'Reminds me of home,' she said. 'It snows every winter there'. She had gone back in her mind, to the hill of the white horse. My mother told me more about her life than I had ever heard before. She had been born in Britannia, outside the empire. I heard stories of dark oak forests and great grassed downs. The spring festival of Beltane and fiery Samhain that heralds winter. She told me about the druids who were the wisest among them. It took twenty years to become one. They knew thousands of lines of verse and all the rituals to appease the gods. They wrote nothing down, it was all contained in their minds. If they arrived at your house, you must offer food and shelter. They made judgements, even kings had no power over them. They sounded a bit like Simon, only they liked poetry more. But she didn't say anything about them burning people alive. The knot on her shoulder was done to mirror her husband's. A swirling design of blue woad. She had met him at midwinter at the Henge, a place she said, where vast stones stood.

'He was the finest man I ever met,' she said. 'Tall and strong, no one could match him with a spear. Like that hero from Simon's stories.'

'Achilles?'

'That's the one.'

Perhaps this man had all four virtues that Plato taught, and I was yet to achieve. She had followed him to Gaul, but there was a rebellion. Her husband, Carmanos, was killed resisting the legions. The Romans took her as a slave, down to the city of Narbo, on the Mediterranean coast. She stood there in the slave market at nineteen. Her fine clothes and torc were gone. Now she wore a sign around her neck with a price of nine hundred sesterces. A discount, because whomever bought her was getting two for the price of one. She was acquired by a slaver and taken to sea with other captives. She thought she was seasick, but miscarried on the boat. Her baby girl was dead and thrown into the water. By the time they docked in Oplontis, my mother had recovered. So, my sister was in the netherworld now.

'She is watching you, Caden,' my mother said. 'Her soul did not perish but will pass to another.'

She told me birds were messengers from that place beyond. The Celts believe that two of the smallest rule the world, the robin and the wren. The robin was the beginning of the sun, the wren the death of winter. They battle on the shortest day and the robin triumphs. She told me how the brave wren bested the eagle by climbing on its back, flying higher than all others.

'You must be like the wren to survive this world,' she said. 'It is not always fair and often cruel.' Then she knelt down and whispered. 'Simon is a clever man. You will grow up to be wise, like him. Your father's business needs merchants who can write, count and speak languages. He has promised he will free you when you are older. If you are lucky, you might even inherit from him.' Then she touched my chest. 'Simon may be teaching you to be clever, to be Greek, but you will always have a Celtic soul. Always.'

The snow lasted a day, the next morning it was gone. Then everything returned to how it had been before.

I'm not sure Simon believed in Gods. Geometry was far more important to him. He said a mind was the first thing to exist, before all else. That was the most important thing in the universe, the source of all knowledge. I didn't really understand what he meant. The closest I got was one day I was leaning into the chest to retrieve a scroll. I found one that it wasn't written in Greek or Latin. The letters were different.

'What's this?' I asked him.

'That one's Aramaic, my mother's tongue. Not spoken really much outside Syria and Judea. It's a prayer. She used to sing it to me as a child. To encourage me to live a life of virtue.'

He spoke it in Aramaic and then translated it for me. *'Blessed is the one who does not walk in step with the wicked or stand in the way that sinners take or sit in the company of mockers, but whose delight is in the law of the Lord, and who ponders it, day and night. For he is like a* tree planted by streams of water, which yields its fruit in season and whose leaf does not wither, whatever they do prospers. Not so the wicked! They are like chaff that the wind blows away. The wicked will not stand in the judgment, nor sinners in the assembly of the righteous. For the Lord watches over them, but the way of the wicked leads to destruction.'

'What does it mean, the way of the wicked?'

'Cleanthes said, a wicked man is like a dog tied to a cart, helpless to follow evil wherever it goes. You will learn more when we study Aristotle's Nicomachean Ethics.'

'Who is the Lord, then?'

'Well, Pythagoras believed there was one who first existed. The true mind who invented reason, geometry and numbers and from that, came all things. For a circle to exist, there must be a point at the centre.'

Perhaps that meant you could prove the existence of a god, using geometry. I wasn't sure.

'I can teach you a bit of Aramaic if you like,' said Simon.

So, I learned a little, translating it to Greek and Latin. It was theoretical knowledge, not useful, as Aristotle might say. But that didn't turn out to be true.

Those words would save my life.

The first half of my day was work, like all the other slaves. Most mornings, I milked the goats and carried the buckets down to the dairy. Then I led the herd back to graze. I had a sling to keep foxes and crows away from the new-born kids. If I ever passed Octavia, I sensed she was furious. She wanted me to toil all day. But it seemed only fair that I worked half the day as a slave.

In the afternoon, Simon taught me. Aristotle said there were four types of learning. We had started with Episteme, the theoretical, like the geometry I drew in wax. Techne meant to build something. Phronesis was judgement gained through experience. Lastly, there was Sophia, or wisdom. Simon said most people didn't achieve the last one, no matter how much they learned. Wisdom and happiness, it seemed, were the hardest things to achieve.

Aristotle knew about the forms of animals and how to group them. The strangest of all was the octopus, it didn't seem to fit in at all.

Sometimes they came up on the fish cart from Oplontis. Their grilled tentacles were Octavia's favourite meal. I helped unload the cart and bring it into the kitchen. My mother did not like handling them. 'Strange slippery creatures,' she said. One was still alive in the bucket and wriggled off the bench. It hid itself behind an earthenware jar and took ages to catch. A cornered creature in a tiny space was dangerous, as I would learn. It bit my hand and tried to blind me with black ink. Just like Aristotle said, it was trying to escape.

Aristotle had lots to say about classifying animals. If something has feathers and wings, it is a bird. The only exception I could think of was Pegasus, the winged horse. But Simon said that didn't count. It was a myth. Simon taught me to recognise birds by their song and observe how they flew. The little ones, like wrens and robins, flapped fast and often. They were never too far off the ground. The robin was brave and would take crumbs from my hand. But I could never persuade the wren to be that bold. It kept its distance on a restless blur of wings. But I liked how it squeezed into tight spaces, creeping out from cracks between the stones. My mother told me it was the druid's sacred bird. I heard some story that a wren had tried to warn Caesar of his demise, but Simon said that was nonsense. We discussed where swallows go during winter. Aristotle said they must sleep in holes or trees. I once spent a whole day one winter, looking in every crevice on the estate. But I never found a swallow.

The largest birds, like eagles, would stay aloft for hours, their wings immobile. In breaks from lessons, we would sit on the grass and watch them. One day, I found an eagle dead on the grass. It had been caught in a snare, there was twisted twine around its feet. We examined the body, as Aristotle would have done. The shapes, the geometry of the wings and tail.

'Even the king of birds can be brought to earth,' said Simon. 'We all have a natural life and die, but our souls can live forever.'

On my eleventh birthday, I was out on the hill with Simon and his goats. That day was never a source of celebration on our estate, a reminder of the murder of Caesar. One goat had birthed early, and the kid was staggering about. A shadow descended, and I heard a shout from Simon. An eagle was lifting into the sky with the kid in its claws.

I threw a stone from my sling, enough to make the eagle swerve. The talons opened, and the kid fell onto the grass. It lay stunned for a moment, then rolled onto its feet and ran back beneath its mother.

Simon checked, and it seemed unhurt. The great bird rose up and circled above us for hours.

I should have known then it was an omen and kept my mouth shut. Instead, I asked a question.

The question that would change everything.

CHAPTER FOUR

W hy can't we fly, Simon?'
'I will let you answer. Use your mind as I have taught you.'
'Because we don't have wings?'
'That's a good reason.'
'But if we made wings, could we fly?'
'Like Daedalus?'
'I don't know who Daedalus is?'
'Have I not told you that story, from long ago in Crete?'
It seems Daedalus was another clever Greek, if not entirely virtuous. Like Archimedes, he was not just a thinker, but a builder. He went to Crete and made many things, including a labyrinth to house a horrible monster he'd helped create. Yet King Minos imprisoned him there, along with his son Icarus. So, he built wings for both of them to escape. But Icarus flew too high. His wings broke, he fell into the sea and died. Daedalus managed to reach land, but then he offered up his wings to Apollo and never flew again.

'So, is this just a story, or did it really happen?'
Simon smiled and shook his head. 'I am not sure we can ever know. But in some of these stories, there can be a grain of truth.'
'Could we build wings to fly?'
Simon rubbed his chin. 'An interesting question. Remember, you need logic, observation, enquiry and demonstration.'

He was setting me a challenge far more interesting than the lines on my tablet.

'If birds can fly,' I said, 'then flight is possible, agreed.'

'Yes', he said.

'The wings of those circling eagles do not move, yet they remain aloft?'

'Can you think of a reason?' said Simon.

'I can feel the wind coming up the hill. Perhaps that pushes their wings upward?'

Simon pointed down the slope. 'This warm wind is the Sirocco, it comes from the south. A wind blowing along the ground is forced upward by a fixed body. It cannot go through a mountain, so it must get over it. Aristotle says everything that is in motion must be moved by something. A sail catches the wind and pushes a boat. Why shouldn't wings work the same way?'

'If we built spars and a sail, then we could be carried upward?'

'Yes, in theory. But it could not be the same as the sail of a boat.'

'How would you know what type of sail to make?'

'What does Aristotle say? Nature makes nothing incomplete, nothing in vain. You must return to your original question. Why can a bird fly but a person cannot?'

'Because they have wings?'

'You would have to study the wings of birds Cadmus, and make the shape of your wings like theirs. Of course, it would be far too dangerous in real life. But as a thought experiment, it has merit.'

It was all very well to think about things, but what was the use if it just stayed in your head? Archimedes wouldn't have been satisfied with that and neither was I. So, I tried a different tack.

'We could make a small one,' I said. 'Like that little sailing ship, we floated on the pond last summer. Start with a toy and see if it would fly.'

Simon smiled. 'Yes, we will start your Techne and build a toy. We can use what you have learned, geometry, physics and natural history. We will combine Euclid, Aristotle and Archimedes. But I am forgetting, this has been done before.'

'You mean this Daedalus?'

'No Archytas, a friend of Plato. He had built a pigeon out of wood that glided in the air.'

Simon agreed we would make a model. If it meant putting my wax tablet aside for a few days and building something, then I couldn't start fast enough.

My mother was busy in the kitchen with the other household slaves when I came back. They were preparing a feast. Her red locks were braided and tied back. She was standing next to an amphora of my father's oil, spooning out something from a pot. It was garum, that strong fish sauce the Roman's love. She sensed I was standing behind her, but she didn't look around.

'As you can see, we are very busy, unless you are here to help?'

'Simon has told me this story.'

'Simon has many stories. You have told me lots of them.'

'But this is the best one.'

She turned her head. 'There is an important visitor coming up from town for dinner. Someone called Aulus. A business partner of your father's. He makes this garum, so we are serving it up for him.'

The earthenware pot had *A. Umbricius Scaurus* stamped on it. I held my nose. 'That stuff stinks.'

She smiled and nodded. 'I'm told it's the very best. They send it all over the Empire.'

I wasn't interested in smelly garum or Aulus Umbricius Scaurus, whoever he was. I wanted to tell her Simon's tale about Daedalus and Icarus. The other slaves had left with the serving dishes and we were now alone. Octavia never allowed either of us in the dining room. It was one of her rules.

She gave a sigh. 'Alright, tell me your story then. I'm all ears.' She kept working, but listened patiently as I neared the end.

'Icarus ignored his father and flew too high. Then he fell into the sea and drowned.'

'There you go,' she smiled, sealing up the jar. 'The perils of ignoring a parent's advice.'

'But they were escaping persecution. The Greeks are the cleverest of all people, don't you think?'

'There are clever people all over the empire and beyond. Some get the chance like you to show their cleverness. Others are not so fortunate.'

'But no Romans have ever flown, only Greeks.'

She turned around and lifted my chin. 'Then you have not heard of Bleydiud, son of Caratauc?'

'Who was he?'

'A Celtic king in Britannia, before I was born. A clever man who cured leprosy with mud and built wings to fly in the sky.'

'What happened to him?'

She frowned. 'He fell like your Icarus, broke his neck and died. He must have offended the gods. You see, if they had wanted us to fly, we would have been born with wings.'

'That doesn't make sense,' I said. 'We ride in carts and sail in boats. The gods didn't give us wheels or sails.'

'That's different.'

'If birds can do it, then why not us?'

She laughed. 'When you are young, you think everything is possible. Then you realise some things are, others are not. It is fate. I have accepted mine.'

'But not mine?'

She held both my shoulders and stared straight at me. She spoke to me in her mother tongue, so only we could understand. 'You are the son of a Roman. With freedom and citizenship, you can travel anywhere in the Empire and perhaps beyond. Even as far as the island of Britannia. There are traders who go there, for tin and gold. You could even return to the place I was born, the hill of the white horse, where the Atrebates live. You might go there one day and teach them what you have learned from Simon. Tell them what became of me. Warn them, the Empire will want to make them vassals.'

As she picked up the heavy jar to replace on the shelf, she grimaced in pain. I took it from her and put it back down. She sat on a stool and looked at me.

'The Emperors of Rome may the rule this land and sea, but some parts of the world are still free.'

I wanted to take her back there, to that hill of the white horse. You think such things are possible when you are young. When you are older, those dreams fade, but sometimes you can still recall them. Then she stared out the door. I followed her eyes to a wren, catching spiders beneath the eaves.

'When I watch those birds, I remember a time before I was enslaved. Someday, Quintus, you will be a free man, and when you are, remember me.'

She used my Roman name. I thought that meant when I was no longer a slave, I could purchase her freedom. But that's not what she meant at all.

She was hiding something.

Simon and I agreed that the shape of the eagle was our template. I drew it on my tablet and Simon asked me what I noticed.

'The head and wings form a triangle?'

'If the angle at the front is a hundred and twenty degrees, how big are the angles at the two back corners?'

'Thirty degrees.'

Simon tapped me on the head. 'Good, you remember your Euclid. The wings will need to be above the body like the eagle, so there will need to be a structure to support a passenger below.'

Simon suggested a little curved stave at the front like the edge of a wing and another straight spar down the middle, like the body of a bird. 'We will make it in linen and wood, like making a little sail.'

The cloth he thought should be held taught, glued and sewn over. Our craft needed a passenger. Something small, but weighty and durable. He proposed we cast it in metal. We made a little mould of a figure in wax, with arms outstretched and legs together. Then Simon enclosed it in clay with a hole to pour on top. Then the wax was heated and flowed out. Simon took a strip of bright metal. It creaked as he bent it into the clay pot he placed on his fire.

'Is that silver?' I asked.

'No, this is tin. It requires less heat to melt. From mines in Britannia, across the sea from Gaul. Isn't that where your mother comes from?'

I nodded. She had said something about mining tin and gold. When it cooled, I broke the mould. My little figure emerged, glinting in the sunlight. His arms outstretched to the sky, like Apollo. He'd been mined out of the earth in a place I'd dreamed of, but never been. Fashioned by fire and ready to be carried into the air. I polished him with a scrap of wool and held him up in my hands. He seemed as eager to start as me.

Simon had a pot of glue made from boiled hooves. I borrowed a strip of fine linen and a needle from the seamstress. How many models did we build? I cannot remember, but it was lots. No matter how many broke, I remained undeterred. I became expert in whittling the wood, rubbing it until it was smooth. I was obsessed with getting it exactly right. Sometimes they fell from the sky like a stone, other times they span and sank. Our little tin figure didn't mind. He was rescued and attached to yet another. If the weight was too far forward, we devised a method of notching the middle spar and adjusting the position of our passenger to achieve the perfect balance. The best results were launching into the warm wind blowing up the mountain. At last, we had one that would glide slowly down. The little craft would bob and float, with Apollo suspended below. I would run and chase it, imagining that I was underneath.

I brought it back and held it up to Simon. 'So now we have proved a person can fly.'

Simon smiled and shook his head. 'These toys are at the mercy of the wind. There is no intelligence.' He pointed up to the shape drifting around the mountain. 'Notice how the eagle turns and spirals, then lifts his wings when he lands. Our little man hanging beneath cannot control his craft. You have proven that these wings could lift a person, yes. But steering and landing safely, that would be impossible.'

Of course, what a foolish boy I was. Our little toy had proved nothing. Like jumping off a cliff, you would be airborne, briefly. You might have one flight in your life, but afterward you would be crippled or dead. Our little tin Apollo, could never prove a person could fly. The only way to do that was to build a wing big enough to carry someone. Then see if you could fly and land.

But Simon would never let me do that.

CHAPTER FIVE

I realised my mother was ill one day when she was breathless, sweeping the courtyard.

'It's just the dust,' she said. 'Never been good with dust, makes me cough. I just need a rest.'

But Octavia wouldn't let her rest, as if she sensed my mother was weakening. She worked her all the harder.

'She's lazy,' I overheard her say to my father. 'Lazy like all these barbarians who live in thatched huts, because they can't be bothered to make anything better.'

Over the next few weeks, my mother lost her appetite and became thinner. I saw her eyes go hollow and there were bruises on her pale skin. Then one morning I heard Octavia shouting. My mother could not get out of bed. The other slaves were trying to pull her up, but she was too weak. Her red hair was drenched in sweat and she was shaking.

Caecilius came and sent them all away, even Octavia. My mother begged him to let me stay, so I sat silent in the corner. He offered her some bread and watered wine, but she couldn't eat. He gave the bread to me, but I couldn't stomach it either, so I broke into crumbs on the windowsill for the birds. A physician from Pompeii arrived, but he could do nothing, other than leave an elixir for her pain. I stayed with Caecilius as my mother lay there. I saw him hold her hand, and she smiled.

'You promised you would free our son.'

He nodded. 'When he comes of age, he will be made free. I will formally adopt him and he will be a citizen of Rome. Then I will pass him my signet ring, symbol that he is my heir. In the meantime, he must continue his education with Simon. I will provide for him and he can work for me as one of my merchants. There is a new plantation of olives we have started in Hispania that I have not seen.'

She coughed as she replied. 'I know you are a good man and will keep your promise.'

Perhaps she was right. He had tears in his eyes. Then she asked if she could speak to me alone. My father nodded, put his hand on my shoulder, then left the room. I was crying, but I will always remember what she told me in the language of her people.

'Remember Caden, you are the son of a free Roman, but you are more than that.'

Around her neck she had a leather thong and twisted inside a knot was her coin. She lifted it off her neck and removed the precious nub of silver, the one with the horse on one side and the eagle on the other. She looked at me. 'I wanted to go back to the place I was born, the hill of the white horse,' she said. 'That's where my people, the Atrebates, live. One day you will visit them, tell them what became of me. The Emperors of Rome may the rule land and sea, but some parts of the world are still free.'

I knew what she said was true. Posidonius had calculated the world was much larger than what the Romans ruled. No one could conquer the whole world. Not even Alexander was able to do that.

She replaced the coin and put the thong around my neck.

'Keep it as a reminder of who you are and your promise to me.'

Then a wren came behind me and chirruped on the windowsill. Scattering the crumbs of bread neither of us could eat. My mother turned to look, and though she was in great pain, she smiled. She said something I'd heard before.

'I love those birds and the story of how they outwitted the eagle. Whenever I see them, I remember the time before I was enslaved. Someday, Caden, you will be a free man and when you are, remember me.'

I knelt down and cradled her head. Then she closed her eyes and died.

They buried my mother on the hillside above the villa. A place where a solitary small oak grew. Beneath it lay a simple stone on which I scratched my mother's name. Sometimes when I passed, I'd put wild flowers there. But it's all gone now.

After my mother's death, my dream changed. I was no longer held in the eagle's talons, but I flew with the noble bird that circled the mountain. I could nearly touch the clouds. Below me, a white horse was carved on a green hill. It was the hill of the Atrebates. I was free, as she had hoped. Then her voice would call me and I'd wake with a jolt, as if I'd fallen suddenly to earth. I'd touch the coin that I kept safe around my neck. On one side a horse and the other side, an eagle. The place where she's been born. I couldn't go there, but my dreams were taking me, anyway. Like the little wren that flew on the back of the eagle.

Another winter was passing. It was very mild that year. No snow, warm winds from the south. It presaged hot summer to come. My mother would have hated it. My father was at home, the sea too rough for ships to sail. The estate was quiet. Most of the jobs were done. Lots of the goats were pregnant, so the milking finished early. I had more time to spend with Simon. I studied hard and crafted more models. It helped me forget about other things. Our little winged man bobbed and floated on the wind. I went and picked it up from the grass and brought it back to Simon.

He held it in his hands. 'I think you have perfected it now. Time to return to our study of moral virtues.'

Then I plucked up my courage. 'You said there was a grain of truth in the story about Daedalus.'

'I did.'

'Aristotle says there is a difference between knowledge that is theoretical or useful. We need to find out which this is.'

'Explain Cadmus?'

'We have built many little models. Now we should build wings, big enough to carry me, to fly, say, a hundred paces over the grass. I will only be a few feet off the ground, not high enough to come to any harm.'

Simon shook his head. 'I am not so sure. If you were injured, how will I explain that to your father?'

'Just think, it will be a feat far greater than Archytas' pigeon. Worthy of Archimedes himself.'

I knew even then I was being mischievous. Invoking Archimedes, perhaps the greatest mind who had ever lived. Simon was silent for a few seconds, but he didn't say no. He was staring at the sky. I could see I had planted a seed. Then he turned.

'I will think about it,' he said.

Nothing more was said for a few days. We continued our usual dialogues. I spent a long time practicing Latin and Greek and having it corrected. Then we started on the Nicomachean ethics. It seemed Aristotle had eleven moral virtues, while Plato had only four. Being a virtuous person was becoming even harder. Eventually, I could not contain myself.

'Have you thought again about our wings?'

Simon looked at me and frowned. 'I have, but I cannot see how it can be done.'

'Why do you say that?' I asked.

Simon shook his head. 'Archimedes built many machines. If it were possible, he would have done it.'

So that was it. Archimedes didn't do it, so it couldn't be done. Simon said he'd never attempted to make anything to fly, as far as he knew. But then Archimedes was killed by a Roman while he was still working. He'd built machines of war to protect his city. That took time. Perhaps he would have got round to it if he'd lived longer? For all I knew, he could have been working on a sketch in the sand the moment the sword that killed him went in.

I'd seen Roman soldiers wearing that sword, the gladius. Titus had one. I was sure it wasn't his. He liked to wave it around and threaten me with it. It made me angry. It had killed one of the cleverest people who ever lived, for no good reason. An evil stabbing weapon. Short enough, so when you killed, you were staring into your victim's eyes. But I would be lucky the gladius was short.

Very lucky indeed.

CHAPTER SIX

I'm not sure why Simon changed his mind. He never told me. Perhaps the chance to do something that Archimedes had not, was just too tempting. One day we were in the middle of a lesson on geometry, discussing the relationship between circles and triangles. He stopped suddenly.

'We will make these wings, Cadmus, enough to glide one hundred paces. But you will tell no one, agreed?'

Of course, I agreed, though I could never know the path on which I had now embarked. So, it started. Like the impetuous child I was, I wanted to race ahead. But Simon was insistent we planned it properly. Based on all we had learned and using the principles of geometry and natural science, just as Archimedes or Archytas would have done.

We had agreed that the wing should be the arc of a circle, elegant and simple. What we couldn't decide was how a person should be suspended below it. A harness like my little tin figure had would not be enough. It needed something more. We had to move the wing like a bird. It was a problem that vexed us for ages. We had no solution. I was beginning to believe that Simon was right. Archimedes had not done it. It must be impossible.

Then one morning I awoke, as if visited by Euclid in a dream. Even before I had gathered the goats, I blurted it out to Simon in my excitement.

'Euclid's first axiom. Things which are equal to the same thing are also equal to one another. The solution is an equilateral triangle. I could hold the horizontal bar and the two sides would connect up to the central spar.'

Simon thought for a moment and frowned. 'The connection would have to be very robust. The apex point would be the most vulnerable to break. It would need to be the strongest joint, reinforced with linen and glue'

I held up my little tin Apollo. 'My weight would be held like our little tin man, in a harness like a swing. I would hang from the spar, in a leather strap like a seat, and buckled around my waist. My hands would hold the base of the triangle.'

Simon nodded. 'I can see that might work.'

'I'll practice on a gentle slope in light wind, just a few feet off the ground to be safe. If my feet don't touch the ground for a hundred paces, then I've flown.'

Simon leaned heavily on his stick and took a deep breath. Then he nodded.

'Agreed, you fly a hundred paces, that's all, then our experiment ends.'

There was a fortnight when both Caecilius and Octavia were both away. She was visiting relatives in Salernum. My father travelled to Ostia to inspect a shipment of wine. Simon was nominally in charge of the household. Titus was still in Rome. It was the happiest time since my mother died.

There was a derelict barn on the side of the mountain. The goats would shelter there sometimes in winter storms. A carpenter from Pompeii had been taken on to repair it and was nearly finished. Simon asked him to do some extra work and explained what we wanted. The best model we had made was a gentle curve. It enclosed a triangle, one hundred and twenty degrees at the front and thirty at each corner. It seemed to float in the air for ages and glide in a straight line.

I sat and watched the carpenter work under Simon's direction. One wood had to flex, the other needed to be stiff. He chose two pieces, one of poplar, the other pine and planed them down. After soaking the pine in hot water, he gave it a gentle curve. He fused them with what he called a lap joint, fixed with glue and tied with linen and glued again. He cut notches in the spar on the upper edge, so we could vary where the harness hung. Then he made a triangle of poplar wood that he bound and glued. We had strong twine that the fishermen used for nets. Simon paid for an order of linen from the sailmaker's in Oplontis. They cut a single piece to the right shape. Simon told me linen was very strong. I tried to tear it, but couldn't. He said Alexander's armour was made of layers of it when he defeated Darius, the Persian King.

The man who worked in the leather shop in Pompeii finished the harness. Made of goat leather, so it was light but strong. He had stitched it exactly as Simon had specified, allowing me to sit securely in. I'm not sure he believed it was a child's swing, but he accepted the money and the last piece was complete.

I swept out the barn and secured the fence. The goats were terrible gluttons. If they got in, they would eat any fabric or leather. It took six days of hard work putting it all together, but it was finally finished. The wing was a gentle arc of a circle at the front and a triangle at the rear. Like pulling a bow with an arrow at full stretch. Below it attached the wooden triangle, all the sides and angles equal. Too simple perhaps for Archimedes, but Euclid would have liked it. Simon said it should it have a name, like a boat. I remembered Zeus had an eagle that sits beside him on his throne. So, we called it Aetos.

'We will keep it safe up here and wait for a warm southerly wind,' he said.

We didn't have to wait long. The following day, the wind was from the south. I thought I would get up and finish my task of sweeping the yard early, before I went to milk the goats. That meant I could spend the whole afternoon up there.

That was a mistake, as I soon discovered.

Valeria was a little sneak. Not that much older than me, but short, with dark wavy hair and piercing eyes. Always trying to offload her work onto someone else. She was Octavia's favourite, and she revelled in it. My mother had warned me she was an informant amongst the slaves. I tried to have as little to do with her as possible. But it was inevitable she would take a dislike to me.

I had just finished sweeping the yard beneath the vines. I took my mother's coin out of the leather thong I kept around my neck. It was turning over in my fingers. A horse, then an eagle, glinted in the sun.

I heard someone say. 'Still staring at your stupid coin?' Valeria had come into the yard and stood in front of me, with her hands on her stout hips.

I put it back around my neck.

'It's a worthless piece of scrap, you know,' she sneered.

'If you say so.'

'Some cloth came up on the cart from Pompeii last week.'

I nodded, trying to keep calm. 'Simon ordered it and paid for it himself.'

'What for?'

'Perhaps you should ask him?'

Valeria frowned and raised her finger. 'Perhaps you should stop lying to me. That crazy old Greek never buys anything. I do his laundry. His room is virtually bare. I am not even sure he owns more than two sets of clothes.'

'He doesn't believe in having anything unnecessary. It's part of his philosophy. He's a Stoic.'

She frowned. 'Stupid, if you ask me.' She started to walk away, then she turned back. 'You're up to something, I can tell. Planning to run away? I hope you try, because I want to see you when they bring you back, all battered and bruised.'

'Why should I do that?'

'Of course, you have an easy life. You think you are better than us.'

'Better than who?'

'The rest of us slaves. Why do you only work half a day?'

'I milk in the morning, then work in the afternoons with Simon.'

She snorted. 'That's not work. You still believe the master will free you?'

'Perhaps, when I'm older and come of age.'

'If you think he'll keep that promise, you're more of a fool than I thought. He might not even still be alive when you're thirty, ever thought about that?'

I didn't say anything but kept sweeping, even though the courtyard was now clean.

Valeria didn't give up. 'You may think you're Roman, but I'm more Roman than you. My mother came from the island of Corsis.'

I wasn't sure I wanted to be Roman, but I knew I couldn't say that. Valeria would tell Octavia and it would used against me, for sure.

'What about your father?' I said. I immediately regretted asking, because Valeria did not know who her father was. He could have been Tiberius himself, for all she knew.

She snarled and bared her little white teeth. 'You scum, your mother was a whore, a filthy whore who deserved to be whipped and die in pain.'

It was like she had lit a fire inside me. I stopped sweeping and raised my hand. That was my next mistake.

She walked up right in front of my face. 'Go on,' she dared. 'Hit me, see what happens.'

She was right, of course. She was Octavia's favourite. No one, not even Simon, would save me from a flogging and then at least a month of the dirtiest jobs on the estate. I lowered my hand.

'See, nothing but a coward who threatens women. The son of a whore. A worthless piece of goat dung.'

She waited for a reaction. She wanted one. Wanted me to lose my temper and strike her. I stood there trembling, remembering all Simon had taught me. Self discipline, endure pain without complaint. It took all my strength to contain that insult to my poor dead mother. A woman who had never chosen her fate, but bore it just the same. I took a deep breath and started slowly sweeping, and Valeria finally walked away.

I would have to be more careful.

I finished with the goats and took the milk down to the dairy. It was quiet, but I stopped myself from running back up the hill. Valeria might still be watching. That first afternoon is seared into my memory. We took Aetos out into the hidden meadow, behind the spur of the mountain. It was too steep to grow much. There had been talk of putting vines on it, but it remained covered in coarse grass. Simon sat on his usual stone and warned me to be careful. The goats were grazing higher up and took no notice. The warm wind was in my face. I could feel Aetos lifting in the breeze, even before I started running. My feet hovered briefly over the grass, then dropped down again. I went back up the hill and did it again and again. I am not sure if it was the excitement, but I barely felt its weight.

We fixed the harness back a notch on the poplar spar so it seemed better balanced. I ran faster as if I was falling forward, but Aetos would lift me up. A couple of times I felt it tilt in the eddying wind. But if I leaned the other way, Aetos would correct itself. I practiced everything I had learned from watching those soaring birds. It must have been the twentieth time I walked back up the hill. Simon signalled that we had done enough. Then I carried Aetos back to the barn. It sat there perched proud, like an eagle. I was covered in sweat, but elated.

Of course, I had barely skimmed the ground, but it felt like I had flown for miles. I was Daedalus, Icarus, Bleydiud or all three at once.

But poor Aetos would have to die to save my life.

The warm south wind blew for another five days. Each afternoon I would go up and we spent the whole time practicing with Aetos. Every time I got more confidence, a little further, a little higher. I began to turn left and right and learned how to deal with sudden gusts. Like the eagles, I'd lift the wing to slow and touch the grass. If I had a choice, I'd do nothing else. The time flew by. It was the fifth day, the last before Octavia's return. It was late afternoon, and I was climbing back up the hill.

'You have gone at least a hundred paces, so we'll call it flying,' said Simon.

I had actually done more, maybe twice or even three times that, so I couldn't argue.

'Am I the first person to fly since Daedalus?'

'Very possibly. Put Aetos away now. We should get back to other things.'

The next day I had finished with the goats. I ran across to the sloped meadow. Simon was waiting for me, sitting on his stone.

'It's a perfect day again,' I said. 'A soft, southerly breeze.'

Simon did not answer.

'Did you see how I landed yesterday? If I lift the wing, I slow to a stop. I can turn by shifting my weight. It was like was dancing on air. I can go further and higher today. I know it.'

Simon said nothing. He looked grave, staring at the ground.

'In a few weeks, I could be up to where the eagles are.'

Simon rubbed his beard and took off his felt cap. 'Remember, I am responsible for your welfare Quintus'

He never called me Quintus, but I did not correct him.

'Your father gave me the job of instructing you in Latin, Greek, mathematics, philosophy and enough poetry to have you pass as an educated Roman, worthy to be his son. But he did not give me permission to endanger your life.'

I was about to speak, but he raised his hand.

'I confess, I have also got carried away with our little experiment. A diversion to teach you the practical application of geometry, natural history, observation and logic. Anyway, we have proved flight is possible. Our task is now complete.'

I stared at him in disbelief. 'Stop now? But we have only just started.'

Simon looked up. His expression had a touch of pleading. Then he touched his temple. 'Think for a moment, use your mind, as I have tried to teach you. Here we are, just the two of us in an isolated field behind the spur of this mountain. Your brief flights are hidden from view. An achievement known to us and us alone. I am talking about realities.'

I threw up my hands. 'What realities? Isn't what we are doing important? The feeling you get when your feet leave the ground, its indescribable. It's like being a bird or a god. I feel like Apollo.'

Simon shook his head. 'Sometimes your thinking is too narrow. Perhaps that is my mistake. You must put what you are doing in the context of our wider world. I am talking of wisdom.'

I know now he didn't want to tell me what to do. He wanted me to reach that conclusion myself.

He pointed upward. 'If you were to fly higher, what would happen then?'

'Someone would see me?'

'Agreed. Do you imagine someone flying over the fields of Campania is an everyday occurrence? What would be the outcome?'

I was a child then; I didn't really understand. 'People would come here? They might steal Aetos?'

Simon shook his head. 'Rome is a military state. Do you think the legions would be happy about a slave having the knowledge of flight? To be able to soar above them? To see their armies, study their cities and their defences?'

'No.'

'You know what happened to that Thracian who rebelled against Rome. What was his name?'

'Spartacus.'

'Yes Spartacus. A slave uprising is what the Romans fear, above all else. Do you think a slave who did something extraordinary, who might have the capacity to spark such a thing, would be allowed to live?'

I hung my head. He was speaking the truth, although I did not want to hear it. 'Probably not.'

Simon stood up. 'I would say certainly not. For all these reasons, you must agree. The only option we have is to stop now. Before we go too far. Trust me, I have your interest at heart.'

'If you think I'm afraid of flying, I'm not.'

Simon shook his head. 'Remember, a virtue exists between two vices. To do more would not be courage, it would be reckless.'

'You want me to destroy Aetos? '

Simon walked over and caressed the wing. 'No, we can deconstruct Aetos back into wood, linen and leather. No one will know its purpose. What we have done here will be our secret. A marvellous thing, something beyond what I thought possible. A feat worthy of Archimedes himself. But remember, even he could not defy Rome.'

'When I am a Roman citizen, perhaps then?'

'Who knows what the future holds? Aetos will stay locked up in that shelter. Later next week, you can choose a quiet day and take it apart. In the meantime, your studies are well behind. We haven't finished our lessons on the Nicomachean Ethics.'

My heart sank. So that was the end of the discussion. Like Socrates, Simon had led me through a dialogue to reach the right conclusion. Of course, Aetos would be my downfall. What was I thinking? I might be clever, but I certainly wasn't wise. Somewhere deep down I should have been grateful, even though every fibre of my being wanted to fly.

But I never did deconstruct Aetos. That day never arrived. As for the Nicomachean Ethics, we never finished those either.

CHAPTER SEVEN

Octavia was back from her trip away. Someone told her about the linen, probably Valeria. She found me carrying the goat's milk into the dairy.

'You are spending a lot of time with Simon up on the mountain?'

'He's teaching me natural history.'

'There's work for you down here. I hear you have been neglecting your chores.'

'But I've done everything the master asked of me. I milk the goats and the afternoons I spend with my tutor, as he requested.'

She hissed. 'Don't you talk back to me. When my husband's away, I'm in charge here. You do as I say.'

'Yes mistress.'

'Don't start thinking you're a Roman. You're nothing but a bastard Celt.'

I said nothing. She was right. At least she hadn't mentioned my mother.

Then she gave me a piercing look. 'I'm told there was some linen cloth delivered here a few weeks ago. The housemaid says she didn't order it. Do you have it?'

'No.'

'You're a born liar, like your mother, and probably a thief, to boot. If I had my way, you'd be sold.'

I gritted my teeth and said nothing.

She turned to leave, then looked back. 'Since you like spending so much time chasing goats, I have a new task for you. You're a sturdy boy. It's time you began working the fields.'

'Of course.'

'Starting tomorrow.'

So, I spent my afternoons weeding the vines and hoeing the ground on the estate. Then carrying wood to heat the bathhouse. It only lasted three days. Caecilius came back and countermanded her order. My afternoons were free again. I could tell Octavia was furious, but said nothing. I tried to avoid contact with her, but whenever I glimpsed her eyes; they glittered with a murderous intent. She was planning something and I wouldn't have long to wait.

One spring morning a week later, it was the day before the Ides of March, my twelfth birthday. Caecilius was away again on business. Octavia sought me out. She seemed strangely excited and was even pleasant to me. That should have made me worried. But the little fool I was, I thought for some reason she had forgiven me. After all, I had done nothing, other than be her husband's son, by a slave.

'There will be a procession tomorrow. An important person is on their way to the port at Oplontis. We all have to look our best, especially you, Quintus. After all, it will be your birthday.'

My birthday had never really been celebrated before, not openly anyway. Perhaps she was getting to like me after all? The next day someone else was sent to milk the goats. They scrubbed my face until I thought the skin would come off. All the dirt from under my fingernails was scraped away. My hair was washed and fashionably cut short. It felt soft and glimmered in the sun. They dressed me in a bright coloured tunic I had never seen before. I felt different, more Quintus than Cadmus or Caden. I have never felt more Roman than that day, before or since.

But like Caesar, I should have feared the Ides of March.

That afternoon Octavia gathered the household, and we lined the road that travelled south to Oplontis. I remember Octavia was wearing her favourite bracelet on one arm. It was gold and shaped like a snake with two heads. Apparently, it was to help fertility and ward off evil. The irony of its failure was lost on me then.

The older slaves and servants were all wearing clean clothes, but none were dressed in my finery. I should have been more worried, but the truth was I was enjoying the attention lavished on me. We must have been waiting on that road for over an hour. The only thing that had trundled past was a wagon from the port, going north, in the wrong direction. It was starting to get warm. There was no shade where Octavia had decided we should all stand.

Eventually I heard someone mutter, 'here they come.'

Octavia put her fingers to her lips and commanded us to be silent. I could hear a horses' hooves on the hard stone and the creak of turning wheels. The tramping of sandals with iron rivets in their soles. I couldn't see until quite late, because Octavia had placed me at the far end of the line. She stood right behind me. Her cloying perfume choked the air.

A cavalryman led the procession. Then there came a detachment of marching soldiers, with red horsehair helmets and scorpions on their shields. A coach followed, with more of them behind. This coach was nothing like anything I had ever seen. Painted in red and embossed with gold. Drawn by two fine white horses, mounted with feathers. Everyone lowered their heads in deference, but I just kept staring. I heard someone shout a command, and the carriage drew to a halt just past us. The rider wheeled round and leaned over the neck of his horse, in conversation with the occupant inside. The soldier sat up in the saddle and pointed at me.

'Come closer boy, there is someone important who wants to see you.'

I felt Octavia nudge me forward. I walked slowly, wondering what I had done to displease them. Perhaps I hadn't bowed my head far enough? I saw two eyes peering out of the darkness from inside the carriage.

'Turn around, boy,' said the rider, 'he wants to see all of you.'

I did as I was told.

'Where do you live,' said the rider?

'At the villa over there, beyond the olives.'

'What is your name?'

'Quintus.'

'You are Roman?'

'My father is Caecilius, a merchant.'

I heard Octavia hiss behind me.

The soldier pointed to Octavia who gave a little bow. 'Is that your mother?'

'No, my mother is dead.'

'What was her name?'

'Orlagh.'

'A barbarian, then, a slave?'

'Yes.'

'That's good. You are invited to the Villa Jupiter on Capri, as a guest of the Emperor.'

'But I have never met the Emperor?'

The soldier nodded. 'Indeed, you have just had the honour. A letter of instruction will be delivered to the head of this estate tomorrow. They will ensure it is followed. Long live Tiberius.'

The carriage and riders moved off. I turned to see Octavia wearing the biggest smile I had ever seen. A smile I had seen once before.

Just as the snake went back into the basket.

Simon seemed despondent when I told him the news.

'They have asked me to visit the Emperor on Capri.'

'Yes, so I hear, interrupting your studies.'

'You told me you had met him once on Rhodes.'

'Long before he was Emperor. He was just another noble Roman then.'

'Why doesn't he live in Rome?'

Simon frowned. 'Rome is a dangerous place even for Emperors. Remember, Caesar was murdered there. He is safer on an island.'

'But how does he rule?'

'By letter and decree. Your father says he has trusted men who do his bidding in Rome, where the Praetorian guard are in charge. The imperial post is very swift, they say. A letter from Neapolis can get to Rome by dispatch rider in less than three days.'

'Will you write to me, Simon? Send my lessons and I can write back.'

He shook his head. 'I will try, but I am not sure they will allow letters to Capri.'

Simon had a flicker of emotion cross his face. I had never seen him cry, but I think he was close to tears. This must be as bad as a burning library. He leaned over and held me by both shoulders.

'You must listen to me. Do nothing to upset him. Obey whatever is commanded of you. I trust you will return soon and we can resume your studies. You must be brave, Quintus.'

He called me by my Roman name again. That made me more worried. I didn't sleep well that night. In fact, hardly at all.

I had a fitful dream. I was frantically swimming in a pool of clear water, chased by a snake. I was searching in vain for somewhere to hide. Then something grabbed me by the leg. I woke up with my foot trapped behind the table. Then I lay awake, staring out the window, watching the slow stars turn, until the soft rain came. I'd never lived anywhere outside the estate. The furthest I had ever been was to Pompeii and the port of Oplontis. I could not remember sleeping in a bed, other than the one I had.

The next day, a soldier arrived early at our estate, with a pony trailing from a halter behind. He had the scorpion on the cheek of his helmet, so I knew he was a Praetorian, the Emperor's bodyguard. He was carrying the expected letter, which he gave to Octavia. Caecilius was still away, so she made all the arrangements. The fine tunic I had worn the day before was gone. They made up a small bundle of clothes with a flask of water that was tied to my back.

The soldier looked down at me. 'You can ride?'

'A bit.'

'You only have to sit and hold the reins on the mare. She's old and not too fast.' He looked at my meagre belongings. 'Is that all you have?'

'I think so.'

'Don't worry. You won't need much. Everything is provided for the boys at Villa Jupiter.'

The boys, did that mean there were more like me? I saw Simon had come down from his cottage. He was leaning on his stick, staring at the ground. Then he looked up at me, but he was grave and silent. Valeria was doing a little dance. Only Octavia spoke and waved. 'Goodbye Quintus, don't forget to enjoy yourself.'

As I mounted the pony, a strange sickness rose in my throat. I felt uneasy as I trotted behind. Octavia seemed so happy and Simon was so sad. Neither was a good sign. I turned for one last look back at the villa. I wondered if I would ever milk the goats, swim in the pond, or visit my mother's grave again.

We descended down on the road to the port of Oplontis. The place seemed quiet and damp. I remember the sombre seagulls circling above. I had done this journey before with my father, to go and visit his ships that had arrived. This time, it was different. I was the cargo to be carried away.

We wound through the wet streets, past the villas, the warehouses and came to the dock. A small, open galley was drawn up, waiting. On its prow was the figurehead of a swan. Our mounts were handed over to a stable hand, a slave not much older than me. I climbed on board. There were some stacked amphorae, but apart from the praetorian, I was the only passenger. The oarsmen started to row out into deeper water. They grunted with effort, but nobody spoke. A little mist had gathered on the sea. I saw the island with high cliffs looming in the distance. It was Capri, the place visible from the mountain behind our home. I had seen it most days when I milked the goats. Simon had said it was a forbidden and that I would never go there. But he was wrong. The oars splashed their rhythm into the still water. One structure stood out at the eastern edge, towering over the sea. I didn't like it as soon as I saw it,

The Praetorian turned. 'That's the Villa Jupiter where Tiberius lives. Impressive isn't it, been completed in less than a year. The height of luxury, no comfort spared to keep our Emperor happy.'

I swallowed hard. There was a still a lump in my throat that would not go away.

'Does everyone on Capri live there?'

'No, but that's where you'll be. There are a few other boys like you, some older. You can play knucklebones and hopscotch. Don't worry, you will have plenty of playmates.'

'Will I have a tutor to finish learning Greek and geometry?'

The Praetorian looked puzzled, as if he had never been asked that question before. 'You'll have to wait and see.'

'Is this boat the only way for my tutor to visit me?'

The Praetorian snorted. 'Unless your tutor can fly, the birds will be the only visitors you get on Capri.'

We rounded the northeastern promontory of the island. There were strong currents, and the oarsmen were sweating. The pale cliffs below the villa were steep, with trees clinging to the edge. On the north side of the island, there was a small harbour and a stone jetty. The rowers drew the boat up alongside and it was secured.

The Praetorian helped me off, and we started walking up the steep path toward the villa Jupiter. It seemed even larger than it had appeared from the boat. It was not a villa like ours, a palace or a small town would have been a better description. With many levels moulded into the forbidding hill. I had a sense of disquiet. It was not a place that appeared welcoming. We reached a gate, heavily fortified and guarded from in front and above. Inside, we wound a maze of narrow corridors that opened into wider halls. I glimpsed rooms and windows and terraces outside. He took me to a small room with a table, a bed, and a chamber pot underneath. It was clean, dry and smelt of vinegar. I felt sick.

The restless Praetorian was looking over his shoulder. 'I expect you are hungry. The matron will come soon. She'll bring you food and water. Then you may meet some of the older boys.'

'May I ask your name?'

He stared at me. The tone of his voice turned to stone. 'Keep that tongue in your head if you know what's good for you. To you we are nameless. You'll get the same answer from all of us. Protection of our Emperor comes above everything else. His word is law.'

I heard shuffling footsteps in the corridor.

'You took your time,' I heard him say.

A large woman entered the room carrying a jug and a small basket. She was wearing a voluminous stola, like the women at the market in Pompeii. Her face was hard and expressionless.

'You are Quintus?'

'Yes.'

She put the jug and basket on the table. 'A few rules. You may call me matron. I'm here to make sure you're washed, fed and clothed, no more, no less. And I'm not your mother.'

'My mother's dead.'

'That's probably a good thing.'

'Did you bathe yesterday?'

'Yes.'

'You may not be used to it, but we bathe here regularly. I have brought you some food and watered wine. I see you already have linen and a blanket.' As she left, she turned. 'Do not leave this room without my permission.'

I wouldn't have known where to go, anyway. The watered wine tasted like Titus' feet. I ate a little of the food. The bread was soft and pale. I'd not seen that before. There was a jar of olive oil and some goat's cheese. I wondered who would milk my goats. What would Simon now do with his time? He was old. I might not see him again. There was no telling how long I had to stay here, or what my purpose was. The journey had taken all day, and it was getting dark. I curled up on the bed. It seemed too large for me. I much preferred my little mattress under the table. I had trouble getting to sleep and lay there thinking. Here, I was confined to one little room. I had not realised how free I had been on our estate. I was the youngest slave. The others treated me like a pet. So long as I kept out of the way of Octavia and Titus, my life was good.

The next morning, I awoke early just as the dawn broke. I was having that dream again, the one where I was in the clouds and the eagle was flying beside me. I was above a green hill, but the white horse had gone. For a moment, I thought I was back at home on the estate. Then I fell to earth. I was in the Villa Jupiter on Capri. I had touched that dream, now it was gone, all in the space of a day. It was all too real, the bed, the walls, the journey across on the galley. The triumphant Octavia, smiling as the Praetorian took me away. Now I knew that look on her face. I did not realise you could have both cruelty and joy together. It did not fit into Simon's world of Aristotle, or Euclid and his triangles. It must be how gladiators or tyrants feel. My only offence was to be the child Octavia could not have. But perhaps it's lurking somewhere, in everyone.

An older boy came to my room to bring me fresh water, clothes, and food.

'Am I allowed to ask your name?'

He nodded. 'Do I look like a Praetorian? I am a slave here like you.'

He told me his name was Linus. He was from Rome, sold to pay a family debt. I asked him how he came to be here. Linus told me it was his own fault. He'd been sent on an errand by his master, but he took a detour to see a festival near the Palatine hill. He said there were men who pretended to be wolves and ran round half naked. Which sounded brave, because it was winter. They'd sacrificed a goat and a dog in a cave, then smeared themselves in blood and whipped women with a thong of leather. Apparently, they wanted to be scourged, so they could fall pregnant. I thought he was joking, but he insisted it was true.

'You must have heard of Lupercalia. It's one of the most famous festivals in Rome. Celebrates the founding of the city by the twins suckled by a she wolf. It had just finished, and the crowd were going home. Then I was grabbed by a Praetorian and taken to Capri. I'm not sure if my master even knows what happened to me.'

'How long have you been here?'

'Three years. We were in another villa until this was one was finished last year.'

'You have not been off the island in all that time?'

'None of us can leave. The Praetorian guard control all the boats. Nothing lands or leaves without their permission. You will notice that even the fisherman are commanded not to come too close. It is all to keep

Tiberius safe. The only way off this island is with the Emperor's leave. When he is bored with you, or finds someone younger.'

'Someone younger?'

Linus could see I didn't really understand. He poured some water. 'You grow up quickly here. He calls us his minnows. Best to accept your fate, pretend to enjoy his attention and hope it's over as soon as possible. For some reason, I was lucky, and he didn't want me. I'm old enough now to sweep the terraces or stack wood for the baths. There are worse jobs. At least I don't have to clean the latrines.'

Then he drew closer and lowered his voice. 'They call him the old goat, he's so hairy.'

'I used to herd goats and milk them.'

Linus gave a nervous laugh. 'Then you have had the prefect apprenticeship. But whatever you do, don't cry or complain. They broke the legs of a Suebian boy who did that. There was another one, a Dacian, I think. He couldn't stand it and cut his own throat. I watched them throw his body into the sea. The Praetorians prefer if he chooses slaves. No one asks questions about us. Most of us so far have survived. But some still scream in their sleep. They are older now. If you are lucky, you will get easier work in the kitchens, or tending the gardens. But don't expect to leave, not for a long time, perhaps ever. What happens here, I don't think they know much about it in Rome.'

'Does no one try to escape from the villa?'

'You're a mad one. The entrances are all triple guarded. Half a legion could be kept at bay outside these walls.'

'But there are terraces to the outside?'

Linus shook his head. 'Didn't you see this place on the boat in? The cliffs are very steep, a sheer drop to the water. If you tried to climb around, you'd fall to your death. If you managed, where would you go? There is no way off this island. Even if you found a place to hide, you wouldn't last long. There's no food outside the kitchens. When they caught you, the punishment would be worse than anything you might endure.'

It was all good advice, like listening to Simon. There were times after that day when I wish I had taken it.

The next day Linus came in with the matron. He was silent, but gave me a knowing stare. As if something was about to happen, but he couldn't tell me. He took my plates and left. The matron sat me down on a chair. She began to go through my hair with a fine-toothed comb, then put in a scented oil.

'When am I going home?'

'Best put that out of your mind. You're the Emperor's property now.'

'I'm not the first one to come here?'

'No, there's some before and I dare say a few will come after. At least you will hope they do.'

'The other ones. Are they still here?'

She turned me round to face her and frowned. 'Haven't you learned yet? The Villa Jupiter is not a place to ask questions. Do as you're told. Manage that and you'll survive.'

Socrates would have been in trouble here. He wouldn't have lasted a week. I was dressed in a white tunic, cut square at the neck, embroidered at the edge with a thin seam of purple. I slipped on sandals of soft calf skin and then I was topped with a crown of woven myrtle leaves. I was being marked out for something special again. That worried me.

A soldier came into the room and tapped the matron on the shoulder. 'He's just gone in. Don't like to keep him waiting.'

'We've finished,' she replied. 'You are going for your bath now, Quintus, like I told you.'

She led me in austere silence through the corridors. The praetorian walked behind me. I was not the first to make this walk and I am sure, not the last. There were mosaics on the floor, but not like Octavia's dining room. These were murals of animals and naked people entwined with each other. I could hear the Praetorian's harsh footsteps echo in the corridor, the matron's shuffle, my sandals slapping on the fresh stone. I noticed every glimmer of light. Birds were singing outside. I was too young to fully understand, but I knew something bad was going to happen. The air became warm and moist. There was a sweet exotic smell, not the oil in my hair. I had smelled this before, myrrh. Simon had told me it was Octavia's favourite scent. He said my father had bought it to placate her.

We entered a large room lined with marble. I was sat on a sumptuous bed with white linen. There were ornate boxes and a small brazier burned where the scent was strongest. The matron said nothing and didn't look at me. She turned, then left and closed the door. My stomach was turning in knots. In front of me was a wall of thick green glass with a gap that served as a doorway. Behind it wafted steam. There was movement, a figure somewhere behind the glass, and then a splash of water. I turned my head away. There was another door to my left. I could see through a window that it led to a terrace, with views over the sea. A curious robin fluttered onto the ledge and stared at me. Why was it that little birds always wanted to witness my worst moments? Perhaps, like my mother said, it was sent from the netherworld.

I could see the faint outline of a naked man, beckoning. 'I am in the bath, boy. Come and join me.' Not an invitation, a command.

I have since learned there are times you make a decision, unaware the fates are placing your life on a different course. But this was not one of them. I knew at once my whole life turned on that moment. I was outside my body, absolutely still. Like the robin sitting on the window ledge, looking down on myself. A sudden realisation of my fate. A choice; be violated and perhaps survive, or run to almost certain death. So many thoughts were rushing through my head. All the wisdom that Simon had taught me, courage, self discipline, to endure pain. The wisest person I knew was telling me to walk into that steam and suffer whatever came next. It seemed everyone who came before me had made that choice. Maybe they didn't even imagine there was one. They had submitted. Perhaps they were wiser than me. Why should I be different? I was a slave. This man was the Emperor of Rome, with the power of a god.

I touched the leather thong around my neck. Then the first line that prayer came to me. *Blessed is the one who does not walk in step with the wicked.* A voice telling me if I went into that bath, I would forever cease to be Cadmus or Caden or even some twisted version of Quintus. My fear of running was less than what awaited me in the steam. I took off a crown of leaves and placed it on the bed. I did not take off my sandals or my tunic, but walked slowly across the room. Then I pushed the door. Perhaps Janus, the god of doorways, smiled on me. It was unlocked and swung slowly open. The pale terrace beyond was empty. I made my way to the edge where tops of the green shrubs emerged from the cliff. Aristotle said that virtue makes the end right. But I had no idea where I was going or what I would do.

In truth, I no longer cared. My fate was chosen.

CHAPTER EIGHT

L inus was right, the cliff below was very steep. White flowering
myrtle grew close to the foundations of the terrace. The same
leaves as the crown I'd left on the bed. They grew too thick to see
if there was a path below. Without a backward glance, I grabbed
the strongest limb I could see and lowered myself down. I dropped
through the greenery and landed on a rough ledge, perhaps left by
masons who had recently laid the stone.

Then I heard heavy feet on the terrace and a command. 'Halt, by
command of the Emperor.'

I crawled underneath the dense shrubs and emerged into the light.
A startled lizard scuttled away from my nose. Ahead, the semblance of a
goat path tracked along the edge of a sheer cliff. I started down, trying to
keep my balance on the narrow ledge. Someone grunted as they jumped
behind me. There was the sound of a branch breaking and cursing as
they tore through the tree. My heart was racing now, thumping out of
my chest. I kept going, grasping whatever vegetation I could find. I could
hear panting following, not far away. Their heavy steps dislodged rocks
that rattled down and splashed into the water.

I didn't dare look back. I followed the track and scrambled over a
spine of rock. The villa was out of sight. I glimpsed Vesuvius across the
strait. My gaze lingered briefly on the southern slope that was once my
home. But it was beyond reach. There was no choice but to keep going. I
descended through the scrub at the edge of the cliff, slowly getting closer

to the water. The sea stretched, glistening to my left. A tangle of shrubs towered over my right.

The path ended suddenly, at a sheer drop over the water. I was trapped. Not even a goat could find its way down. I crept back and huddled beneath the dense shade, hoping if I lay quiet, my pursuer might pass. There was a deep breathing somewhere close. I closed my eyes, unable to move. For a while, I didn't hear anything. I prayed he must have missed me. Then I felt a sweaty hand seize me and pull me up roughly by the collar.

'You little rat. Don't you realise the Emperor can have you killed for this?'

He pulled so hard he was choking me, I couldn't breathe. I twisted, trying to escape the hold. He leaned forward to grab me with both hands. Then I felt my captor lose his footing. The last thing I heard him say as we toppled off the cliff was... 'You stupid boy.'

I kicked out and fell free. My feet hit the waves first, but the shock knocked the breath out of me. I struggled back up to the surface and gasped for air. I had fallen into deep water, but the guard had not been so fortunate. There was a glint from his breastplate where he lay unmoving in the shallows. I started to swim away from the place where he had fallen. I looked up at the cliffs, but could see only dazzling sun. A current was taking me further away from the island. I was drifting out into the channel we had crossed only two days before. There was nothing I could do but try to stay afloat. As I rounded the northern head of the island, the mainland came into view, but it was far further than I could ever swim.

The water was icy, and the sun began to burn my face. I spat the sea out of my mouth and kept kicking. I could swim for hours in the pool on the estate, but there were no waves there. Seagulls circled overhead, and I wished I was with them. I thought of Icarus who had had fallen into the sea. I wondered how long he had floated there, watching his father fly away. Now I would share his fate to drown. Was that the better choice? I did not know.

I was not sure how long I drifted. All my strength was used to stay afloat. I remembered asking Simon why the sea was salty. He said Aristotle believed that sweet water was light and lifted up, leaving the heavy salt behind. But Empedocles thought the sea was the sweat of the earth. I wasn't sure I believed him. After all, he jumped into a volcano to prove he was a god.

I coughed salt water, trying to stay above the waves. My lips swelled. The island drifted further and further away. I wondered what Octavia would tell my father. Valeria would laugh and Simon might weep. The leather thong floated around my neck and in it the tiny silver coin. The promise I made to my mother would sink with me, like my dead sister, to the bottom of the sea. I was very cold and preparing to die. All the things Simon had taught me would go to waste. For some reason, I started reciting Simon's prayer over and over while I kicked my legs. *'Blessed is the one who does not walk in step with the wicked or stand in the way that sinners take, or sit in the company of the scornful.'* How many times I repeated it, I do not know. It ran in a never-ending circle round my mind.

A splash of salt water suddenly brought me round. A sail, moving closer toward me. I raised a hand into the air, but I could not speak. My throat was swollen and dry.

I heard someone shout. 'Hey, there's someone in the water.'

Oars emerged. I saw a rope curling above me like a snake, then slapped on the water in front of me. I gripped it with all my strength. They pulled me through the waves, brine flooded my nostrils. I turned on my back, holding the rope behind my neck. Then I felt hands reach down and pull me up. I lay on a hard deck, gasping. Fish slapped beneath me in the hold. Lots of faces crowded around. Someone threw a blanket over me, sat me up, and gave me some water. My lips were so dry I could hardly open my mouth and most of it dribbled down my chest. I vomited a bitter yellow phlegm mixed with seawater, but felt better after that.

Someone knelt down next to me and pushed the others away. 'Give him space. He's just a kid. Where are you from?'

'Just north of Oplontis,' I spluttered.

'Well, it's your lucky day. We are heading back to drop our fish there. What were you doing in the water?'

I hesitated for a moment. Looking back until that time, I had always seen myself as honest. Simon thought that truth was the most important thing. But if I had listened to Simon, I would be in Tiberius's bath. After Octavia's betrayal, my world had changed. The truth was dangerous. Only a fool would think otherwise. My life of lies began, half drowned, on the deck of that boat. I hoped Simon would forgive me. I had overheard a story on one of my trips to Oplontis, so I knew it contained a grain of truth.

'I was gathering shellfish on the rocks, a big wave washed me in.'

'Just you, no one else?'

'I was on my own.'

'Wearing your best clothes, it seems. Well, the currents have taken you a long way. How long have you been in the water?'

'Since this morning.'

'Well, you're safe now, a lucky day, one you won't forget in a hurry. We're only coming back because we've caught all we can carry. Cheer up, lad. Neptune has smiled on you.'

I had cheated Poseidon or Neptune, or perhaps both of them. They gave me more water and a crust of bread dipped in oil, which I ate. The boat rocked gently, and the wind filled the taught sails. I must have fallen asleep because one of the sailors was shaking me. The boat had stopped moving, and the sail was furled. They were tying up on the dock.

'We are back in Oplontis. Time to find your family. Where did you say they lived?'

'Just north of here on an estate on the edge of the mountain.'

'We've got someone going that way with fresh fish. We'll put you on their cart. What's your name, anyway?'

'Cadmus.' That was a small enough lie, I hoped.

'Well Cadmus, if they asked who saved you, it was Lucius, the fisherman.' As the cart pulled away, I heard Lucius call out. 'You can keep the blanket.'

I never did discover what happened to Lucius. But I prayed Neptune was also kind to him and he didn't live to regret pulling me out of the sea.

I made an excuse and got off the cart early as it neared the edge of the estate. I wound my way around the olive groves until I got to Simon's cottage. Simon wasn't there. But I took a bag of dried figs, walnuts and a skin of water. I went up to the barn where Aetos was. It was still as I had left it, covered in an old blanket. I was so tired, I wrapped myself up and fell asleep.

I must have slept there all night. In the morning I heard the hurdles shifting. Someone gave a shriek. I glimpsed the stunned face of Valeria, before she disappeared. My tunic was dry, but it smelled of fish and salt water. I got up. I could hear someone else walking slowly up the path.

It was Simon. 'In the name of Zeus, how did you get back here?'

I had never heard him invoke Zeus before. I didn't know what to say.

'We were told not to expect you back for some time.'

'I escaped from the Emperor's villa on Capri.'

Simon looked grave. 'Caccilius is away, but it would not have mattered if he had objected. No one can countermand the will of the Emperor. How did you get away?'

'One of his guards chased me. We fell from the cliff. Some fishermen picked me out of the water.'

'And the Praetorian?'

'I think he drowned.'

'Did anyone see this?'

'I don't know.'

'When I lived on Rhodes, I heard rumours of other young boys taken for Tiberius. Terrible things happened to them. No one dared complain. But the death of one of his personal guard. I do not know what the consequences will be.'

'Can't I hide here?'

'The fisherman will talk. Saving a boy in the water is a story that will reach the ears of the authorities.'

'Valeria has seen me.'

'Then there is even less time. We must get you away.'

'How long do I have?'

Simon looked flustered. 'I don't know, less than an hour perhaps.' He sat down. 'We need horses, but they are all in use. The sirocco has started blowing again. It will be warm for the next few days. We will need food and plenty of water.'

It seemed hopeless to me. An elderly cripple and a boy wouldn't get far on foot. Then it suddenly became clear. If I was going to die, I wanted it to be like Icarus or Bleydiud.

'You can't come with me Simon, I have to go myself.'

Simon shook his head. 'They will block the roads for miles. Everywhere will crawling with soldiers by tonight.'

I pointed to the craft behind me. 'You are forgetting Aetos.'

For the first time I can remember, Simon didn't have an answer. He didn't even pose another question. Aristotle probably would have accepted his fate. Archimedes, I know what happened to him. At least one of the Zenos would have gone down fighting. The unwashed Diogenes wouldn't have appealed to Tiberius, anyway. But Daedalus had a plan. The risk of dying flying Aetos was better than any option either he or I could think of.

He nodded. 'How far do you think you can get?'

'I've no idea. Past the mountain maybe. The wind is from the south, so as far north as I can go.'

Then Simon closed his eyes. 'Perhaps the gods have given us a reason to defy them.'

⟿⟿⟿ ⟿⟿⟿ ⟿⟿⟿

Simon brought my sandals and a winter cloak. He put a leather bag on my back with food and water. Around my neck hung the thong with my mother's coin. I carried Aetos outside and buckled the harness around my waist and thighs. Simon was really crying now.

'Goodbye Cadmus. Remember, fly like Daedalus, not too high.'

The warm wind was at my back. I could feel it lifting the fabric as I carried it higher up the slope. A nanny goat gave me a curious stare, before resuming grazing. I climbed as high as I dared on the foothill of the mountain. I then glimpsed something on the road, perhaps half a mile below. It was a helmet glinting in the sun. I saw a horse stop, then the rider turn. I had hoped to reach the grassed slope where I had practiced, but now there was no chance of that. Below me was a rough descent, then a sheer drop from a spur. For a few moments, I hesitated. The rider was coming closer. I took a deep breath, gripped the baton, and ran down the slope into the wind. I reached the stone outcrop, my feet fell into nothing and I launched into the air.

At first, I went into a long slow glide down the mountain, straight toward the mounted man. I could see the rider struggling to draw his sword. Then I swept up and over the horse. There was a look of astonishment on a face that disappeared below and behind me. The breeze buffeted Aetos. I had never been this high. The wind rushed past my face as I turned. The wing flexed and creaked, but did not break. The taut linen fluttered at the edges. Simon had built her well. There was a danger I might crash into the side of the mountain. I swung my body away. An obedient Aetos turned. I spiralled upward, circling. The sun flashed in my eyes. My heart was pumping, and I felt dizzy and sick.

When I dared look down, Aetos had climbed a long way. The world below was a patchwork, like standing on the highest place in the world. I could see the estate, the villa, dark fields of olives and the rows of vines. The pond where we swam was tiny. Fields, a forest, a river, a road, and the vast expanse of sea. In the distance lurked Capri.

I saw an eagle flying in front and then alongside me. Eyeing me, curious, like a brother envious of my larger wings. Then it veered away, as if a sign from the gods. The eagle of Jupiter had given me his blessing. I had a feeling of exultation. This is what it must be like to be a god, but which one I did not know. Perhaps all of them at once.

I looked down into the crater at the top of the mountain, green to its edge, then darkness at its core. I swung back and was carried away, eastward, around the edge. Then the wind gathered and pushed me past the mountain. The plain of the Campania stretched below. I was too high to glimpse any movement on the ground. Could Simon ~~could~~ still see me? I must have seemed like a strange bird. To my left lay the shimmering sea and the city of Neapolis. Wisps of cloud were not far above. Then I was within their soft embrace. It seemed like I was in my dream. I cannot remember how long I remained this strange state. Until the gods reminded me that I was flesh and blood. The leather creaked, the wind was no longer warm. I did not melt like Icaurus. I was shivering. My hands ached. I could not feel my toes and my fingers were like ice. Exhilaration turned to fear.

I had escaped, but now I would surely die like Icarus. I had never landed from such a height. All those times I had turned and touched the grass, I had been but a few feet in the air. Was it better than being subject to the horrors on the island of the Emperor? The thought of Tiberius' touch made my skin crawl. I fell below the cloud. Ahead in the distance there was another mountain, standing alone, like Vesuvius, near our home. I was sinking now, too low to fly above it. The ground was closer, coming up fast. Not like the gentle fields and soft grass that I had skimmed. It was uneven, with small trees and rocks. Perhaps it would be quick. I would break my neck like Bleydiud. Then I glimpsed a patch of grass coming up beneath my feet. I lifted the wings like the eagles I had seen. Then I felt my feet touch the ground, but too fast, I was running. My foot struck a stone, and I tripped and tumbled. I heard the spar snap, then nothing.

When I awoke, I was lying on the ground, staring at the sky, through torn, fluttering linen. My left shoulder and leg ached. A gust of wind was slowly dragging me along. I untied the buckle and slipped out of the harness. Aetos slipped away, turned over once, then disappeared.

How long I lay there I wasn't sure, but it must have been ages. I hardly dared move. My tunic was torn. I tried lifting my shoulder. My right hand moved down my leg. As I lifted it up, blood dripped from my fingers. I rolled over on my knees, then slowly stood up. My left leg was sore, but it could take my weight. I was a few steps from a deep ravine, where Aetos had gone. I still had my sandals. My right thigh was bleeding. The leather bag clung resolutely to my back. The thong with the coin still hung around my neck. Not far away, a stream tricked down into the ravine. I hobbled back, following it through the meadow and into a thicket of trees. Further up, it formed a pool. On the other side, a dark-haired woman, in a pale yellow tunic, was filling a skin with water.

She looked up and then jumped in surprise. 'Goodness, where did you come from? Have you fallen from a horse?'

'I am not sure where I am?'

She offered me a drink of water and looked me over. Then she made me bend all my joints. 'Well, no bones broken, some nasty grazes, but you'll live. I am Panya. What's your name?'

'Cadmus.' Only Simon called me that, it that seemed a safe name to use.

'Well, Cadmus, our camp is just up the hill. We have a fire and some food.'

I limped around the pool and followed her back on a track that led upward to an open space and a fire. It was evening now, and the sun was low. Nearby ran an empty road with a mile marker.

'Where are we?' I asked.

'You must have had a nasty knock on the head. We are just short of Teanum. The wind has settled down now, so we decided to camp here.'

'Teanum, that's north of Neapolis, then?'

'We passed Neapolis a few days ago, maybe fifty miles back, a little less.'

Out of the trees came a muscular young man wearing a cap like Simon's and carrying a huge load of dead wood.

'Who's this?' he asked. 'Gathering strays again, Panya?'

'This is Cadmus, he's not a dog, but he's lost. Ariston is from Athens, I'm from Crete. As you can tell, we Cretans have far better manners.'

'Where did you say you're from?' said Ariston

'Near Neapolis.'

'Cadmus is a Greek name?' said Panya.

'My father was an admirer of their philosophy.'

'What are you doing up here?' asked Ariston. 'You look as though you have had a nasty tumble.'

It was no good telling the truth, like my story for the fishermen. Only another lie would suffice. I hoped Simon would forgive me.

'I was travelling to Rome to see family. I had a ride on a cart, but they threw me off when I couldn't pay.'

'They threw you off a moving cart,' said an outraged Panya. 'You must tell an official at the next changing station.'

I shook my head. 'I'm not sure they would believe me.'

Ariston tossed the wood onto a pile. 'Nothing will come of it. Who's going to take the word of a boy? Best to forget and thank the gods you didn't break your neck. Money talks nowadays, no one's interested in justice. It's how big your purse is that matters. Anyway, you are welcome to spend the night here. Panya has made a habit of saving hopeless cases.'

She turned and laughed. 'Well, you're the best example of that. Perhaps I should have left you in Paphos to rot.'

He held up his hands. 'You see, she can't help herself. It's a fine night. We are sleeping outdoors. Lots of firewood in that patch of forest and fresh water from the stream. The inns are all full anyway, or charging outrageous prices to bed down with fleas. There's safety in numbers, but best not to travel too late. Though this road is better patrolled than most, there are still bandits about. This warm wind from the south is a blessing.'

So, I took up their offer, and they kindly shared their food. I washed the dirt out of the graze on my thigh. Panya rubbed some lavender oil on it that stung.

Ariston told me I'd come down near a road called the Via Latina, southeast of Rome.

That warm wind had carried me a long way.

CHAPTER NINE

I had never heard of the Via Latina. At breakfast, Ariston told me it was the oldest road to Rome. A bit slower and less busy than the Via Appia further west. I remember Simon telling me the Via Appia was where they crucified slaves after a rebellion. Ariston was more concerned about the mosquitos in the marsh that the Via Appia ran through.

'As big as your thumb,' he said. 'A wonder I had any blood left, after they finished with me.'

'Too many soldiers there pushing you out of the way,' said Panya.

Ariston nodded. 'Those dispatch riders, they stop for no one. One nearly rode over us near Neapolis. You still have to be careful on the Via Latina, but it's much quieter, with good places to stop along the route.'

'Have you been to Rome before?' asked Panya.

I shook my head.

'The greatest city in the world,' said Ariston. 'Makes everywhere else look like a village. Romans love a spectacle. We can make enough money in a week there to live for months.'

'That's what we do,' said Panya. 'We're acrobats. We met in Cyprus. Ariston had to leave, or he'd get conscripted. We left and went to Crete and then on to Syracuse in Sicily.'

'Syracuse,' I said. 'That's where Archimedes lived.'

'Was he Greek?' asked Ariston.

'Yes, a famous inventor.'

'Never heard of him,' said Ariston.

'Do you see those mile markers?' I said. 'Archimedes invented the machine that measures the distance on the road. Although the Romans built it and put it to use. It proves the Greeks are the cleverest people in the world.'

'I'm starting to like you, Cadmus.' said Ariston.

Panya began to gather her gear. 'We've been working or way north for summer and then south for the winter the last couple of years. This will be our third time in Rome. Acrobats don't need to carry much. Just the ability to bend yourself backward. Shall we show him Ariston? Usually, we only do it for paying customers, but let's treat this as a rehearsal.'

'Sure, but then we must get going.'

Panya ran several steps on the grass, then, after a flurry of forward tumbles, leaped into the air. Ariston caught her feet and lifted her up. She balanced upside down with one hand on his head. Then he turned in a slow graceful circle before she leaped down.

'We have lots of variations, Cadmus, but you get the idea. There's a long tradition in Crete. I've been doing it from the age of three.'

I couldn't remember what I was doing at age three, perhaps following ants or watching spiders, not doing somersaults.

Ariston gathered up his gear. 'Well, if you're going to Rome, you might as well come with us. Your mile marker shows we have a hundred and eleven more to go.'

I started off quite stiff, my left leg still ached, and I was sure I had a huge bruise on my shoulder. The Via Latina might have been a minor road to Rome, but it was bigger and busier than the road to Oplontis. With a deep ditch on either side and a gentle camber to the middle. We passed carts and horses going south. A flock of sheep grazed on a nearby hill. The shepherd didn't look much older than me. Tracks led to estates on either side, past fields of wheat just starting to sprout in the spring sunshine. At one point, we stepped off the road to make room for several soldiers riding south. I kept my head down, but none of them even glanced sideways.

'My younger brother. You remind me of him, Cadmus. Such a gentle soul.'

'Is he in Cyprus?'

Ariston gave me a sharp look.

'It's alright,' said Panya. 'My little brother's dead. About your age when he died. Fell off a cliff and drowned in the sea. My mother's favourite. You are lucky to have a family. You must be looking forward to seeing them?'

'Yes, I am,' I lied.

'When we get to Teanum, we'll do a performance in the forum,' said Ariston. 'You're welcome to watch. What would be really useful is if you could hold out a cap and gather some money.'

I needed to blend in and being discreet. Now I had hooked up with performers who needed the attention of a crowd. I wasn't sure my decision to travel with them was wise. But some strange fate was guiding me. I had got this far. What choice did I really have?

'Of course,' I said. 'Anything to help.'

We walked past orchards and fresh sprouting barley. Birds were singing. I heard the first cuckoo echoing over the valley. Panya must have heard it, too.

'Do you know Zeus disguised himself as a cuckoo Cadmus, to win the heart of Hera?'

Simon had never told me that story, but I knew the cuckoo. The bird whose young pretend to be something they are not. Perhaps that was what I was, receiving kindness from others I did not deserve. We came to a busy junction. Ariston pointed to the road that went west.

'That's the way to Suessa and the Via Appia, but we're keeping on the Latina to Teanum.'

The Via Appia. I kept getting that image in my head. Where they crucified Spartacus and his followers all along the road, nearly a hundred years ago. A reminder of the fate of rebellious slaves.

Teanum was built on the edge of a mountain like Vesuvius. Surrounded by sweet chestnut trees and vineyards. Comfortable and quiet, prosperous, but not too gaudy. As we entered the town, I kept my head down. No one took the slightest notice of me. There was an aqueduct, large baths and a theatre. A temple to Apollo, Simon said Daedalus had built one when he hung up his wings. I strangely felt at home. It reminded me a little of Pompeii. I had left that place behind. In my heart, I knew I would never see it again. You remember things from strange angles. The place you grow up is part of the geometry of your mind. Romans love their straight lines and rectangles. Their towns were full of them. A square forum in the middle, arches formed of semicircles, pediments of triangles. Roads so straight they seemed to go on forever. Simon said even the water that flowed in the aqueducts depended on geometry. But this precision was a reflection of something older. Laws that were indisputable and forever true. It was really Euclid and the Greeks that designed all this. The Romans just worked out ways to build it.

Panya and Ariston set themselves up in an open space at one end of the market. I sat to one side and watched. They did some stretching and waited until a small crowd had gathered. Ariston held Panya upside down. She held his feet and they flipped backward like a wheel over each other's heads. Their tumbling and lifting were flawless and there was lots of applause. I went round with the conical cap and collected the coins.

Ariston looked pleased with me. 'That's more than we got last year. Must be your doe eyes Cadmus.'

I wasn't sure what he meant by that. I'd just held the cap in front of the best dressed spectators and waited for them to respond.

Panya nodded. 'It's good practice for when we get to Rome. They have hired us for Floralia, but we are practicing some new tricks. We can't do all the same ones as last year.'

Panya bought me a new tunic cut in the simpler Greek style. Pale yellow, just like the ones they wore. I dumped the torn one I had worn all the way from Capri. The tunic the matron gave me that fateful morning. It felt good to get rid of it.

'That's an expensive tunic you have just thrown away,' said Panya. 'Even though it's ripped, you could have it repaired.'

'It made me itch,' I said. 'I like this one better.'

I envied their freedom. They travelled where they liked and made a living wherever they found themselves. I might know how to calculate the angle of a triangle or how big the world was, but I would starve if I tried to do what they did. Ariston threw me some coppers from the money I had collected. Every one was a loaf of bread, I thought, as I managed to catch them all.

'Not bad,' said Panya. 'You should try juggling.' She took me to a market stall selling toys for children. Carved wooden horses, toy carts, little wooden swords and spinning tops. She bought some coloured balls filled with dry beans in a bag. It would be wrong to say that Panya taught me to juggle in an afternoon, but after a couple of hours, I could keep three balls aloft.

'It's a useful skill,' she told me. 'Find yourself in a market, whether you speak the language or not, you can buy your lunch in under an hour.'

I wasn't sure why juggling appealed to me so much. When the balls are in the air, you think of nothing else. Your mind is wiped clean and your worries vanish. As Aristarchus claimed, we were all spinning in one great circle around the sun.

We spent the night there in a cheap lodging next to a tavern. A storm arose in the darkness and woke me. Spring rain rattled against the shutters. I lay awake for a while, listening to Ariston's snores. It was the first time I had slept indoors since I had fled from Capri. The week seemed like a year. My life of goats and geometry had come to a sudden stop on the road to Oplontis. The ides of March were as unlucky for me as they were for Caesar. What I would do when we reached Rome? I still had no clue. But I was thankful I was alive and free at the end of each day.

In the morning, Ariston came back with some oil and bread for breakfast. 'Well, we're lucky we started out north when we did.'

'What do you mean?' said Panya.

Ariston tore open the loaf and handed me a chunk. 'I overheard a dispatch rider near the stables. They've blocked the road where the Via Appia meets the Latina south of here. Someone murdered an imperial guard at the Emperor's Villa on Capri. There's a rumour it was an attempt to kill Tiberius himself. It's taking hours to get through. They are checking everyone and every wagon. Only imperial riders get priority.'

I took a deep breath. If I thought Teanum was safe, it was an illusion. Nowhere was. I should have guessed they hadn't given up. An escaped slave from the Emperor's villa, and the death of a Praetorian, that would never be ignored. My pursuers had set their circle too far south, but for how long, I could not be certain. I wondered whether I should strike out on my own. But we looked like a little troupe that had been together for ages. I might even pass as Greek if questioned. Though I wasn't sure what my companions might say if we were challenged? But alone, I would be far more conspicuous. Achilles had disguised himself as a woman to avoid a war. Though he couldn't keep it up and went off to Troy in the end. I felt someone from the netherworld was watching over me, guiding me north to Rome. At least there would be safety in the crowds there. Simon would have approved of my logic.

Even though it turned out to be wrong.

Tusculum was the sort of place I would have avoided, but Ariston was keen to stop there. Like Teanum, they had built it on the edge of a mountain. Surrounded by rich estates and vast villas that made our place near Pompeii look very modest. We took a branch road, marked by well-ordered cypress trees wavering in the wind as we wound up to it.

Tusculum wasn't large, but had old walls, a forum, and a massive temple of Jupiter on a hill. I sensed more military presence than Teanum. Venerable men wearing togas, like I had seen my father wear. With a bearing that they were important people who had to be kept safe. I felt their scrutiny weigh heavily on me.

'This is where wealthy Romans come to escape Rome,' said Ariston. 'Politicians and retired officers, we found last year they can be generous.'

'Are we staying long?' I asked.

'We won't stay the night, just a quick visit,' he replied. 'A good place to earn some extra money before we get to Rome.'

They repeated what they had done in Teanum. Found an open space near the forum. A wealthy crowd soon gathered. They gasped at Ariston's strength and the improbable positions Panya could adopt. As I finished gathering the spectators' money, I came to the edge of the square. A cool breeze crept around my ankles and I looked up. A statue stood above me, hand outstretched. Fresh carven, the plinth triumphantly announced... *Our illustrious Emperor, Tiberius.*

There he was, the man with the power of a god. He had been so close twice, almost to touch me, but whose face I'd never seen. According to Simon, he was an old man now. This must be a younger version of him. Carved in marble, waves of hair cut short. Thin nose and jutting chin. His eyes stared down as if the whole of Tusculum was under their gaze. It seemed that stone figure could reach out and crush me in his grasp. As I brought back the cap, I realised my hand was shaking.

'What's the matter?' asked Panya. 'Are you cold?'

'There's something about this place. I don't like it.'

Ariston laughed. 'Tusculum is the safest town this side of Rome. More security here than anywhere. Never once been worried we might be robbed. Anyway Cadmus, you've done us proud, another good haul.' He ruffled my hair with his huge hands. 'You are our lucky charm.'

I gave a weak smile. That was the first time someone had ever described me as lucky. I hoped it wasn't something he would later regret.

Ariston poured the coins into his purse. 'We are leaving now, anyway. Tusculum may be safe, but it's far too expensive.'

We started back toward the road down to the Via Latina. I noticed a soldier on gate. He was keeping a watchful eye on those moving in and out. I held my breath and kept walking. They were looking for an escaped slave, not a member of an acrobatic troupe. He let Ariston and Panya pass, then I felt a hand on my shoulder.

'You boy, where you from?'

There was a lump in my throat. I couldn't speak.

'Come on lad, I haven't got all day.'

'He's with us,' said Panya. 'We're acrobats from Greece. Been here performing just today. We're just leaving to go to Rome for Floralia.'

Then he stared at me. 'What's your name?'

'Cadmus.' I stuttered.

'Greek, eh?'

I nodded. 'Nai.'

He frowned, then shrugged his shoulders. 'Right, move along.'

Panya waited until we were well clear of Tusculum. 'I didn't know you spoke any Greek, Cadmus.'

'I had a Greek tutor. I can write a bit, but not as good as my Latin.'

'You are full of surprises,' she replied.

Ariston pointed to dark clouds gathering in the north. 'I think we might afford another room tonight.'

Panya nodded. 'I don't fancy bedding down in a puddle.'

They came across a sheltered hamlet away from the busy road. A hostel, with a fire in the hearth and food.

'Why didn't you tell that soldier you were from Neapolis?' asked Panya.

I shook my head. 'Those soldiers frighten me.'

'No matter,' she said. 'Stick with us and you'll be fine.'

The next morning was dry, and we made an early start. Ariston set a quick pace. He wanted to reach Rome before dusk. The road climbed further on past oak and chestnut trees. The scent of warm fennel I remembered from Simon's garden. We passed a vineyard on a rocky slope, then we came over the shoulder of the mountain. On the other side, I got my first glimpse of Rome.

'Well, there it is,' said Panya. 'The greatest city in the world.'

It must have been over twenty miles away, but it still seemed huge. Girded by immense walls, with hills covered in red-tiled roofs. There was a haze of smoke drifting above. I remembered my father had called it a cesspit. If it was, then it was a vast one.

'Come on,' said Ariston. 'We need to get down to the Latina gate on the southern side. If we hurry, we'll make it before it shuts. We have a place to stay inside.'

Once I was among all those people, I might be safe. But like Teanum, the gates were sure to be guarded.

We kept a good pace and made the Latina gate well before dusk. It was busy with crowds moving in and out. Goods were being inspected on the way in and tolls taken. The traffic slowed to a crawl as we got closer.

'Will we have any trouble getting in?' I asked.

Panya shook her head. 'Not now, you look more respectable. Ariston has a letter with the Aedile's seal in case of difficulty. The only people they regularly turn away are beggars. I am sure the Praetorians want Rome purged of them.'

A guard stepped out in front of me. I froze for a second, but he was more interested in the contents of the wagon behind us.

'Come on,' said Panya, tugging at my shoulder. 'Quickly now, or you'll be crushed.'

We entered the street behind, inside the walls of Rome. I had never seen more people in my life. If you took Pompeii and multiplied it by twenty, you wouldn't come close. How they all lived together in one place I couldn't comprehend. And the noise. There was constant shouting, clattering carts and braying mules. No one smiled or took notice of anyone else. A dense mass of people pressed me from behind. They herded me along in a wave through the narrow streets. Feet trampled me from all sides. One man jabbed his elbow into my ribs. Someone glanced me with a sedan pole. A wine cask nearly clashed against my head. Thankfully, Ariston knew where he was going, and his immense bulk pushed through. On one square we passed through, two Praetorians were standing in one corner. The horsehair plume on their helmets gave them away. One glanced at me momentarily, then looked away.

'Is it much further?' I asked.

'Not far now,' replied Panya. 'We have space in a tenement on the eastern side, near the Esquiline hill. Not too far out. But it's on the seventh storey, so cheap. Owned by a merchant from Syracuse, he lets it out to travellers he trusts.'

We traipsed the streets in Ariston's wake until we reached a congested row of apartment buildings. Ariston finally dropping his bag in front of a tavern.

'Well, this is it,' he said. 'Nicer inside than it looks from here. I'll get the key left with the taverner. Panya will get us some food. Not the quietest I grant you. The floor below us is a brothel. At least it was a year ago.'

I had a vague idea what that meant.

'Nice ladies mostly,' said Panya. 'Just stay away from the man who runs it. He's a brute. Wait here, Cadmus. We'll be back in a moment.'

'And leave the whores alone,' said Ariston.

I just stood there, not knowing what to say.

'It's a joke, Cadmus,' he smiled. 'Don't you have a sense of humour?'

A whore, that's what Valeria had called my mother. As I waited, I wondered what had happened to Simon and the others on the estate. I was sure that Praetorian had seen me as I passed over his head.

Ariston came back with a key and a jug of wine. Panya returned with some bread, olives, and cheese. We walked through a passageway, past the tavern, then into an atrium lit by the open sky above. There was a cistern with a pipe from the roof, just like the villa at home. Next to it stood some plants in huge stone pots. The apartments stretched to seven stories. A staircase wound upward on one side. I followed them up the flights of stairs to the top floor, then onto a landing. Ariston handed me the jug of wine and opened the far door.

'Here it is, a bit musty, but the last tenant seems to have left it clean.'

There was no furniture, just a bare floor, some hemp mattresses, and some crockery stacked in one corner. One set of shutters opened onto the street, another set opened inward with the view of a wall. The next apartment block next door was only a few feet away. The window fell into a dark narrow alley.

'Well, not much better than camping, but safer than the street outside,' said Panya.

'There is plenty of space to practice our holds and stay supple,' said Ariston. 'We can practice our lifts downstairs.'

Panya handed me a jug. 'This one looks clean, but rinse it anyway. We'll need some water from the cistern in the courtyard, Cadmus. Be a treasure and bring some up. If it's empty, there's a fountain at the end of the street.'

I took it down to the cistern. There must have been recent rain, as there was plenty of water. I rinsed the jug and poured it onto the roots of the plant. I recognised that scent from the leaves. It was a myrtle, just like the one I had climbed down on Capri. I filled the jug to the brim. As I climbed back up, I could hear shouts from the tavern across the hall.

Ariston mixed it with wine and poured into a shallow bowl. He took a drink and gave it to Panya, who did the same and offered it to me.

'Well thank Zeus, we are back in Rome, safe and sound.'

'Where does your family live?' asked Panya.

I had never been to Rome, so I gave the vaguest answer I could. 'In the northern part of the city.'

'What near the Colline gate?'

'I think so.'

'Nice part of Rome, not too crowded,' said Ariston. 'Your family rich then?'

'I don't know them that well. It's my uncle.'

'Perhaps they'll pay us for getting you here?'

Panya shook her head. 'I am sure they will be grateful just to see him back. We have done a civic duty, we shouldn't expect payment. Beside Cadmus is part of our troupe now, at least while we're here.'

Ariston laughed. 'You're too soft. Anyway, we've got work to do. First thing is to find the Aedile who hired us for the entertainment and let him know we have arrived. I was told in the tavern he was inspecting the bathhouse down the street. I'm overdue a visit there, anyway. Might as well combine business with pleasure. I'll find out when they admit women and let you know. What about you Cadmus, fancy a wash?'

I felt much safer in the apartment than in the crowded street. 'I'll wait until tomorrow.'

'Please yourself,' said Ariston. 'Just a warning. Don't go out after dark. Rome can be a dangerous place, particularly at night. The vigiles are supposed to ensure law and order, but you won't find them around here much. Some are as bad as the thugs who roam the streets.'

It seemed these vigiles had a lot to do. Put out fires, catch lawbreakers and escaped slaves. Which was interesting, because Panya told me some used to be slaves themselves. It was noisy outside. A few drunks were turned out from the tavern quite late. It took me a long time to get to sleep. I lay there, my mind turning over. I was safe for the moment, but how long could I stay? Like the libation that Ariston had offered, I was at the mercy of the gods.

The next morning, I ventured out onto the street with Ariston. There was an endless stream of people coming and going. It would be easy to get lost here. I was just another face in the crowd. No one knew me, at least that's what I thought. I watched them practice some of their act in the atrium downstairs. It was just before Floralia, a festival to ensure fertility and a good harvest. They were not the only entertainers who had come to take part. People threw flowers and petals littered the street. It was a good time to be here in the spring, Panya had told me. Not too warm. The Tiber stank in late summer and many wealthy Romans left for the countryside. My father said he hated Rome. I still wasn't sure whether I liked it or not. It was a world away from our quiet villa on the edge of the mountain. It might be dangerous at night, but during the day if you were careful, it had wonders like nowhere else.

I went with Ariston to a nearby bathhouse. I'd been once with my father to the Stabian baths in Pompeii. It was dark there, and the steam was scorching. I couldn't wait to move into the cooler pool. This one was bright and large. We went inside and paid to put our clothes in a cubicle. The attendant gave me a linen towel and thick wooden sandals because the floor was hot. The walls and ceilings were covered in marble. There were mosaics on the floor. Only simple trees and flowers, not like the ones in Capri.

Half hidden in the steam, I scraped my oiled skin to remove the dirt and grime. Ariston left me to do his stretching. 'It's a good place to keep supple,' he said. I sat on the step half in the water. My leg had healed, there was a faint scar on my thigh. My towel waved in the warm air, like fluttering linen on Aetos before it tumbled into the crevasse.

We finished, and Ariston left me queueing at a shop. He wanted the skewered lamb they wrapped in bread. He gave me enough money to buy a meal for all of us. I was jostled, but managed to hold my own. Ariston wanted two. He said it was the best grilled lamb outside of Athens. I brought them all back to the apartment. It was a long climb back up the stairs. On the floor below ours, a bald, thickset man was arguing with a woman. He turned and scowled at me.

'What are you looking at, boy?'

I turned and hurried up the last flight. When I reached the apartment, Ariston was back.

'What took you?' he asked.

'It's popular, this lamb. I was nearly pushed out of the line, twice.'

Panya took hers. 'So how are you liking Rome so far?'

'Nice to visit, not sure I would want to live here.'

Panya smiled. 'Take my advice. Don't stay too long in Rome or it will steal your soul.'

I wasn't sure how a city could steal someone's soul. Plato said the soul is reincarnated, but your previous life is forgotten. It is only through philosophy, apparently, that you eventually remember.

'Ah, depends where you live,' said Ariston, taking both in one hand. 'Down here in the Esquiline amongst the plebs, it's noisy and crowded, I agree. There's free bread for the poor, there would be riots otherwise. But a nice place on the Viminal Hill, well, that would suit me fine. Panya and I did a performance up there last year for some rich Romans. Afterward we drank Falernian wine and ate stuffed peacock.'

She nodded, as her mouth was full. 'It was in a garden. I remember they had pruned a shrub, so it had grown in the shape of a bull.'

Ariston took another gulp of wine. 'That's what you do when you have too much money in Rome, Cadmus. You pay to have your trees trimmed into any shape you like.'

Panya wiped her hands on a cloth. 'Bulls are sacred on Crete. In ancient times, they used to jump over a bull's horns, but it's far too dangerous. No one would dare do it now.'

'It that where King Minos lived, with the labyrinth and the minotaur?'

'Well, you know your Greek stories, Cadmus,' she said. 'You had a good tutor.'

Ariston nodded. 'Half man, half bull, then slain by Theseus. When I was young, they used to tell it by the fire, so the shadows scared the children.' Ariston had finished his first and started on the second. 'Well, if we are lucky after Floralia, we might get another invitation up there. In the meantime, we must do as the Aedile asks.'

After we'd eaten, we refreshed ourselves with water. Panya pinned flowers in her hair and gave me a garland to wear around my neck. We were given a space near the temple of Flora, on the Aventine hill. Ariston and Panya gave six short performances a day. My juggling was improving. But it was a sideshow, a minor distraction before they started. Any applause was really for them. I watched their graceful lifts and tumbles with awe. It made my little feats seem very tame. But they gave me a little share of what they took. I began to wonder if I might earn enough money to get to Gaul.

In our free time, we went to see the sights. I started to get used to the crowds and the jostling. Even forgot that I was a fugitive. There were spectacles, perhaps beyond what Simon knew. Dancing bears and giant flightless birds, a monkey that could ride a goat. I wasn't sure what Simon would have made of that. We saw a huge grey animal in a square, with a long nose like the tentacle of an octopus. I remembered those huge ears in a mosaic on the dining room's forbidden floor. Panya told me it was an elephant from Africa. They had been used in war. But this beast was peaceful and garlanded in flowers. It stood on its hind legs and sat on a huge stool. Children fed it fruit, which it gathered with its nose.

We passed the temple of Vesta that held the sacred fire. Ariston said if it was ever extinguished, Rome would fall. Simon had told me it kept the statue of Athena, that Odysseus stole from Troy. At the western end of the forum was a bronze milestone glittering in the sun. This was the spot from where all distances were measured. Rome was the centre of the world, a restless Empire that was ever expanding. Eratosthenes said a line that went due west would eventually curve and come around east and join itself. The legions could travel in one vast circle and arrive back again. I wondered how long would it take to cross twenty-five thousand miles of land and sea? The world was far bigger than their Empire. I wasn't sure if it was even as big as Alexander's. Rome controlled just a small part. But only a Greek could tell you that.

There was a theatre constructed in one square. I saw, for the first time in my life, a play. Panya explained that it was written by a Greek slave called Livius, who had come to Rome. I recognised part of Homer's story that Simon told me. The victorious Greeks prepare to return home from Troy. But it did not go well for Odysseus. There was hardship and many deaths. It made me think of my journey to the hill of the white horse. The one I had promised to make. But my mother had also wanted me to be Quintus. A freedman at thirty, a prosperous merchant like my father, dealing in oil and wine. My slave's, I would be sure to educate and release them all. All had been perfect in the little world I had created in my head. Now it would never happen. I was doomed to follow a different path. In time, I would learn everything about my old life was really an elaborate and seductive myth.

On the final day, we finished. I was sitting on the temple steps with Panya. She turned and smiled.

'It has all gone well, Cadmus. Ariston is off to see the Aedile to collect our pay. Tomorrow we will take a trip up to the Colline gate to find your people. They must be worried. How long since you last saw them?'

'Not for quite a while,' I said.

I didn't know it then, but all my lies were about to spectacularly unfold.

CHAPTER TEN

We got back to the apartment. Panya sent me downstairs to the tavern to buy some wine.

'Ariston will be thirsty when he gets back,' she said. 'We all deserve a little celebration.'

I went downstairs to the tavern carrying the coppers. The taverner filled my jug, and I turned around. A figure was standing in front of me. I stopped so suddenly, a little wine splashed to the floor and onto their feet. I looked up. It was Titus. He had a puzzled look on his face, then he raised his finger and grinned.

'Quintus, my clumsy little slave boy. Here you are at the tavern below my favourite brothel.'

I looked away. 'You have the wrong person. My name is Cadmus.'

He leaned down. I could smell his sodden breath. 'I know you, Quintus,' and he pulled back my tunic. 'You still have that little mole on your neck when you knelt before me.' He rubbed my face and hair. 'Didn't know they had sold you. Caecilius got rid of you at last, eh? Strange, I thought aunt Octavia would have told me the good news. How much did they get for you?'

I turned to go. I felt his hand placed a hand on my shoulder, which stopped me.

'Don't ignore me. Octavia got me a job with a Questor. They enforce the law.' He gripped my shoulder harder. 'You are staying here, then?'

'No, in an apartment down the road, with my new master.'

'Ah, so Caecilius saw sense and sold you on. What did you do to displease him?'

'Nothing.'

He grinned. 'I guess Octavia finally convinced him. What's your new master's name?'

'It's none of your business now.'

He grabbed my face with his hand and rocked my head from side to side. I glimpsed people turning, staring. Titus leaned down.

'Don't forget who you are, little Quintus. You may have a new master, but you are still a slave. I could twist your puny neck now and just have to pay your price. Not much more than a week's wager on the chariots. The only thing that stops me is upsetting the other patrons here. I like the wine this place serves, not to mention our lovely ladies upstairs.' He let my face go. 'I'll let you off cleaning my feet on this occasion, but next time be more careful.' Then he staggered away.

I made my way back up to the top apartment. Ariston was out, but Panya immediately knew something was wrong.

'Are you alright Cadmus?'

'I have your wine, but one of the patrons bumped me on the way out. It spilt a little. I'm sorry.'

'A splash of wine is no matter, but you look as if you have seen a ghost.'

'I saw someone I knew, where I used to live.'

'Is that a problem?'

I didn't answer. She knelt down and placed both hands on my shoulders.

'You are in trouble, I can tell. I will do my best to help, but be honest with me.'

I took a deep breath. I had no choice but to come clean. 'I am a fugitive slave trying to get to Gaul. My mother was captured there.'

'You have seen someone who knows you have escaped?'

'It's worse than that.'

'Really? How bad?'

'Worse than you can imagine.'

'If I am going to help you, I need to know.'

'I escaped from Capri, from the Emperor's villa. I was taken there, chosen to accompany him, to his bed.'

Panya took a deep breath. 'Are you the one they are looking for, the one they say murdered a guard?

I gave a silent nod.

'That explains the purple trim on your old tunic.'

'One of his soldiers was chasing me. He fell from the cliff. I didn't murder him. Panya, if they catch me, I will be killed, or worse.'

She stared into space for a moment, as if she wasn't sure what she was going to do. Then she turned and grabbed some bread and cheese, put them in my leather bag and pushed the bundle into my chest.

'If you want to get to Gaul, you have no time to waste. The vigiles may be here soon. Your best chance may be to get to the port at Ostia and find a boat. The city closes its gates at sunset so you don't have long. Go down the stairs. There's an exit out the back of the courtyard into the lane. When you reach the main street, go right, that will take you south to the Triple gate, near where the Tiber flows out. Be careful, there are lots of beggars and pickpockets that collect outside. If you are lucky, you'll get through unnoticed in the crush. On the other side is the road to the port at Ostia, where the river flows into the sea. You will know you are on the right road because you will pass a pyramid tomb. There should be ships there, you might find one to take you. It's a full moon. If you walk briskly all night, you might get there before dawn. If you leave now, you have a chance.'

'What will you tell Ariston?'

'Yes, what will you tell me?' asked Ariston, standing at the door. 'What in Hades is going on? The tavern is full of vigiles, and a Praetorian giving directions. Someone said they are looking for a fugitive slave and are starting a search floor by floor.' I saw him stare at me. 'He sounded a bit like you, Cadmus.'

'It is,' said Panya. 'We are going to help him, Ariston.'

Ariston shook his head. 'It's too late, Panya. They are downstairs. What can you or I do?' Then he pointed at me. 'What exactly has he done, anyway?'

'He's an escaped slave from somewhere near Napoli.'

'Then he'll be locked up and returned to his master. Happens all the time.'

'You should know what prisons are like, Ariston. Remember Paphos?'

'I haven't forgotten. Neither has the Governor there.'

Then you agree, we are both safer if Cadmus isn't found here.'

'But he's been seen with us, all over the city Panya.'

'We will tell them he left to go up to the Colline gate. With any luck, they'll head there first.' She pressed some coins into my palm. 'I have a few denarii. It's not enough for passage, but you might be able to talk yourself on board as crew if they are desperate. If you are caught, we must deny everything, but I hope you make it, Cadmus.' Then she furrowed her brow. 'If that is your name?'

'It is one of them,' I said. 'I'm sorry, you have been kind to me.'

I poured the coins into my bag. Panya stuffed my cloak in and pulled the bag over my shoulders.

Ariston put his ear to the door. 'Hurry, I can hear them coming up the stairs.'

Panya pulled me over to the other side of the apartment. 'Then we'll get him out the window, over the alley. He can get onto the floor below. I doubt they'll look there. Hold my legs as I lower him down.'

I climbed up onto the window, into the shadow of the adjacent apartment.

Panya nodded to me. 'Trust me, Cadmus, and hang on tight.'

I climbed onto the sill and gripped Panya's slim, strong hands. She lowered me down. I could see she was outside most of the window herself. Ariston must have held her ankles. My feet touched a ledge. I could see shutters in front of me. My forehead touched the lintel as I leaned forward. I pushed the shutter with my foot; it opened inward and my legs slipped in.

'Good luck Cadmus,' she whispered and released her hold.

I tumbled down onto a mattress in a dimly lit space. It was an empty bed, surrounded by a curtain. There was a smell I recognised, rosewater. I dragged the fabric to one side and looked out. They had divided the room into cubicles with wooden screens and curtains. I could hear shouting. A large bald man and several half-clad women stood remonstrating with someone at the door.

'We've got no boys here, I tell you. I'm on this door all day. I know everyone who goes in and out. You are disturbing my clientele. I know a senator. He'll hear of this outrage.'

The bald man chased the vigiles out. The women retreated back into their cubicles. One of them must have glimpsed me. She raised one eyebrow as she disappeared behind the wall of fabric. I crept out into the corridor of curtains and made my way silently to the door. The vigiles were escorted down to the bottom floor. I waited until I heard them descend the final flight of stairs and enter the tavern. I could not stay much longer here. So, I crept down behind the brothel keeper as far as the atrium at the bottom. There were more footsteps. I hid behind the cistern and the myrtle growing there.

Someone growled. 'Forget the brothel. Have you searched the top floor?'

Through the leaves I could see a man with a thin face reply.

'Not yet. We need your authority to get access. He won't let us up.'

There was an angry retort. 'Do I have to everything myself? Take your men and search this tavern and the shops outside.'

Then I saw Titus, an official in a toga and a grizzled thickset soldier, enter the courtyard and ascend the stairs. The praetorian had a horsehair helmet, and one of his eyes was scarred white. I waited until the atrium was empty. Then I crawled out into the lonely back alley, toward the crowded street. Lots of people were moving in both directions. I had no idea if any of them were vigiles. In my panic, I couldn't remember what Panya had said. The sun was behind me, so the south must be to the right. I pushed myself into the crowded street and walked as fast as I dared. A couple of times I felt a hand on my shoulder, but it was just impatient people pushing past. I kept glancing behind, then I saw him again. The man with a thin face. As his eyes met mine, he knew I'd seen him. He grimaced and pointed at me, shouting, 'stop that boy'.

The street was so full I could hardly move. I ducked down and dashed around people's legs. I could hear the complaints of people being barged behind me. A stationary cart was parked in front. Hard against the kerb and stacked with roof tiles. I crept under and lay still. The outer rear wheel had a tile behind to prevent it rolling backward on the slope. There was a crush of feet around me. I could hear shouting somewhere in the crowd. 'Let me through. I'm after a fugitive slave.'

Then I felt something grab my ankle from the kerb. I turned to see his face crawling under the cart. I struggled and kicked. Then I heard grinding as the tile behind the wheel dislodged. The cart began to move. His grip on my ankle released, and I leapt back into the street. The cart rolled backwards, and I heard a scream. I didn't turn, I just kept running. I was several blocks away before it felt safe enough to stop at a covered stall. A vendor was packing up his unsold onions.

'Which way to the Triple Gate?'

He didn't look up, but pointed down the road. 'It's over there between the Aventine Hill and the river. You should be able to smell it before you see it boy, it's next to the cattle market.'

It smelled like the goat dung I helped Simon spread on his garden, only worse. Wooden barricades were filled with doomed cattle, tethered together. Beyond, I could see the arches of the triple gate and the walls above. A crowd crawled toward the nearer arch where traffic was leaving.

As I drew close to the gate, the throng thickened again and slowed. Then it stopped. Nothing seemed to be moving. I climbed up a little way on some scaffolding. I noticed there were soldiers on duty, monitoring the traffic coming in and out. Outside, I glimpsed a group of beggars being kept at bay. There was some commotion from in front. I climbed down and pushed my way forward.

I saw one of the soldiers wave his hands to the crowd. 'We are closing the gate early, orders from the Tribune.'

'But there's still nearly an hour of light left?' someone shouted.

'We don't know why,' he replied, 'but its orders, alright.'

His comrade nearer me shook his head. 'If we're not careful, there will be a riot here.'

In the commotion, I was pushed over and fell at one of the soldiers' feet. I looked up, and he was staring at me. Then I remembered something Panya had told me. I held out my empty hand. The soldier grabbed me by the collar.

'You're on the wrong side lad, there's enough beggars in Rome already.'

To my relief, he dragged me to the gate and threw me out. I landed on my hands and knees. Someone tried to pull at my bag. Everything I had in the world was in there. I leaped up and punched someone hard. I got a curse and a kick in return. But I didn't stay to argue. I ran down the cobbled road. The marker said Ostia, and I saw the glint of the setting sun on a marble pyramid. Once I was free of the walls, the traffic thinned. A few empty carts on their lonely trek back to the port. It was beginning to get dark. I had a lump of bread, some cheese and six denarii to my name. As Panya said, it was full moon, and I had to walk all night.

But I couldn't have slept, even if I wanted to.

Ostia was on the northern edge of the Tiber. I could see the masts of ships before I reached the port. I lingered until dawn, then merged into the traffic as the gates opened. A place not unlike Oplontis, well ordered blocks of streets, but there was lots of new construction and the warehouses were larger. One of them was my father's, but I did not know which. It was easy to follow the streets down to the harbour, where half a dozen ships berthed. Further out, a war galley lay anchored. I had little idea which ship was from where, and there wasn't much time. If I tried to get on any ship, I might find myself somewhere like Alexandria, even further away from Gaul than Rome. But even that might be a better option than waiting for the vigiles to catch me here.

At the farther end of the wharf I overheard someone speaking, it sounded like my mother's tongue. I moved closer and crouched behind some boxes. Two slaves were standing by a cart, they had paused for a rest, holding an amphora between them. The smaller man was arguing with the taller one.

'I'm tired and my back is aching. Can't we stop for a rest? These dammed things are heavy and someone's taken the crane. It should have gone on before the boxes, anyway.'

'We can't stop Suadurix. The ship sails soon to catch the tide. This space is promised for the galley out there. If we get this last one on, it's fully loaded and can leave.'

'She's a little low in the water for my liking and Narbo's a long way.'

'That's the captain's problem, not ours. Now lift.'

The pair grunted as they struggled onto the ship. Narbo, I knew that name. It was the city where my mother was taken to in Gaul. Then she'd been bought by slavers and transported to Oplontis. I touched the coin in the thong around my neck. A reminder of the promise I had made. If I could get there, I was part of the way to keeping it. They carried the last amphora on and lowered it down into the hold.

'Right, I'll let the captain know we've finished. You go back to our quarters and get us something to eat.'

The slaves left, and the ship was silent. I lifted myself over the bow and crept on board. They had left the hold unlocked. I lowered myself down. In the dim light I could make out boxes, sacks and rows of amphorae, secured with ropes between the handles. I was adept at crawling into small spaces. There was a crevice between two amphorae and I fell in behind. I pulled my bag and some sackcloth over me.

Then I did what I had done my whole life. I curled up in that small space and went to sleep.

When I woke, the boat was pitching. I could feel the bow shudder as it hit the waves. Then I heard the hatch open and saw sunlight streaming in. Someone was climbing down.

A voice shouted from above. 'Make sure the cargo's stable. I don't want any of that wine rolling around and crushing the delicate stuff.'

'Looks like it's alright, Captain.'

'Make sure you check them all. I've had problems with loads from Ostia before.'

Steps were moving around, coming closer. Then the sack that was covering me was roughly pulled back. A man was staring straight at me. 'Son of Neptune, what are you doing here? Captain, we've got a stowaway, a kid.'

'That's all we need. Bring him up before he damages any of my cargo.'

I was brought before the captain, a man called Talos. He asked me what I was doing on his ship, which was called the Salvia. I told him I was trying to get to Gaul, where my family came from. I think he knew immediately I was an escaped slave, but he said nothing. He didn't even ask my name.

'Can you swim?'

The sea looked rough. I didn't know what the best answer to that question was. I shrugged my shoulders.

He leaned over. 'As we go past the northern coast of Corsis, there's a bay with a long, shallow beach. I don't want any trouble dealing with officials. That's time wasted and delay on a voyage costs money. If you can swim, we'll drop you off in the water. From there, it's a short paddle to shore. Or I can turn you over to the harbour master at the next port. Your choice.'

Corsis, that's where Valeria had come from. That wasn't a good omen. But I couldn't argue. If he handed me to a harbour master, I was as good as back in Capri.

'I can swim,' I said.

'Good, then offer a prayer to Neptune. In the meantime, stay on deck with the sailors so we can keep an eye on you.'

So, I was going to take my chances again in the water. I'd kept myself afloat for hours off Capri, but I had no idea what his idea of a short swim was. I stayed out of the way of the crew. The deck was familiar. She was square-rigged, with rings on the sail, similar to the ships my father had shown me. Well loaded, slow but stable. The billowing sail reminded me of Aetos. Now smashed and lying in a ravine somewhere south of Rome. It all seemed like a dream from long ago. Hard to believe it had really happened at all. Now the wind was carrying me away again. What had happened to Panya and Ariston? I thought of Simon too. I wasn't sure how far I'd have to swim or how cold it would be. But I tried not to think about it and save my strength.

The sun sank to our left. I spent that night on deck under the stars. There was a clear sky, we were making steady progress. We followed the north star that Simon had shown me. I saw the serpent and Apollo's cup. I asked one of the sailors where Corsis was. He told me it was the northernmost of two large islands between Rome and Gaul. It had high mountains, and the people there had accents so thick he could hardly understand them. It was reputed to have the finest honey in the world. I wondered if I'd made the right choice. Even if I made it to shore, getting to Gaul would be difficult. There might be ships from there. I hoped they liked honey in Narbo.

The next day, I woke up to a steady swell. We were progressing in a wide channel. I was told the emerging mountains to the left were on Corsis. Today was the day I was going to swim there. Someone offered me some food, but I pushed it away. I felt sick, with no desire to eat. That time in the water off Capri had made me really fear the sea. The current had taken me then. I'd not really swum anywhere, other than stay afloat. I thought of my stillborn sister, sinking in the water. Perhaps it was fate that Neptune would claim us both.

I felt even sicker. The waves were getting larger and the wind stronger. What started as a sudden squall became a storm. Talos was a hard man. Surely he wasn't going to put me over in this? But would he let me change my mind?

The storm was as big as any I could remember, but far more frightening out on open water. There was lightning and thunder. I heard someone pray to Zeus and another sailor curse Jupiter. The ship was heaving, waves started crashing over the deck. Talos had taken the steering oar and was shouting like a man possessed. The crew were hauling on ropes to trying to furl up the sail. But one of the ropes was jammed somewhere high up on the mast.

The wind screamed, and the ship lurched sideways. The mast began to creak and groan. The sail billowed and flapped, then the Salvia swung sideways in another gust. A crack came from the steering oar. Waves were now pouring freely over the deck. Talos was shouting for someone to free the jam, but his crew were all hanging on for dear life. Another big wave crashed behind me. I was washed across the deck and found myself clinging to the mast. The spray stung my eyes and flooded my nose. I didn't want to be back in the open sea again. That fear gave me a strength I didn't think I had. I hauled myself up to the place I thought the rope was stuck. My hands were shaking. I could barely use my fingers, they felt so cold. I reached out. The rope felt like it was snagged around a twisted toggle. I pulled and tugged, then finally, it released.

The sail furled upward, and the ship righted itself. I slid down that mast like a drowned rat. It was still rough, but the ship felt more stable. I could tell Talos was relieved. A sailor took me to the deckhouse out of the wind, wrapped me up and gave me strong wine. It warmed me, but still tasted of Titus's feet. After the storm had passed, Talos invited me to share his meal of pork and bread. I was ravenous. He watched and waited until I could eat no more.

'Storm hasn't spoiled your appetite. You've sailed before?'

'No, but my father had merchant ships. They showed me how sails work.'

'Your father was a merchant?'

'Yes.'

'Was he married to your mother?'

'No.'

He sighed. 'We've blown well past Corsis. Can't drop you there even if I wanted to.'

I wasn't sure if that was good or bad.

Talos rubbed his chin. 'You've saved a valuable cargo. Wine and garum, not to mention perfume from Egypt. The ladies of Narbo do like to smell sweet. You're a slave, aren't you?'

I nodded.

'I'm not going to ask your name. My father was a freed slave from Istria. I detest the pirates that supply the trade. But there are severe penalties for assisting slaves to escape.'

Talos was silent for a while. It was to be the harbour master in Narbo, I thought. Then he pursed his lips and nodded.

'I'll drop you off at Narbo. Pretend you are part of the crew when we disembark. Then you're on your own. But if anyone asks, you never travelled with us.'

'Of course.'

Talos poured some wine 'The gods have been kind. I'll make an offering to Neptune and Mercury when we arrive. I suggest you do the same.'

I think I had heard that somewhere before. Gods were capricious things. Sometimes, like Apollo and Athena in the Trojan war, they take sides. But perhaps I shouldn't complain if one or two of them appeared to be on mine.

The next few days were uneventful, with a fair breeze and a calm sea. They repaired the steering oar. Talos gave me a sheltered place to sleep, behind the deckhouse and out of the wind. The crew were kind. One of them said he was certain we'd lose the mast in the storm if I hadn't freed the sail.

Talos asked me up into the deckhouse. 'Early summer is the best time for sailing. That storm was unusual this time of year. Some of the crew have asked if you can stay on. They think you're a good omen. But I know that's not possible, is it?'

I shook my head. If the crew knew who was after me, they might change their mind.

'Shame. You might have the makings of a sailor. So, tell me, where are you going?'

'Narbo.'

'Then what?'

'I'm trying to get to Britannia, outside the empire, where my mother's people are.'

Talos sucked in a deep breath. 'That's a long way. Never taken Salvia outside the pillars of Hercules. Not many ships do that trip, it's dangerous out in the open sea. No one knows where the water ends out west. Some say it flows off the edge of the world, into a bottomless abyss.'

I knew that couldn't be true from what Simon had taught me, but I kept quiet.

'Your best bet is to take the road that goes northwest out of Narbo, the Via Aquitania. It goes all the way to the west coast of Gaul, a place called Burdigala, where two big rivers run into the sea. There's a port there. You can get a boat up the coast of Gaul and over the sea to Britannia.'

'How long is the Via Aquitania?'

He shrugged. 'Two hundred miles or more. Like all the roads in the empire, well marked with taverns and places to stay. But Gaul's a colony, so there's lots of military traffic. If you are careful and lucky, you might get to the end in a couple of weeks, maybe more. I'll give you some fresh clothes to help you blend in better.'

The next day I got my first glimpse of the coast of Gaul. Narbo was on a hill next to a river that emptied into a wide lagoon. A small tug rowed out and Talos paid them to pull us in. The dock differed from Oplontis, or what I had seen of Ostia. A series of islands joined by wooden jetties, stretching back to the mainland. They were busy with carts loading and unloading amphorae, boxes, and sacks. Talos gave me some woollen trousers and a fresh tunic. He handed me a leather purse with some silver denarii, patted me on the head then said, 'right, good luck and get lost.'

We had to pass a slave market on one of the islands. Perhaps the place my mother had been taken sixteen years before. There were large cages filled with people. I had seen slaves, but this was different. If you were born into it, you knew nothing else. These were the faces of people recently enslaved. Men with chains around their necks. Despondent women with children clinging to their legs, staring at me with doleful eyes. I tried, but it was hard not to look at them. A few seemed defiant, but most looked resigned. They had a dazed look, as if they didn't quite believe it. There was nothing I could do but walk on.

Narbo had solid walls. I passed through the gates with some of the crew in a cart carrying cargo. The interior looked like Pompeii, or any of the places I'd seen on the way to Rome. It seemed hard to believe I was actually in Gaul. Established Roman houses with tiles and paved streets. A forum, temples, bathhouses. Lots of retired soldiers with dignified limps. I'd glimpsed that type in Tusculum, grizzled men with scars from their service. I avoided any eye contact. The sooner I was out of Narbo, the better.

I spent some money on some bread and cheese from a stall. Now I had to find the gate that led to the Via Aquitania, the road that led northwest. I was unsure of where I was going, other than to reach Burdigala at the end. I followed the traffic around the wall until I got to the northern gate. It felt conspicuous walking alone. Just outside, there was a merchant who had stopped his cart to tie down his load. He supplied wine to taverns along the route. I hitched a ride out of Narbo with him and agreed to stay on the back to ensure the amphorae didn't come loose. There was a fort outside. We passed cavalry with oval shields, practicing manoeuvres on a field.

'What legion is that?' I asked.

'Local lads, auxiliaries attached to the Tenth,' he replied. 'They keep the road secure from bandits. I'm grateful for them. Rumour is there's trouble again on the Rhine. Just hope they don't get sent somewhere else.'

'How far to Burdigala?'

'I only go as far as Torlosa. That's a hundred miles. Burdigala is a hundred and fifty beyond that.'

Two hundred and fifty Roman miles. Then a ship to somewhere outside the empire and I would be free. That didn't sound impossible. At least that's what I thought then. But it would be far harder than Talos had led me to believe.

It would make a swim to Corsis look easy.

CHAPTER ELEVEN

I was learning the truth was overrated. There was nothing better than a good lie. One that was modest enough to be accepted without question. Like a myth, with a grain of truth that made it plausible. The merchant asked me what I was doing in Narbo. I told him I had been on a trading trip with my uncle from Burdigala, but he had become ill in Narbo. I was returning along the Via Aquitania to my mother.

At first, everything was going well. It was warm. We passed the first toll without question. The first mansio with a changing station was about a day out of Narbo. We had gone about twenty miles. I could have probably walked faster, but this seemed safer. After the amphorae were unloaded, he paid for my assistance with a meal. He started to ask questions about my uncle. His name, where we lived in Burdigala, what sort of trade he was in. I gave a few vague answers, but it was clear. Another day in his company and my story would unravel. A settlement had grown up nearby. He was staying in accommodation I couldn't afford. Probably filled with Roman officials asking more awkward questions, anyway.

I spent the night in the stable with the horse and early the next day I made off on my own. There were various groups on foot, doing short distances between places up and down the road. I lagged a little way behind them, like a petulant child. Far away not to be bothered by them but close enough to be taken for one of their party.

The following day, I met a boy called Berduc herding sheep on the north side of the road. Two years older than me, but I was nearly as tall. He was taking them to the next settlement. They were proving difficult to shift from patches of fresh grass, and some were wandering too close to the ditch. He needed to keep them on the north side of the road, before a horse or cart hit one of them.

'Your accent's strange,' he said. 'Where are you from?

'My people are the Atrebates in the north.'

'I've never met anyone from there,' he said.

I offered to help him and found myself a stick. Sheep were easier to herd than goats. Keep the lead ewe moving and the rest would follow. Progress was slow, but I could move unnoticed and keep an eye on traffic on the road. At the end of the day, we reached a settlement. We herded the sheep into woven pens. Berduc shared his food with me. He was walking back to his village tomorrow.

'I'm going to the end, to Burdigala.'

He shook his head. 'Never been that far. I've been to Torlosa, that's the next big town along here. Next to a river, the Garumna, that comes up from the south. It flows all the way to Burdigala, but winds a lot more than the road. Be careful in Torlosa, my uncle was robbed there.'

I thought if I had survived in Rome and negotiated Narbo, Torlosa shouldn't be too difficult. The next day, I set off again. Keeping up the pattern of blending into the traffic. I wasn't attracting the gaze of passing cavalrymen. It seemed my chances of getting to Burdigala were good. Most nights, I would find myself a hidden spot to sleep, away from the noisy geese that patrolled the settlements. The weather was fine, and the nights were warm. I juggled my bags of beans to earn a few coppers, enough to buy some bread. But I needed to save some money for the boat in Burdigala. I couldn't risk stowing away again. A good two hundred and fifty Roman miles. If I kept to twenty a day, it would take me two weeks, just as Talos had advised. I told myself the worst was over.

How wrong could I be?

I reached Torlosa after six days. I reckoned that was a third of the way to Burdigala. It was a Roman town, no doubt of that. On the Garumna, a river running north west. Both the road and river ended in Burdigala, but like all Roman roads, it took the more direct route. Torlosa had an imposing wall with gates, similar to Narbo. Sleeping out had left me weather stained and dirty. It had turned hot, so I washed my face and hands in the water upstream of town. I was running low on food. I debated for a while whether I should skirt Torlosa. But I wasn't sure of the distance to the next settlement. So far, no one had challenged me. It was a chance to earn a bit more money. One of the leather straps on my sandals had snapped. They were never meant for hard travel. I needed new ones. So, I slipped inside, following a swineherd bringing pigs to market. I had a nagging doubt just before I went through the gate. But there was a cart pushing behind me. To turn around would have drawn attention, so I kept going.

Most of the buildings were built of brick. A bathhouse which I probably needed, but kept away from. There was a forum with food stalls. A noisy cock fight was taking place at the far end. There were cheers and groans as money changed hands. My juggling earned me enough to eat for a couple more days. I bought myself some replacement sandals. They were expensive, with thick riveted soles and straps made of goat leather. Strong, like the ones we had used on Aetos. I was standing there, thinking back to that time on the mountain, when a woman approached me. She dropped some coppers into my hand.

'I was watching you. Nice little flourish at the end into your bag.'

'That's kind,' I said. 'I need more practice.'

She turned and pointed down the street to a large, imposing building. 'There's a wedding just on the other side of the temple to Minerva. I've come to ask if you would juggle for the guests. Just a short performance, a few minutes. They'll pay three times what you've taken here.'

I would have enough money to pay for the food to get me to Burdigala. A short performance, then I could leave. An offer too good to refuse. Minerva was the goddess of wisdom. It's a pity she didn't impart any to me, or I would have realised something wasn't quite right.

As I walked past the temple, a few thin dogs lay panting in the shade. I turned into the street. Someone hiding in a doorway grabbed me from behind. Then my legs were taken from under me. I didn't stand a chance. They pushed me down to the ground and held me there. I struggled, but it was no good. They were too strong and there were three of them.

I heard a rough voice hiss in my ear. 'If you fight like a little boar, we will truss you up like one.'

They tied my hands and feet together so I could hardly move. Then lifted and tossed me into a cart onto a thin bed of straw. Then there was a lot of backslapping and congratulating. The rough voice I couldn't quite place. One had an accent from Gaul. The other sounded more familiar. They pushed the cart a little way until we entered a courtyard with trees. Then a figure leaned over the side. A thick set man with huge hands and one white eye. He seemed particularly pleased with himself. Around his neck swung the emblem of the scorpion. A Praetorian, like the ones I'd seen on Capri. Not as tall as some, but very strong. Then I realised where I had seen him. Ascending the stairs in the apartment in Rome.

He gave a sneer. 'Ah little Quintus, we meet at last.'

'My name is Caden,' I said with my best impression of faltering Latin. 'Let me go, I'm a swineherd from a village east of here.'

'Sure you are and I'm the Emperor Tiberius, well his envoy Praetorian Cato, anyway.' He had a very unpleasant laugh. Another face appeared beside him, square jawed, wearing the same helmet I had seen the cavalry wear outside Narbo.

'This is my comrade, Acco, and someone else, an old friend of yours.'

A familiar face appeared. Bare headed with his tufted beard. It was Titus. His smile reminded me of his aunt Octavia. That day we had waited for the Emperor on the road. A triumphant smile, a glee at my despair.

'Well, well, well, if it's not the cursed little Quintus. You don't seem pleased to see me?' he mocked. 'You've travelled a long way from when we last met in that tavern. Even further from my aunt's estate.'

'Are you sure?' said Acco. 'He smells more like a swineherd. Shall we can beat the truth out of him?'

I felt Titus jerk back my collar. 'Look, he has a little mole on the back of his neck. When he was kneeling down, cleaning up the mess he'd made. I would contemplate taking off his head with my gladius at that very spot.'

I was silent for a moment. Titus knew me. I couldn't maintain the pretence much longer. Perhaps it would be best to cooperate before they really hurt me.

'My regards to aunt Octavia.'

Titus snorted. 'I'm sure she'll be happy about your recapture. You've been a bad boy, I hear. Caused lots of trouble for all of us and made the Emperor very angry. Now he'll be appeased and our lives can return to normal.'

A normal life for Titus, Octavia, and everyone else, but not for me. I watched them hitch the rough cart to Acco's horse. They must have bought it in Torlosa once they'd seen me. It still had feathers in the straw from its last load of chickens. They left the city via the eastern gate I'd walked through that morning. We started back down the Via Aquitania the way I had come. I lay in that creaking cart and kicked myself. Berduc had warned me, if only I had avoided Torlosa. All my efforts were now undone. The road was rough, and I did my best to tuck myself into a corner on the straw, to stop my head rattling. Trussed up, I had nothing to do but think and listen to scraps of their conversation. Acco spoke like a local Gaul. I presumed Titus had come over with Cato to identify me. Of course, he was more than willing to come. They were talking about a reward, I couldn't quite hear. Cato was describing a villa somewhere. Titus was whispering and chuckling. Then I heard Cato reply, 'put it away, keep it as a surprise. Wait 'till we're on the boat'.

The first night we made camp close to a tavern, just off the road. It was warm and windless. They lifted me out of the cart but left me tied. Acco took my purse, Titus tethered the horses. Cato amused himself by throwing his pugio into a nearby tree. He held the short knife at the point. The blade quivered in the trunk each time he threw it. I remembered Simon had told me it was the weapon that killed Caesar. Plunged into him by his assailants on the Ides of March. Sixty years before I was born, on that ill-fated day. Seventy-two from when Tiberius saw me on the road to Oplontis and my world ended.

Acco returned with some food and wine to celebrate my capture. The Gaul tossed my purse to Cato and the remaining coins jangled in his fist.

'Thank you, Quintus, for our feast,' Cato teased. 'Seems you had enough money for all this, with some left over.'

Acco raised his cup. 'Yes, very generous. Cheers.'

'He probably stole it anyway,' said Titus. 'My aunt told me he was a thief, just like his mother.'

I was not allowed to have my hands untied to eat. They fed me mouthfuls of my food, still tied up. Acco brought me back from relieving myself in some bushes and allowed me to sit up next to the fire.

'I never thought I would be wiping a slave's arse, but I'm not untying you, boy, not from the stories I've heard.'

'What stories?' I asked.

'Seems you killed one of the Emperor's guards, then jumped into the sea.'

Titus nodded. 'This little scum was nothing but trouble on my aunt's estate. But killing a Praetorian, that's a surprise, even for you, Quintus.'

I am not sure who claimed I was a troublemaker, but I guessed Valeria told tales about me.

'It gets better,' said Cato. 'They thought you'd drowned. Then someone heard you were picked up by fishermen and dropped at Oplontis. Tiberius sent a Praetorian to your estate, the same one who brought you over to the island. He told the Emperor you flew off like a bird. He kept insisting he had seen it with his own eyes. Tiberius ordered his tongue cut out and Sejanus threw him out of the service. He's probably begging on the streets now, the fool.'

'So, did you fly like a bird?' asked Acco, making flapping movements with his hands. 'Shall I check him for wings?'

'Of course not,' said Titus. 'He's a born liar.'

'Why would a Praetorian make up a story like that?' said Acco.

Titus spat. 'I don't know. Perhaps he went mad?'

Cato took another gulp of his wine. 'I heard a story once about a Tribune whose wife tried to poison him. She put henbane in his wine. Didn't die, but it sounded nasty. He thought he was a bird flying in the sky. Now perhaps someone on your estate, Titus, poisoned that guard.'

Titus sat back, affronted. 'Everyone was loyal on my aunt's place he insisted. Never had any problems there.' Then he pointed at me. 'Apart from this one. The only person who might have done that was his bitch mother, and she's long dead. Or perhaps that old Greek. What was his name, Quintus?'

'Simon.'

'My uncle kept a decrepit old Greek in the cottage at the back of the estate. You used to spend a lot of time with him, eh, Quintus?'

'He was my tutor.'

'You were a slave. You didn't need a tutor,' snapped Titus.

'Simon used to be a slave himself.'

Titus scowled. 'You think you're so clever, because you can spout a bit of Greek and some worthless philosophy. But you've forgotten my Roman lessons. Aunt Octavia was smarter than you, wasn't she?'

I bit my lip. Octavia's unexpected birthday present was like the snake she released from the basket. I was unsuspecting then. Such things were beyond my grasp. I was wiser now.

Cato drained his cup. 'Either way, Tiberius wasn't happy. Dangerous thing, slaves making a fool of emperors, killing bodyguards. It can't be tolerated. Who knows where it will lead? A threat to the social order.'

Just as Simon had warned me. Slaves had to do as they were told. I took a deep breath.

'What will you do with me?'

'Ah,' smiled Cato. 'We were told not to draw too much attention to our task. What happened is too embarrassing to be made public. These lads are sworn to secrecy. I have the authority to do whatever is necessary. Roman soldiers take an oath to faithfully execute all that the Emperor commands. There are a special cohort of us, the speculatores in the Praetorian guard. We have additional responsibilities. We keep our ears to the ground, sort out problems, eliminate troublemakers and get the Emperor whatever he needs. I'm told he likes boys, young, before they begin to develop into men. Thin and muscular, like you. My boss, Sejanus, has given me signed orders. He's now the most powerful man in Rome. It appears Tiberius wants you back alive. They were his explicit instructions. Alive and unblemished. A good number of the speculatores are out looking for you. I dare say half the imperial riders are carrying letters with orders to assist them. Tiberius sent a message to expect us to governors in every province.'

Titus rubbed his hands. 'There's serious money for whomever captures you.'

'Not to mention early release from military service and a political position if you want one,' said Cato. 'Acco here will get full citizenship and a promotion. When we get to Narbo, I'll file a report for immediate dispatch, so the Emperor will know you're coming. Don't worry. He'll keep your bed warm, Quintus.'

'Cato's the best slave catcher in Rome,' said Titus. 'No one has ever escaped from you, have they?'

Cato was enjoying this sickening adulation. The old soldier leaned over and put his finger to his nose. 'Well, I've got out of some tricky situations in my time. I might have only one eye now, but I still see better than most with two. I know the best places to hide and how to escape, because I've had to do it myself. Only a handful of the Seventeenth got out of Germania alive. I swore to Mars that if he let me live, I'd worship at his temple on the Capitoline hill. I'd be his avenger to seek out those who defy Rome. Did as I promised and joined the guard. In time, I commanded the vigiles. I know every back street and brothel in the city. We knew you got to Rome, Quintus. Titus saw you there, juggling with some acrobats. Followed you back to the tavern near where you were staying. Then he heard you were wanted and did his duty. Reported you to the questor for the reward. They thought you'd got out the Colline gate and gone north. But soldiers searching all the roads there, they found nothing.'

The thought that Titus had been rewarded was depressing, but I bit my lip. Cato was telling me lots of very useful stuff, confirming some things I had guessed, but there was a lot I didn't know. I'd been very foolish thinking my escape was a trifle, that would be forgotten.

Cato leaned over. 'Those acrobats, were they friends of yours?'

I felt sick. 'They knew nothing about me, apart from letting me join their act.'

'Yeah.' said Cato. 'That's what she said. I interrogated the woman myself. It's amazing how long she could hang upside down.'

My stomach felt like a stone. Poor Panya had risked everything to help me. She and Ariston had saved my life. Without them I'd have been nabbed on the Via Latina. Like Lucius, who'd plucked me from the ocean. I hoped he hadn't suffered a similar fate.

'They didn't know anything. I ran off once Titus spotted me.'

Cato nodded. 'They both maintained that at the hearing. I wasn't sure I quite believed it. In the end the Aedile vouched for them, said he'd employed the pair and the Magistrate let them go. We'd wasted too much time on them, anyway. One of my best vigiles was found down near the Aventine hill. He'd been crushed by a cart. Dead when we found him. His leg had been nearly severed, and he bled out in the street. Not sure what he was doing there. Then I thought, perhaps he was chasing you, Quintus?'

Cato took another swig of his wine. 'Titus here told me he thought your mother came from Gaul. I had a hunch you might try to get back here. The Aventine hill is on the way to the southern gates of the city. The Latina gate, the way your friends said you all came in, that was one option. But I guessed you slipped out the other gate, to Ostia, before they were ordered shut. You took a ship, didn't you?'

I didn't answer. I didn't want them to know I had been on the Salvia. It was like I had the plague, anyone who met me was in danger.

'But you didn't pay for it,' said Cato. 'There were no records of anyone like you booking a passage. My guess is you stowed away. A vessel had recently left for Narbo. I know this part of the empire. Used to be stationed here years ago.'

I stayed silent. I had to admit Cato had guessed well.

'Your old friend Titus agreed to come with me. Just like his father, a loyal Roman to the core.' Cato rubbed my old adversaries' hair. 'You'll get your commission in the equites now, Titus. After that, who knows? Easier than the slog to centurion. It's the shortest and smartest way to a safe command.'

So that was what Titus was after. I'd seen him in the saddle a few times. I didn't think he had the makings of a cavalryman. My guess was he'd spent more time betting on horses, than riding them.

Cato was on a roll. He couldn't stop telling me how clever he'd been. He took another swig and wiped his mouth on the back of his hand.

'First night in Narbo, some sailor told us a story he'd heard about a kid who had stowed away from Ostia. Pity he was too drunk to remember the boat. It had probably left port by that time, anyway. Where you went after Narbo, I wasn't sure. Gaul's a big place. I had your friend Titus and another speculatores, Gamo, a big Batavian with me. We went to the Governor and showed him our orders. He gave us three men from the local legion with horses, money and supplies. I reasoned you would want to get to western Gaul, further from Rome. Titus and Acco here, we took the Via Aquitania west. Gamo took the other two and went south, down the Via Domitia toward Portus Veneris.'

I kept quiet, but it wasn't far from the advice Talos had given me.

'At changing stations, taverns we asked a lot of questions about a lad travelling alone. People tend to tell Praetorians the truth and we reward those with good information. Then we heard about this kid who juggled balls for a few coins or food.'

Titus poked me. 'You got a bit cocky, Quintus, thinking once you were in Gaul, you'd escaped. That juggling trick, it marks you out, makes you memorable.'

That skill that Panya had taught me kept me fed, but I had overused it. I couldn't feel my hands. The bonds were so tight. I doubted they would ever juggle again.

Cato leaned back. 'Rome controls nearly everywhere now. I have to admit, you are a sly little wretch. You got much further than anyone thought. Almost to the edge of the Empire, but not quite, eh? You didn't reckon on old Cato tracking you down. I've been around a bit too long to be outwitted by a boy.'

'A barbarian,' added Titus. 'A traitor like Armenius.'

Cato grimaced at the mention of that name. Then he took a deep breath and sighed. 'I remember it too well. It was my first year, a munifex, the lowest of the low. As we marched through that forest, I had a bad feeling. There's a just a few of us left. We went to Hades and back. I crawled for three days through the trees. Titus' father here served with me. He wasn't so lucky. I lost a lot of good comrades in that foetid swamp. I hate forests now. Chop them all down, I say. The open plain and dry dirt is all I want under my feet.'

'But it was avenged by Germanicus,' said Titus. 'He slaughtered the barbarians and regained the eagles. Then came back in triumph to Rome. That's what my aunt told me.'

Acco shook his head. 'I was in the Fifth then. I saw that place in the forest, it was littered with bones until we buried them. There's another rebellion brewing on the Rhine. I've orders to report as soon as we're back. My legion might be moving again.'

Cato spat and rubbed his clouded eye. 'Tiberius sorted that filth out last time. Now he's Emperor, we'll do it again. Pity Germanicus is dead, he was the best general I ever served.' Cato turned back to me. 'As for you, boy, you're as slippery as an eel. I'm taking no chances. You'll be tied like this for the whole trip in the cart. Your comfort is of no concern, so get used to it. If you start to get noisy, we'll stuff and gag your mouth. When we get to Narbo, I'll have a slave ring put round your neck, and a cage made to ensure you stay on the boat. I'm not going for a dip in the sea and I certainly don't want to disappoint our Emperor. I've an idea to sail back directly to Capri. We'll get you there, well before the autumn storms start.' He grabbed me by the cheeks and shook my head. 'Just be thankful I can't brand your pretty face.'

I briefly closed my eyes and saw those white cliffs shining in the sun. I felt as desperate as the day I fell and floated for hours in the ocean. Perhaps it would have been better to drown then, rather than hear all this. Then Cato turned the knife. His hideous eye flickered as he smiled.

'I don't know what our Tiberius has got planned, but he has a reputation for cruelty. When you meet him again, I wouldn't want to be in your shoes. I think I'd prefer to be a galley-slave, than what he's got in store for you.'

I tried not to let them see how frightened I was. The truth was, I was on my own trip to Hades, with no hope of escape.

'Sorry to have put you all to so much trouble.'

Cato smirked. 'You're a cheeky wretch. But don't worry about me. I'll be enjoying my retirement in Tusculum. Seems you've visited there already, I hear. He stretched back. For a long time I've had my eye on a villa nearby. I always fancied it. Now I've heard it's up for sale. Lovely views and lots of land. It's not cheap, but once you are back on Capri, it's mine.'

I thought back to my brief time in Tusculum. Where the guard on the gate had questioned me as we left. Not too far from Rome, but not too close. There was money there, Ariston had said. Safe city walls and a temple of Jupiter. A statue of Tiberius in the forum. Lots of retired dignitaries and senior soldiers to swap stories. Cato thought he would fit in well. I knew there was a reason I didn't like it.

The old praetorian stretched out with his hands behind his head. 'I've given my whole life for the Empire. These old bones need a rest. This is my last adventure, then I'm done. Time for Cato to put up his feet. The only thing I'll be riding is a pretty slave.'

I closed my eyes again. I didn't want to stare at their grinning faces anymore. My luck had run out. My own careless fault. I'd eat all the henbane in the world before going back to Capri. Or dive overboard rather than meet Tiberius again. Cato had it all planned, taking no chances with his key to a new life. Acco would get citizenship and promotion. Titus would get his commission, everything else would return to normal. I had to escape before they caged me and put me on that boat. But with my hands and feet tied together like a pig for slaughter, I couldn't see how it was possible.

'I can see you need your beauty sleep,' said Cato. 'We have a long way to go tomorrow. Put him back in his chariot, boys.'

Acco and Titus picked me up tossed me back into the empty cart. Cato threw an old horse blanket back over me. I thought for a moment he had some thought for my welfare. Then he laughed. 'We need to keep you nice and warm for the Emperor.'

I didn't sleep well that night. I had strange dreams. Dreams of my dead sister, floating in the ocean, fought over by seagulls. A goat's head emerging from a cloud of steam. A crow with an eye in its blood red beak, following my every move.

Cato shook me roughly in the morning and fed me some bread and water. They hitched Acco's horse to the cart and started down the road. I lay there for a while, contemplating all the things that had gone wrong in my brief life. Poor Quintus was feeling very sorry for himself. The floor was uncomfortable, so I shifted position again. Then I felt something beneath the straw, sharp against my wrist. I touched it again. It was too rigid to be a splinter. It must be a nail in the floor of the cart, but it was protruding less than the width of my thumb. I remembered something that Aristotle said. During our darkest moments, we must focus to see the light.

I wasn't sure if Simon believed in luck, but I was getting one last roll of the dice.

The cart shook and rattled relentlessly on the hard stone. I tried to rest as much as I could. I managed to doze off and when I woke up, the movement had stopped. It was near dusk. I lifted myself up, enough to look out. They must have been in such a hurry to get back to Narbo, they had passed all the inns. Cato had decided to camp outside again. They had pulled over in a dusty spot, near a small hamlet. I glimpsed some trees, just to the north of the hovels that stretched back from the road. It was quiet. Soldiers camped next to a Roman road. No one would bother them.

Titus fed me a few mouthfuls of rancid cheese and watered wine. Then they took me out to relieve myself. Then I was dumped back in the cart with the dirty blanket tossed over me. I had to wait for night and hope they slept soundly. I heard them agree watches. Cato went first. The fire crackled and I saw sparks drifting in the sky. A dog barked. Then the flames died down, and it went quiet.

I waited until it was fully dark. Then I managed to squirm until I felt the nail touch my wrists. The cord they had used was very tough, like the linen we'd used on Aetos. I worked slowly, trying not to make too much noise. It must have been well after midnight when I felt the first big strand finally crack and sever. I heard someone grunt, stand up, and come over. I tucked my hands under my body and feigned sleep. They pulled back the blanket.

'You are doing a lot of wriggling, boy,' growled Cato.

I opened my eyes. 'I must have been dreaming.'

He laughed. 'Of what, you reception on Capri? Don't worry, you'll be back there soon enough.'

I closed my eyes again, and he left. I heard him wake Titus up. Then I waited until I heard his heavy snores. The next cord seemed to take even longer than the last. But then the whole rope loosened and unravelled. Once my hands were free, I started working on the knot they had tied around my feet. My fingers and wrists throbbed. Eventually, I managed to loosen and untie the last bonds. My shoulders and knees felt swollen and strange after being tied together for so long.

I lay there for a little while, listening and deciding what to do. A thin moon was rising in the sky. There was enough light to find my way, but following me might be difficult. I remembered what Aristotle had said. He who overcomes his fears will truly be free. I had the clothes I was wearing. The blanket might be useful, but my feet were bare. My new sandals Cato had removed and tossed somewhere in the cart. I groped around and found one and then the other. I fastened each one slowly on.

I must have made too much noise because I heard someone get up and walk toward the cart. If they saw me, it would be obvious the rope was cut. I took a deep breath, gathered the blanket in one hand, and rolled onto my feet. Then I leaped out of the cart. Panya would have been unimpressed. It tipped over as I jumped. I collided with Titus. My knee struck his head and he shouted. We both fell onto the ground and the cart crashed on top of him.

I landed on all fours, but he gripped my ankle. I grabbed a handful of dust and threw it in his face. He swore, then released my leg. I snatched the blanket and started running like a hunted animal. I wasn't sure where I was going. There was shouting behind me. I just needed to get as far away from their fire and the houses as possible. I was heading along to the edge of the road, back toward Torlosa. That was probably the first place they would look. So, I changed direction, over the ditch and onto the grass, north and away from the road. I ran toward shadows that I thought were trees. I nearly fell over a hurdle fence, but kept going. Suddenly there was more noise behind me, shouting, dogs barking. I ran and jumped over a stream and through a meadow.

I passed between the dim shapes of cattle, lying down in the darkness. The dense trees obscured everything in front, so I skirted the wood. The moon was setting in the west, so I knew I must still be heading north. Once it was daylight, the pursuit would be mounted. I had to get as far as I could before dawn. I was very thirsty now. Cursing myself for not drinking when I had the chance. The moon had set, but there was a faint glimmer of light in the east. Daylight was not far away. There were hills emerging in the distance. On a flat plain they would catch me quickly, but on higher ground I hoped there might be places to hide. I came to a steep valley filled with a thicket of pine trees. I forced my way past the stabbing branches, then waded up a stream. It was getting lighter. I stopped for a few seconds to drink some water, then kept going. It was a slippery and difficult ascent.

Halfway up the ravine, I had gone as far as I could. A large tree blocked my way. There was no way forward and I could not go back. There was no choice but to climb it. It was getting lighter now. When I was as high in the tree as I dared, I stopped. It was about halfway up. I tied knots in the blanket and wedged it in the forks of branches, then huddled inside. They would not follow me up here, so I lay there for a while. I must have dozed off. The sky was getting brighter. Horses were galloping, and a dog barked in the valley below. The sound of horses got fainter until there was only the sound of the breeze.

I spent the whole day in the tree and saw nothing but a strutting pigeon. A cow bellowed after a lost calf, somewhere down in the fields. I was very thirsty in the warm wind. I could hear the trickle of the stream below, but I didn't dare descend. After waiting until twilight, I untied the blanket and climbed down. I splashed the cool water over my face and drank as much as I could. It tasted like nectar in my cupped hands.

I scrambled up over some exposed rock in the last of the light, then crawled to the top of the rise. Once above the skyline, I took care to keep low. I could see the road like a ribbon behind me. In front was the small hamlet and the fields I had run through. I hadn't come very far, less than two miles. There was no sign of horses. I could just make out what looked like the cart, unhitched next to one of the dwellings. A dog barked once and far away.

I turned and started north, at my best guess. It was getting darker. I moved between the cover of trees as far as I could. As night fell, I found myself walking through open fields. I followed the great bear and kept the pole star in front of me. Like the Greeks say, Orion escaping from Scorpius. I must be like the swift Orion and never be in the same sky. I knew I could not let myself be caught again.

Cato would not make the same mistake twice.

At dawn, I came to an isolated house in a valley. Part of a small farm, surrounded by fields planted with barley or wheat. It looked like it had been built as a Gaul's house, angular and wooden. One side was for livestock under thatch, the other had been replaced with roman tiles. There was a trickle of smoke from the chimney. A few cattle grazed in a meadow. I sat there for a while in a thicket, watching. There was no sign of Cato or any of the others.

I was hungry, thirsty, and tired. I had lost count of the days, but it must be somewhere in the middle of May. At least the weather was warm. That was something to be thankful for. I wasn't sure what I should do. I hadn't stolen before, but I was desperate. A young man emerged from the house, took a horse from the stable and rode away. At first, I thought it might be Titus. But it wasn't. He rode too well. I watched him follow a track westward and disappear through the trees.

I went down closer to the edge of a woven fence where a solitary pig was enclosed. The trough was empty. It came over and eyed me. When no food was forthcoming, it grunted and flopped back down into the mud. There was nothing to eat outside the house. I would have to look in. The shutters on the windows were still closed. I must have stood on the threshold for some time, uncertain what to do, when the shutter opened. I saw a woman. We stared at each other briefly, then she closed it again. My legs wouldn't take me much further, so I sat down with my head in my hands. If Cato was inside, I was done for.

I heard the door open and someone say, 'well, aren't you going to come in?'

Inside there was a fire on the hearth and a cauldron. A loom near the entrance where the light was best and a quern for grinding grain. At the far end was a raised platform for sleeping, covered in pelts and blankets. She could see I was starving, so she brought me some food. Bread and some stew. I ate it all. I tried to maintain my manners, but I must have looked like a ravenous beast.

'What's your name?'

'Caden,' I said.

'You're covered in scratches and bruises. You look like you have fallen out of a tree.'

The truth is that wasn't the only thing I was covered in. I was crawling with lice. I wasn't sure whether it was the blanket that Cato had given me or whether I picked them up somewhere on my journey. Enora was her name, and she took pity on me. She shaved my scalp with a sharp knife and threw my infested locks in the fire. She boiled my tunic with soap along with the trousers and the blanket, then dried them by the fire. Only the tough sandals I had were still serviceable.

'What's that thong around your neck? Is it an amulet?'

'It has my mother's coin inside.'

'Show me.'

I took it off and gave it to her.

'You're left handed,' she said. 'My husband was the same, but he learned to hold a sword in his right.' She took the coin out and she held it up to the light. 'A horse and an eagle. Not a roman coin. It's Gaulish silver, I think. Quite old, not seen one like this before. What tribe is your mother?'

'Atrebates.'

'I think they are a long way north of here.'

'I am trying to get back to them.'

'Rome controls all Gaul now. Even if you reach them, they will send you back to whoever you escaped from.'

'My mother's tribe is in Britannia. At a place where a horse is carved into the hill. I am trying to get to the coast, get a ship there.'

'Someone after you?'

'Yes, three horsemen. They caught me in Torlosa. I escaped on the way back to Narbo.'

She took a deep breath. 'Where's your master, Narbo?'

'No, I come from an estate south of Rome. My father's Roman, my mother's dead.'

'So how did you get here?'

'By ship, from the port of Ostia outside Rome.'

'These people are sent to bring you back?'

'There is a Praetorian called Cato, who leads them.'

Her face fell. 'A Praetorian?'

Then the story or a version of it came out; being taken to Capri, the fall off the cliff, the rescue by fishermen and stowing away. Most of it, except Aetos. She was silent for a while after I finished.

'My son's due back the day after tomorrow. He's off to buy an ox from a farm west of here. I can give you some food and water, but you are best gone by then. Assisting an escaped slave is severely punished. My son wants to join the legion like his father. He won't want any mark on our reputation.'

She went over to a box on the other side of the room. 'I've got some old clothes here, too small for my son now.' I was dressed back in trousers of wool and my tunic that had dried by the fire. A cap of rabbit fur covered my denuded head.

'If you are caught, tell them you stole this.'

'You are a Gaul then?'

'I am Arverni, well we were. Our last chief was Vercingetorix, who was defeated by Caesar. We are part of the Empire now.'

'Wasn't he captured and taken to Rome?'

'He was. Is that what they want to do with you?'

'They want me back. There's a reward.'

'A lot of trouble to go to for a boy.'

'They have told me I am certain to be punished and then probably executed.'

'You have a long way to go to get to Britannia. The Atrebates do like horses, from what I hear.'

At that moment, I heard urgent galloping outside.

Enora whispered. 'Quick, climb up that ladder into the loft, cover yourself in straw and stay still.'

I did as I was told and squeezed myself hard into a small space behind a rafter at the edge of the eaves. I heard Cato's distinct rough voice call from outside.

'We are soldiers on the Emperor's business. There are no inns for miles, so we need food and rest for the night.'

I heard Enora murmur agreement and open the door. There were footsteps and the noise of baggage deposited on the floor. 'There's hay next door and a trough of water for your horses,' I heard her say.

Cato told Acco to tether their mounts. There was the sound of wooden plates clattering on the table. The hair on my forearms was standing on end. I could hear them all distinctly, as well as when we had sat around the fire.

I heard Cato clear his throat. 'This is Acco and Titus, my colleagues.'

'It's unusual to have a Praetorian visit this part of Gaul,' said Enora.

'We are looking for a fugitive,' said Cato.

'Is he dangerous? Should I be worried?'

'A boy about twelve,' Cato grunted. 'An escaped slave, the personal possession of someone important. He's a sneaky sort who might steal things. Have you had any clothing or equipment gone missing? Food taken, that sort of thing?'

'Not that I have noticed.'

'That blanket by the fire. Where did you get it?' said Acco.

My heart sank. I should have left that lice ridden rag behind.

'It came from Narbo, from a stall in the forum. My son's away, so I thought I would wash it for him.'

'It's army issue,' replied Acco.

'I know. They sell them off from time to time.'

'Mind if we have a look around?' asked Cato.

'Of course,' she replied.

I heard Cato ask Acco to search the adjacent barn. It was dark, but I heard someone climb the ladder. It must have been Titus. He grunted and had a cursory look, then climbed down.

'Nothing up there but straw.'

A door opened and shut and I heard Acco's voice. 'Just livestock. If he was hiding there, he's scarpered'

Cato grunted. 'Where's your husband if I may ask?'

'He's on the Rhine, an optio with the Eighth.'

I heard Cato murmur with approval. 'Augustus, eh, a fine legion, with a great reputation. Was with Caesar in Gaul, I believe. Was serving in Germania myself, before I joined the Guard.'

'Which legion did you serve with?' asked Enora.

Cato hesitated before he replied. 'The Seventeenth. It's gone now. Still a few old survivors like me, in other legions.'

'A traitor,' muttered Titus, 'betrayed them.'

'We were led by a trusting fool,' said Cato. 'But that's all in the past. Let's not get distracted. We are looking for this slave. You haven't had any visitors then?'

'Apart from yourselves, no. But the magistrate might pass by here tomorrow.'

'You know the magistrate?'

'A close friend. He is very kind, making sure I am safe while my husband is away.'

Not sure if I have met him, remind me of his name,' asked Cato.

'Titus Pollianus.'

'I met the Governor, but not him,' Cato replied.

'Of course,' whispered Enora, 'I tell you this to avoid embarrassment. His visit is not an official engagement, you understand.'

''Yes, I understand,' murmured Cato. 'Well, with your leave, madam, my comrades and I will bed down near the hearth. We are used to sleeping rough. We will bid you a good night, and we'll be away first thing in the morning.'

There was a storm overnight. Rain hammered the tiles over my head, but stopped before daybreak. Cato snored all night. I slept fitfully, hardly at all. I heard them gather their gear and leave in the morning. I glimpsed Enora go out and return to dump wood next to the hearth.

'You can come out. They are gone, for now.'

I brushed off the straw. 'You have taken a big risk helping me.'

'I don't know much about the Atrebates, other than I heard they were betrayed. One of their own was working for the Romans. Their rebellion ended in disaster, as all do against the Empire.'

I noticed there was a small shrine in one corner. A bronze figure of Mercury, smaller than the one we had. A larger one of a woman, flanked by two horses.

Enora touched it. 'This is Epona, the horse guardian. One of the gods of Gaul. Like the horse you have on your coin. Seems the Romans have adopted her so the cavalry have her as their patron now. If you are being chased by horsemen, she may not favour you. A prayer to Mercury might be a better bet. You will need to leave as soon as it's safe. Where are you going?'

'I need to get to the northwest coast of Gaul and catch a boat onward to Britannia. I've been told that traders travel there.'

Enora shook her head. 'I've never been up that far. The Romans call that province Gallia Lugdunensis and boats travel there, from Burdigala, up the coast.'

'Burdigala, the town at the end of the Via Aquitania?'

She nodded. 'It is the main road in this part of the world.'

'I can't use the Via Aquitania again, it's not safe. They captured me at Torlosa, but I got away. I have to get to Burdigala in a different way.'

'There are some big rivers that also flow there, but they are miles north. It's a long rough walk across country if you don't take the road.'

'Isn't someone visiting you today?'

She laughed. 'I didn't want them thinking they could take advantage of a woman on her own. They have a reputation these Praetorians, to take what they want. If they thought a magistrate was visiting today, they might think twice.'

'Then your husband isn't in the legions either?'

'No, that part is true. At least it was. Statius was killed a year ago on the frontier. My son wants to join his legion, but I am doing my best to dissuade him. I need him here to work the farm his father bought us.'

It seemed Simon was wrong. The truth wasn't important. It was what people believed was the truth that mattered.

Enora turned and opened a box. 'I'll give you another blanket, a better one, and keep yours. I don't want to have to explain where it's gone if they return.' She brought out a leather bag. 'I've put some food in, enough for a few days. I have a small axe and an old knife I can spare. A bronze handled bowl, a wooden spoon and a skin for water. There's also a flint to start a fire. Do you know how to use a sling?'

'Slaves are not supposed to carry weapons. But as a goatherd I was shown how to use one.'

'Well, it just needs practice. My son had this one when he was younger. Tuck it in your belt, it weighs nothing. It may be a child's weapon, but used properly, it can stun a bear. When you leave, there's a window at the back that's shaded. That will be safer. Further north of here, the ground will climb into the Black Mountains. You need to be doubly careful. There are wolves there and brigands. Though the snow will have melted, it can still be windy and cold. If you go far enough north, you will come to a river called they call the Tarn. Follow it west and it will eventually take you to Burdigala. Slower than the Via Aquitania, but perhaps safer for you.'

The bag was heavy, but I knew in time it would lighten. She tossed me a purse. 'Your Praetorian friend left me something to pay for my hospitality. I don't want his money, you can take it.'

I looked in the bag. It was the same pouch Talos had given me. I weighed it in my hand. Cato had been generous. It was more than they had stolen from me in Torlosa.

I left just before dusk and a good thing, too. I slipped out the back way as she had suggested and hid in a line of coppiced trees. Three distant horsemen were heading west over the fields. There were hoof marks everywhere in the fresh mud. It looked like Cato hadn't quite believed Enora and they must have patrolled the outer fields and forest all day. I stayed there and waited until it was dark and the sky was clear.

Then I followed the polestar all night.

I think it was my second day in the hills. I realised I was being followed. Not by Cato, but by wolves. I would catch them out of the corner of my eye. Slinking just behind the trees. I wasn't sure how many, but they looked hungry and desperate. Linus had told me Rome's founders had been fed by a she wolf. These looked like they wanted to feed on me.

I cut a staff and sharpened one end. The small axe and the knife I kept handy in my belt. I was following a deer track north, further into the hills. There were a lot of smooth stones in the bed of a dry stream. I gathered up about twenty or more, just the right size to fit the sling. At night, I found shelter in a shallow cave and lit a fire at the front for my protection. I was unsure if wolves would attack me during the day. But by night I could take no chance. Even if the smell of smoke might help the horsemen.

Enora had given me some dried fruit, hazelnuts and a sausage of salted pork. I had to be careful with it. There was no telling when I'd find more. The next day, I noticed the wolves were following me again. I loosed a couple of stones, but they kept following at a distance. It was getting late. I was looking for a safe place to spend the night. I thought I'd found a suitable cave until a brown bear wandered out. I made a rapid retreat back to the path and kept going. Then something suddenly bounded ahead of me. A young deer. The wolf pack was howling, chasing it down. Now they were pursuing me. I looked to climb a suitable tree, but none seemed sturdy enough to take my weight. I was running blindly, in panic, with no coherent plan.

Then I fell. The ground gave way, and I slithered down into a pit. The breath was knocked out of me. I narrowly missed a sharpened stake that grazed my cheek. There was growling from the ledge above. I held my knife in one hand and my makeshift spear in the other. A wolf was staring at me from the edge of the pit. I jabbed my stave, and it snarled and circled. Then I saw a spear take the wolf, straight behind his shoulder, and it dropped dead. The rest of the pack yelped and scattered. Someone reached down, grabbed me, and pulled me up. I lay on my front, still holding my knife. There was a man standing over me, tall, dark-haired with a tinge of grey in his beard. His cloak was weather stained, and he wore trousers and boots to his ankles.

'They are gone now. Are you hurt?'

I rolled over. 'I don't think so.'

He knelt down to inspect the wolf. It was motionless, grey and glassy eyed. He pulled out the spear and wiped it on the fur. 'Anyone else with you?'

'No, I'm alone.'

'You fell into my deer trap. Lucky you weren't spitted. What are you doing up here, anyway?'

'I'm on my way to the river Tarn.'

'That's a long way north of here. Is that where your people are?'

'I'm trying to get to Burdigala, then the west coast of Gaul.'

How old are you?'

'Nearly thirteen.'

What's your name?

'Caden'

'You shouldn't be out here, you know. If you are going to Burdigala why didn't you take the Via Aquitania?'

'I did, it's a long story. There are people looking for me there.'

'A fugitive eh, well you're in good company. My name is Alban. We'll take this carcass back to where I can skin it safely. Then you can tell me your tale.'

He gave me the spear to carry and hoisted the dead wolf onto his shoulders. We walked some way up between the trees. It was a long, hard climb. Close to the top there was a trunk of an ancient oak, shattered by a previous storm. It threw out green shoots and behind it there was a cleverly hidden cave. There was a low fire at the entrance and another man sitting there. Younger with lighter hair, but dressed the same. I could tell immediately they were brothers. He jumped up from the fire and pointed at me.

'Who's this?'

'A boy I found. Fell into one of our traps and was surrounded by the pack. Calls himself Caden.'

'We agreed not to bring people here,' he hissed.

Alban heaved the dead beast off his shoulders, onto the ground. 'I can't leave him surrounded by wolves in a pit to die. Anywhere there's a good pelt there. You were grumbling the other day about the cold.' Alban turned to me. 'Please excuse my brother, Yann.'

Yann scowled. 'You've told him our names, showed him where we live and you say I'm the reckless one?'

'Caden's by himself and on his way north. He can spend the night here, then be gone tomorrow. I wasn't going to leave him in a trap, any more than I'd leave my own brother. We haven't seen anyone for weeks. Seems like he has a story to tell. Might be a bit of news about the world outside. Anyway, now we have plenty of meat to share.'

Yann knelt down and felt the fur. 'Wolf meat is tough, needs to be cooked a long time. Not much fat on it either. Venison or pork, that's what we really want.'

'Stop complaining,' said Alban, 'and put it in the pot.'

Yann was right, stewed wolf meat was still tough, but I was hungry and didn't care.

Alban poked the fire with a stick. 'So, what are you doing in the Black Mountains?'

'I'm trying to find my way to my mother's people, the Atrebates.'

'Where are they?'

'She came from Britannia, but there's some in northern Gaul.'

'Then you are an escaped slave,' said Yann.

'Yes.'

'Our tribe was the Averni,' said Alban. 'We had a small farm west of here. Cattle, a few sheep, some grain. The Romans raised the tax again. We couldn't pay, so they plundered our herd, then confiscated the land. We were starving, but they took my wife and son into bondage to pay the tax.'

Yann nodded. 'Those Roman swine stole all we had.'

Alban threw a bone on the fire. 'There's a stone villa where our house once stood and some retired soldier now owns our land. We exist here hunting what game we can, fish, wild boar, a few deer.'

Yann nodded and picked out some of the stringy wolf meat from between his teeth. 'Occasionally we relieve a few Romans of their coin.'

Alban pointed at me. 'My son would be your age now, but I have no idea where he is.'

'They took my mother from Gaul to Campania, south of Rome.'

'What happened to her?' asked Alban.

'She became a domestic slave. In households, they are mostly treated well, as long as they do as they are told. Some of them, if they are lucky, might even be freed. If they can read or write, they can be useful in trade.'

Alban shook his head. 'I've seen the fate of slaves from the Averni. They use them to clear forests further north. Others, I'm told they work in mines or pull the oar on a galley. Their life is even worse.'

'Better to be here in the mountains and hunted like wolves,' said Yann. I saw him staring at my neck. 'What's that in the leather thong?'

'It's a coin of the Atrebates, my mother's tribe. I'm trying to get back to where she was born, the hill of the white horse in Britannia.'

'Show me,' grunted Yann.

I pulled out my precious coin and handed it over. He stared at it and turned it over.

'Not seen one like this. Horse on one side, eagle on the other. Perhaps we should keep it. Payment for the meal.'

Alban shook his head. 'The Romans melt these and mint denarii now. Give it back. It's not worth anything to us.'

Yann hesitated.

'I said give it back.'

Yann tossed it toward me. I caught it and put it back in the leather knot.

'Well, you can sleep here,' Yann grunted, 'so long as you're on your way tomorrow.'

I made my bed in the corner, grateful for a full belly and the warmth of the fire. I kept my coin tucked down where I was sure it was safe.

The next morning Alban roused me. The fire was cold. Yann was standing, staring out of the cave, holding a spear.

'Wake up,' Alban whispered. 'I've just been out on our morning patrol. There are three horsemen further down the valley. They look like Roman soldiers. Luckily, we haven't re-kindled the fire, or they might have seen the smoke.'

'I'm not happy about you leading Romans up here,' growled Yann. 'They could stumble on this place. Maybe he's a ploy sent to find us?'

'Don't be stupid,' muttered Alban. 'He's an escaped slave. He hates the Romans as much as we do. Slip your sandals on Caden. I'll take you down to a spot where we can see them safely.'

The brothers took spears. I followed them down to the edge of a wooded cliff, with views down into the steep valley. I could see three horsemen. They were immediately familiar. Acco, with his long cavalry sword and oval shield, was in front. Then Cato with his horsehair helmet. Bare headed, Titus was lagging behind. A few yards in front of them, a huge black dog with a spiked collar nosed the grass.

'Friends of yours?' said Yann.

'That one in the middle. He's a Praetorian called Cato. The lead rider is Acco, assigned by the Governor.'

'I'd say he's an exploratores, a local scout from the cavalry,' said Alban. 'We need to be careful.'

'A filthy traitor,' whispered Yann.

'They've got a war dog,' murmured Alban.

'Vicious brutes,' said Yann. 'The Romans use them to hunt us. Lucky, they have just one.'

'Who's the third?' whispered Alban. 'He doesn't look like a soldier. He's got a sword, but no armour.'

'That's Titus. He knows me from the estate where I worked.'

'We should kill them,' hissed Yann. 'Solve your problem and ours.'

Alban shook his head. 'Not easy. The dog would warn them before we got close. If any got away, they would have a cohort up here in two days. They don't usually come this far into the mountains. Must be keen to find you?'

'I'll get my bag and leave now.'

'No, watch and wait,' said Alban. 'They won't get horses up here. They will either have to turn around or continue on foot. If that happens, Yann, you may get your wish.'

I saw Acco, then the others, dismount and lead their horses a short way up the track. It became so narrow and steep, they turned back. Acco called the dog, who returned to his feet. I watched with relief as they climbed on and rode off the way they had come.

Alban waited for a while to make sure they were gone. 'Hmm, a praetorian, you said. Sent all the way from Rome to find you?'

'So he told me.'

'Why would they come all the way from Rome for one slave boy?' said Yann. 'Doesn't make sense. You're not likely to lead a rebellion?'

'I escaped from the Emperor's villa.'

'In Rome?' said Yann.

'No. The Emperor doesn't live in Rome. Most of the time, he's on an island off the coast. It's safer for him.'

Alban frowned. 'So how does he rule, then?'

'He writes letters to the people who serve him, just like the rest of the Empire.'

'You seem to know a lot for a kid,' said Yann.

'I had a tutor, a Greek who taught me.'

Yann scowled. 'Sure you're a slave? I'm beginning to think you're a Roman spy after all.'

'Romans educate slaves for trade and other tasks.'

'Is that what you were doing for the Emperor?' asked Alban.

'No, they selected me for a different reason.'

I am not sure how Yann guessed what my purpose was. But he smiled. 'Didn't fancy the Emperor's bed, then?'

'No.'

'So how did you get off the island?' queried Alban.

'I went off a cliff into the water. Some fisherman picked me up, floating in the sea. They took me to the mainland. Managed to get away to Rome and then by boat to Narbo. Got as far as Tolosa, where Cato and his friends caught me. I slipped my bonds and escaped one night, before they got me back to Narbo.'

'Who did you steal the axe and the knife from?' said Yann.

'I was given them, by a Gaul. A woman who helped me after I got away.'

'Next he'll be telling us he killed a Roman,' snorted Yann.

I said nothing, but my silence betrayed me.

'Did you kill a Roman?' asked Alban.

'The Emperor's villa is on a cliff edge. One of the Praetorian guard came after me. In the struggle, we both fell off into the sea. He must have hit his head. I didn't see him come up.'

'Well, you two have got something in common,' said Alban. 'Yann here killed the tax collector.'

Yann scowled. 'He had it coming. That crook was keeping half the money himself.'

Alban stood up and took a deep breath. 'Well, looks like they're gone now and hope they don't come back.'

I followed the brothers back to the cave. Alban leaned his spear on the wall.

'You've been to Rome?' said Alban.

'Only for a few days. It's a vast place filled with more people than you can imagine.'

'It's where all our grain goes,' said Yann. 'There's a granary in Narbo where it's stored before it's shipped out.'

I nodded. 'The Romans get grain from all over the empire, even as far as Egypt.'

'I don't even know where that is,' said Yann.

I wasn't sure how to explain where Egypt was. I just repeated a version of what Simon told me. 'If you took a ship from Narbo and sail as far east as you can, you'd get there. The bread is free for those Romans who can't pay. The city needs grain to keep the peace. If there's not enough, there would be riots.'

Yann scowled. 'Here they put insurrection down by force. If Gauls don't have enough bread, we starve.'

Alban shrugged. 'If you collaborate with the Romans, you might live. Those who resist are persecuted or enslaved. They've taken most of the best land. Many have no option but to join the legions if they wish to eat. I am told they have fearsome weapons. Engines that can fling stones into cities. A giant crossbow that can pin a man to a tree.'

Yann spat. 'I'm not fighting Rome's wars. I'd rather die first.'

Alban turned over the ashes with a stick. 'They're clever, those Romans. From what I can see, they recruit people from one part of the Empire to subdue another. Have to hand it to them. They've got it all worked out.'

'Yeah.' said Yann. 'I understand it perfectly. People in Gaul starve to feed Romans who don't work.'

Alban stood up. 'The safest thing for us is to get this lad out of here, north to the Tarn if that's where he's going. For his sake and ours, the sooner he's on his way, the better. We should leave this place for a while, Yann, just in case.'

Yann yawned. 'I don't fancy a long walk. You can take him if you want to. I'll stay here and keep an eye on the traps. I need to scrape this pelt and dry it out.'

'Are you sure?' Alban frowned. 'This is the longest we've stayed anywhere. We had a close call today. They could be back.'

'Thanks, but I can look after myself, big brother,' grunted Yann. 'If they're after the kid, you're the one that needs to be careful.'

Alban shook his head. 'I can't force you to come, but don't sleep here for the next few nights. Move to one of our other camps and leave me a sign, like we agreed.'

'Please yourself,' replied Yann. 'I'll see you in three weeks. Just remember, we've no salt left. I'll have to eat any venison that I catch myself.'

I was relieved that Yann wasn't coming. I didn't quite trust him. If it has been in his interest, I'd be back as Cato's captive. Whereas Alban, I thought, was different. Aristotle might have said he was a noble man, enduring his misfortune.

But perhaps he should have left me in that pit.

Alban was keen to start as soon as possible and gathered his gear into a bag. He armed himself with a knife, an axe, and a spear. He tied his boots over his ankles. 'You need to be careful with those Roman sandals. There are vipers in the grass.'

'I don't like snakes,' I said.

Alban nodded. 'Then follow my steps and be careful where you put your feet. I once saw a reaper in a field bitten by one. His whole leg swelled up before he died.'

He cut me a staff of birch and cut one end to a crude point. 'Best keep a sharp stick, just in case.'

'How far is it to this river?'

'The Tarn? Never walked it straight through, eight nine days if you can keep up. I've got some friends who move into the hills in the summer. If we are lucky, we'll get shelter and some food from them.'

Alban looked across at Yann, scraping his pelt. 'See you in three weeks, my brother. Spend the night at one of our other camps.'

Yann didn't answer, but raised his hand and waved us away.

Alban set a fast pace. 'I want to put some distance in today. The praetorian, he may be past his prime. But the other one, you said you knew him.'

'Titus?'

'He's no soldier, you can tell. It's the auxiliary I'm worried about, the Gaul. They're used to tracking in rough country for weeks at a time. I've got a few tricks to keep that dog off our scent. But we will need to keep moving and choose paths their horses won't like.'

The Black Mountains were craggy hills, a little like Vesuvius behind our estate, but they seemed to go on forever. Overhead, the clouds rolled over the unforgiving cliffs. There were deep gorges, forested valleys, peat bogs, and steep rocky slopes. The warmer southern sides were covered in brushwood, gorse and chestnut. The northern flanks had darker stands of pine. We crossed fast-running streams and shallow rivers where beavers swam. In places, boulders balanced on one another, like silent acrobats.

Sometimes Alban would deliberately track up a stream. 'Confuses the dog,' he said. 'We enter one place and come out as far upstream as we can.'

Perhaps that's what Heraclitus really meant when he said you never step into the same river twice. Alban was what I imagined Odysseus might have been. Swift-footed, cunning and brave. I learned a lot about which paths to choose, what trees gave suitable cover and how to pass silent and unnoticed in a landscape. He picked woundwort and sorrel, which were good to eat. In one grove, he stripped young linden leaves and handed them to me.

'Keeps the hunger away and good for the stomach,' he said.

They tasted nearly as good as the lettuce I remembered Simon grew. Alban showed me how to spear a trout in a stream. He must have learned every trick there was to stay alive for so long. Just off the path, we found the undergrowth rooted up. Alban knelt down and lifted a clod to his nose.

'Boar, lots of them. Here this morning. If we had time, I'd hunt a few. Might try my luck on the way back to keep Yann quiet.'

Later that day, we climbed higher, following the tracks of a goat. I glimpsed one with curled horns, perched on a cliff.

'Do you hunt those?'

'Not unless we are desperate,' Alban muttered. 'They are more difficult than deer. They'll take you onto a ridge and leave you there.'

I think Simon had given me a similar warning. Never underestimate a goat.

'You were unlucky with those wolves,' he told me. 'They will normally leave an armed man alone. As will a bear, unless it's a mother with cubs. I've never pushed my luck with them. You must keep your wits about you living out here. It's knowledge of the place that keeps you alive.'

Simon had told me about the four types of knowledge. Episteme was the theoretical, like the geometry I drew in the wax. Techne, was the craft to build something as we did with Aetos. Phronesis was the action and judgement learned through experience. Perhaps that was what I learned on my brief flights and now navigating with Alban. But was I acquiring the last and most elusive one, Sophia, wisdom? That I did not know.

We broke free of the trees and I spotted an eagle, soaring, like the ones I'd seen at home. It was the emblem of the Romans. The symbol their legions carried into battle. It seemed to have followed me across the sea, though I knew that couldn't be true. I recalled the newborn kid I saw the eagle take when I was eleven. Like me, it hadn't given up the struggle to be free. Even when I was in Cato's claws, I'd managed to escape.

All that now seemed more like a dream. What had Simon thought when he watched me soar? Maybe he thought like the little tin figure, I was helpless, at the mercy of the wind? Or perhaps that his whole life had led up to that moment. The myth of Daedalus became real before his eyes. We had achieved something that even the great Archimedes did not dare. Simon told me that thought itself moves nothing. There must be a desire to see it realised. Simon had the first and my ignorance supplied the second. If I had really understood the danger, I might not have taken a single step. The notion of death had never occurred to me. I imagined myself immortal, like Apollo. Such is the ignorance of youth. Wisdom then, was still beyond me.

One evening we came to a high valley in the mountains, filled with grass and wildflowers. In the meadow there were tents with shepherds, where Alban was welcomed. They had brought up small flocks to graze on summer pasture and were penning them in for safety overnight. They hadn't seen any Roman troops or horsemen. We sat round the fire and ate the bread and cheese that was offered. Then someone played a flute. A sad tune. Someone said it was about lost lamb, wandering in the wilderness, crying for its mother.

I sat there listening as sparks fled up into the darkness. I doubted the player had ever heard of Pythagoras or that music could be explained by numbers. Yet those shepherds knew it brought harmony to the soul and composed the mind.

We left the shepherds' camp at dawn and kept heading north, toward the Tarn. We now had food that would last a few days. One morning Alban stopped suddenly. At first, I thought he had seen horsemen. He pointed to a snake sunning itself on a stone above the path. I wondered if Euclid had ever seen one. He might have liked the triangles etched along their back.

'They're more common now the weather's warmer,' said Alban. 'Sometimes in spring you see them three of them twisted together. Be wary, I was told it's a warning from the gods.'

I was always wary of snakes. Since that time Octavia had fed my frog to hers. Titus knew I didn't like them. He would hide it under a blanket in his room and uncover it when I least expected.

It was nine or ten days since we had started walking. I'd lost count. It was drawing close to the end of the day. Normally Alban would be looking for somewhere to camp. But he was pushing on.

'I think we are getting close,' he said.

I heard rushing water somewhere below. We came through some trees, Alban stopped and pointed.

'Down there in the gorge, that's the Tarn.'

It was far bigger than anything we had forded. Certainly, the largest river I had seen since Torlosa. Alban stood gazing down into the tight valley.

'This is where I said I would take you. The water slows here, as it turns a bend. It's easier to cross, but we must be careful. The level is steady for this time of year. It often floods in the spring and early summer, but seems quiet enough now.'

I wasn't sure when I reached the river exactly what I would do. Enora had said the Tarn went west, but I doubted she'd been here herself, let alone walked it. We found a path that snaked down the precipice, closer to the river. Trees had fallen on the southern side, at the edge of the water. A kingfisher sat on a stick watching us. Alban waded in, but it got deep. I followed him in a short way. But he ushered me back to the edge and pointed downstream.

'There's a track higher up, along the northern bank. If you follow it downstream far enough, it will eventually take you to Burdigala. It's getting too dark to cross now. We should wait until tomorrow.'

We went back some distance from the bank and lit a fire in a secluded hollow. Alban took a stick and pointed toward the opposite bank.

'There are lots of high cliffs there, but further west it breaks out into more open country. You will need to be careful, the going will be easier, particularly for horses. Further north, there is another big Roman town, Segodunum. Last time I visited, there was a legion stationed there, with lots of soldiers. Stay well away from it. Beyond that there's another river, the Olt, six, maybe seven days walk further north. It also runs west to

Burdigala. Then another, even bigger river beyond that. But I don't know its name, never been that far. But I'm told they all flow west to the sea.'

We broke out our food, there wasn't much left. Alban prodded the fire. He seemed pensive. As if our long walk had let things he'd forgotten, revive again. He looked up at me.

'So Caden, once you get to Burdigala, what then?'

'I will try to get a boat further up the coast, then to Britannia.'

'A bold plan. How old did you say you were?'

'Twelve, on my last birthday.'

He nodded. I've met grown men with less pluck than you. Done my bit to resist the Romans, but what you're doing takes real courage.'

I took heart from what he said. For long periods, I had doubted myself. I had never heard of a slave escaping the borders of the Empire. Entire armies of vigiles in Rome could hunt them down. There had been rebellions, but they had always failed. Perhaps Alban was the first person I'd met who believed I might succeed.

'What are your plans, you and Yann?' I asked.

He stared upward into the dark trees.

'We have no plans Caden, just survival day to day. We've spent four years in the hills, avoiding capture. Sooner or later, the legions will catch up with us. My wife and son are gone, I don't know where. There's nothing left for me now in Gaul. So many have been lost to war, towns burned, many died or were enslaved. At the siege of Avaricum, I'm told, Caesar killed forty thousand. It's a wonder there are any people left, but still Rome wants more. They won't stop until they reach the end of the earth, wherever that is. Your plan to get to Britannia seems as good as any I've heard.' Then he lay back. 'When you get there, just remember Alban helped you.'

I thought back to what Simon told me. Eratosthenes said the earth was a sphere. If they marched and sailed twenty-five thousand miles, those legions would come back to the place they started. Perhaps one day, they would conquer the whole world. Alban was right about one thing. I would remember him.

But not in a way he would have wanted.

CHAPTER TWELVE

Alban woke me in the morning. We ate a little of the food from the shepherds and he insisted I take the rest.

'I still have some friends in these parts. I can get more on the way back. My brother will have something waiting for me. He's probably gorging himself on venison as we speak.' Then he pointed to the river. 'I never asked, can you swim that far?'

'Yes, of course.' When I thought of sea I had floated in for hours, this river looked easy.

'Let me go across first and set you on the path, then I'll come back. The river is deep and slow here, it gets faster further on.'

Alban found a log to float my gear. Everything of value I packed in my bag. I had some hazelnuts, cheese and some dried meat. I sheathed the knife and wrapped the axe and flint together. Then I rolled the blanket under the straps. Alban went first to test the current. I could tell it was quite strong in the middle, because he drifted downstream to a sloped pebbled beach on the other side. He sat down and motioned me across.

I put my bag on the log, touched the coin around my neck and pushed out into the river. I remember it was very calm and bright. The kingfisher from yesterday had gone. The river was cool, but the day was already warm. I wasn't worried. My clothes would dry soon enough, on the other side.

Two-thirds of the way across, I saw a black dog run out of the trees. I shouted something, then Alban turned and tried to stand. The dog snarled and leapt at him, and they both rolled together on the ground. The brute had his arm in its jaws. Alban drew a knife and plunged it into its guts. Then a rider came out holding his sword. It was Titus. Alban stood up and shook off the limp dog. By the time he turned around, Titus was nearly on him and he ducked. Titus swung his gladius and missed, then struggled to turn his horse. Alban sprinted for the water, but another horseman emerged, Acco. He threw his spear through Alban's back, just as he was waist deep. I watched in despair as Alban collapsed, face first. The spear quivering in his limp, floating body.

Then I heard Cato shout, 'the boy's in the water, get him.'

I turned and kicked myself back into the current, the deepest part of the river. There was a splash as Acco encouraged his horse in and began swimming after me. I kicked as fast as I could and paddled with my arms. The water was getting rougher, and I picked up speed. When I looked back. Acco had given up and was guiding his horse back to the bank.

I was going faster now, bouncing between rocks and pouring water. The log slipped away, but I clung to my bag. The river fell over stones, water rushed over me. Then I was sucked under, spinning down. I held my breath and tumbled. My hip bounced off something hard, then I was spat out at the bottom. I came up and gasped. There was gravel under my feet, then I was carried away and under again. I kicked and fought, trying to get free of the current, bobbing up again for air. The river finally slowed in a wide arc. I was deposited, breathless, on the northern bank, bruised and shaken. There was a gorge above me. The horses couldn't follow the bank, they'd have to go around. I stared at the southern side, but I had no strength left to cross back again.

I stumbled under some trees, pulling my precious bag, dripping up the bank. Grateful I was intact, nothing broken or bleeding. The thong with my mother's coin was still around my neck. The trees grew thick here up the steep slope. I climbed my way up as quickly as I could. I shivered in the shade, but it was the safest place to be. Out in the open, someone would surely see me. There was shouting, somewhere below and to my right. Eventually, I reached the tall grass at the top of the slope.

There was a track there leading west, high along the river. The route Alban had suggested I took to Burdigala. There were fresh hoof marks in the dust. On the other side there was a gentle slope down to dark oak, and clumps of pale birch. I couldn't see anyone in either direction, so I took the chance and staggered across. I was not far into the trees when I heard horses. I dropped still, under the trembling bracken. One horse came from the west, riding fast. I guessed it was Acco. It met the other two, not far from where I had crossed. I prayed I hadn't dripped too heavily on the path. I was close enough to hear them. Cato's rough voice was unmistakable.

'That little wretch must come out somewhere.'

'He's not in the river,' replied Acco. 'Not that I could see, and I've been at least a mile downstream. You get a good view up on this path. I didn't see him swim back to the southern side. Now if Titus had held onto the dog, we'd have had both of them.'

'Has he drowned?' I heard Titus reply.

'I hope not,' growled Cato. 'He's no good to us dead. If his body washes up at some point downriver. We'll see it sure enough. If he's alive, he's heading west, but which bank, north or south?'

'We could split up, patrol both sides,' said Acco. 'If I take my horse across, you and Titus can stay here.'

'We might lose each other in these wretched trees,' complained Cato. 'Once he gets to the open country west of here, we'll find him again. There's no way he can outrun horses. I knew he had some help, couldn't have got this far without it.'

'Well, both of them are dead now,' said Acco. 'The one at the cave was a well-known outlaw. Wanted for killing a Roman official. The one back there was his brother. The Governor's been after both for years.'

'Worth a commendation to you, I'm sure,' Cato grunted. 'But the boy is the one we're after. Shame about the dog. We could have done with it now. What do you suggest Acco?'

'I say we patrol this side. You get the best view of the river. He's got to come out somewhere.'

'Fine,' said Cato. 'Titus, make sure you keep up.'

Then I heard the horses trot off westward along the path. So poor Alban never knew his brother was already dead. They must have come back to their cave sometime after we had left. Perhaps the dog was on our trail after that. They must have lost the scent and crossed the Tarn too early. Acco seemed to know the lie of the land. He rode like he was born on a horse. Titus must have got impatient, or they would have had me as well.

I moved deeper into the forest and lay there for a while, eating some of the damp food. I had a difficult choice, to stay where I was and wait for night, or keep going? In the end, the weather decided for me. I could hear rumbling in the east. A thunderstorm broke in the early afternoon. I had begun to dry off, but now I was wet again. The forest would be too dark to walk by moonlight. Best to keep moving and use the darkness to cross open meadows if needed. I couldn't hear anything other than the coo of sodden pigeons and the relentless rain running in the leaves.

At twilight, the rain eased, and I emerged from the forest into a meadow. I could see smoke somewhere west, not too far away. There was no movement, but three horses were grazing nearby. I sat there waiting for sunset. Then I saw two figures return and throw wood on the blaze. I took my chance, crossed the meadow in the gathering darkness, and left them behind me.

If Cato thought I would follow the Tarn west, then my best chance was to go north. Alban had said it was at least six days' walk to the Olt. A bigger river, though I had little idea what I would find there. I needed to find somewhere dry and warm, but I couldn't risk a fire. So, I walked as far as I could in the remains of the light. A couple of miles at most. In a dense copse of trees, I found a dry crevice amongst a pile of stones. It stank of fox, but I was too tired to care. My damp blanket was better than nothing. I rolled myself up and fell into a fitful sleep.

By the time I awoke, it must have been mid-morning. The sun was up and there was a warm wind from the south. My clothes, blanket and bag were nearly dry. It all seemed quiet apart from the slight rustle of leaves in the wind. I drank the last of the water from my skin. I'd need to find a stream and replenish it before it got too hot. There were a few hazel nuts at the bottom of my bag. I cracked and ate them. That was all the food I had. I reached down to tighten my belt and touched something. The sling, I had forgotten it, knotted there. Once I had crawled out of the copse, I flitted between trees, keeping out of the sunlight. I stayed low in the patches of scrub and heather, using all the skills poor Alban had taught me. Careful to avoid open places where I might be seen. Or pass through them as quickly as possible. I found a stream, filled my skin and gathered some more smooth pebbles from the bed. Later that day, I managed to stun a hare with the sling, as much by luck as skill.

That evening, I found a sheltered glen with a little recess into the cliff. If Cato and his band had gone west, then I hoped they would be miles away by now. After digging a hole with my stave, I waited until dusk to start a fire. I copied my mother, who I saw take out their entrails and remove the skin with a single tug. That hare roasted on a stick, the first fresh meat I'd had for ages. It singed a bit on the outside, but that didn't matter. I gnawed it down to the bones and licked the fat from my fingers. The fire burned down. I'd gathered plenty of wood in case I needed to get it blazing. There was no sign of wolves or bears, but that didn't mean they weren't out there. The only noise in the darkness was a persistent owl. It was Athena's bird, the symbol of wisdom, according to Simon. For some strange reason, it soothed me.

The next morning, I was careful cover the fire and erase all traces of where I'd slept. I had a good six days of walking ahead. If the Olt was bigger than the Tarn, there might be settlements there. Cato might have guessed what I'd done and be waiting there again. Without the dog, I hoped they would find me more difficult to follow.

It was high summer now, and the days were long. The grass grew tall in meadows and the trees were in full leaf. There were patches of farmland and fertile fields. I came to a Roman road. There were slow-moving carts and the occasional horseman. I warily tracked it north for a short way. Then waited until it was empty and crossed at a lonely spot. Further west, small flocks of sheep were sheltering in the shade at midday. I still had some money that Enora had given me. I traded a few sesterces for bread and ewe's cheese and got directions from shepherds. They told me the road led to Segodunum, the Roman town Alban had told me to avoid. The shepherds said if I veered northwest I would come again to hills, only good for grazing goats. Eventually I would reach the river Olt, but they did not know how far it was.

I came to hills again. Not as difficult as the Black Mountains, but it led me down into a wide valley and back up again. It was country that was difficult for horses and away from larger settlements. The days were getting very warm.

I followed the shepherd's example and slept the afternoons in cool hollows, then walked long into the evenings, until dusk. The streams began to wither to a trickle in the heat. My water skin I filled as often as I could. I took smaller paths and tried to avoid anything with traffic. My ears were primed for every rustle in the grass. At the first sound of hooves, I'd vanish into the undergrowth until they'd passed. Sometimes the shimmering haze would play tricks with my eyes. I imagined horsemen on the distant summits, then with another glance, they were gone.

Food was difficult to find. I kept away from anything that looked like a Roman has built it. I bought bread from the most isolated farmsteads. The poorer and more run down, the better, hoping they had less contact with their overlords. The long days meant I could travel twenty or thirty miles. My sandals from Torlosa had stood up well. But the tracks I took were rough and overgrown. After a few days, my legs were showing the strain. Even legions rested on the fourth day of a march. I had cuts on my ankles and blisters on both soles. I couldn't afford to rest, but my feet wouldn't take me much further.

Sooner or later, those horses would catch up with me.

I think it was on the afternoon of the sixth day after leaving the Tarn. I could hear fast flowing water. It had been raining off and on all day, with thunder rumbling somewhere in the north. Aristotle said clouds colliding caused that noise. But clouds felt soft when I'd flown in them. Not solid, like stones that would grind and clash. Thorns had torn my feet and I had blisters. My left ankle was swollen after I had twisted it in a hole. I'd tried strapping it to bear my weight, but was painful. I really needed a day's rest or more, but I didn't dare stop.

Then I came suddenly to a cliff edge and glanced down onto a wide river. This must be the Olt. I spent a long time scanning the northern bank, trying to convince myself that Cato wasn't there. I could try to follow the river from here, but it was difficult on the southern side. There was dense wood and gullies, with no obvious path. With my wrecked ankle, I'd be slow and risk further injury.

Eventually, I hobbled down to a small pebbled beach. I risked bathing my throbbing feet in the cool water. The trees rustled on the other side, so I crept back behind a log and stared across. Nothing moved on the opposite bank, but I still wasn't convinced. My food was nearly exhausted. How far it was to Burdigala, I did not know. I sat there for ages. I couldn't bring myself to cross. What had happened at the Tarn was seared in my eyes. Alban floating face first in the water and Acco's spear quivering between his shoulders. I was certain he was dead.

It seemed better to remain on the southern bank. I camped in the trees a safe distance back from the water, to wait for the next day. It was warm. There was no need for a fire. I couldn't smell smoke, so if Cato and the others were waiting, they might have done the same. I took my knife and lanced my blistered feet. Then ate the last of my food, wrapped myself up, and slept.

When I awoke the next morning, the river had risen. Flowing high and fast and lapping at the bank near my feet. A snake swam in the turbid water. A mess of smashed and twisted wood floated past. Bundles of thatch were carried on the angry current. A house must have collapsed into the river, upstream. It was too dangerous to swim across now. I had missed my chance.

Then I saw an oval shape turning in the torrent. I grabbed a broken branch and hobbled up the bank. I reached over and dragged it to the edge. It was a small boat, wrenched loose from its mooring. A crude rope tied to a wooden spike was floating alongside. It was four feet long and three wide, with ribs like a wickerwork basket. Covered in dark hide and sealed with pitch. A brace of wicker was woven at the front end. It seemed undamaged and dry. A paddle still lay in the bottom, along with a twisted line and a hook. The boat was big enough for one or two at most.

I wasn't sure which god of the river had delivered this gift. I called it Argo after a story Simon had told me about some Greeks sailing in search of a Golden Fleece. It fitted me and my modest bag. Not swift, but it was stable. Tricky to row a distance upstream, but as I was going west and downriver, it was fine. This might be safer and quicker than walking. A chance for my feet to recover and my ankle to heal. If Cato or any of his band saw me from the bank, they would have to swim after me. I would be difficult to catch and could escape on the opposite side.

So, I began my journey with Argo. I had to be careful, there was lots of floating debris, logs and branches that had washed into the river. But it meant the Olt was flowing fast, the only effort I expended was to steer. My feet were grateful for the rest. The first night I spent on an island in the river. The line proved useful. I hooked a perch, just like the ones I'd seen caught in the river near my old estate. I cooked them as Alban did, on a stick over the fire. The moon was beginning to wax again. I curled up on the boat hidden under the trees. The next morning, there were ducks diving within a few feet, oblivious to my presence. I found a clutch of eggs, which I roasted in the ashes and ate.

I launched Argo and started out again. It appeared I was alone on the water. Herons patrolled the wide shallows where I could touch the bottom with my paddle. Long strands of green weed undulated below the surface. A larger boat might have grounded, but my little boat floated freely on. I could see ahead where the river fell over rough stones. Debris had caught in the shallow rapids. But Argo was light enough for me to carry it up the bank and back down to settled water. I drifted past miles of tall white cliffs, as high as those on Capri. The water was deeper and a curious otter swam alongside. This part of Gaul seemed empty in contrast to further south. Surely, the Romans could not have killed and enslaved them all.

Eagles circled above. I thought of Simon and the mountain behind our villa. So far away now, I would never see that place again. Those few weeks seemed like years. Aetos lay broken in a gully near the Via Latina. I wondered what had happened to Talos and Enora. I prayed they were not in trouble for helping me and paid the same price as Panya, or poor Alban.

As I went further west, the river became gradually wider. Grazing cattle came down to the bank to drink. Now there were other craft on the river. Little villages scattered on the banks where the water slowed. Some on stilts, with boats moored below, much like my own. I avoided their attention, but for how long, I did not know. My fear had started to subside. I was warm. My ankle had recovered, and I caught fish to eat. I was reliant on no one but myself. Moving slowly toward what I thought was freedom. I had almost forgotten the Romans existed.

Then I came to Cadurcorum.

As I drifted westward, there were more boats and some rafts of lumber. Some men were wearing tunics cut in the Roman style. I gave them a wide berth. I paddled more slowly now. There was something coming up ahead. I could sense it. A lone fisherman sat on the bank, holding a thick line. A Gaul, not a wealthy one, given his ragged dress. I manoeuvred Argo close and held a branch to arrest my progress on the current. He looked up at me.

'Caught anything?' I asked.

'Damn otters keep stealing the fish out of my traps,' he snapped. He hauled one up and showed me where he had repaired the damage. 'They break them with their teeth, see. Too lazy to chase their own fish. I've tried spearing them, but they're so quick.'

'Are there Romans down river?'

He nodded. 'Keep going and you'll come to Cadurcorum. Plenty of soldiers, if you want to meet some. They're building a new town. If you try to pass their bridge, they'll make you pay a toll. That's why I stay up river. Won't be much for your little boat, but if you had cargo could be expensive. Very good at collecting tax, these Romans. They worship lots of gods, but gold is the greatest.'

He told me that Cadurcorum was one of the last places in Gaul to hold out against the Romans. A year after the surrender of Vercingetorix, Caesar cut off the hands of all who held out there.

He furrowed his brow. 'You're not from round here, I can tell.'

'No,' I said. 'I've come from the south.'

'Even more Romans there,' he said. 'Still, if I mind my own business, they leave me alone. But give them the wrong look and you're in for trouble. I sell my catch to a trader that takes them into the town. I stick to trapping fish, leave selling them to the merchants that knows their ways. Not that I'll have any to sell, if these damn otters keep pinching them.'

I thanked him for his help. As I paddled away, he called out. 'Stay away from them soldiers, lad, if you know what's good for you.'

Cadurcorum might be a place that Cato would visit, or soldiers could be stationed. Cato said they had sent messages all over. Either way, it didn't seem sensible to linger there. The moon would be waxing, nearly full. If I arrived just before night, I could stay upstream and scout around. I might carry Argo around the bridge and continue on, perhaps even as far as Burdigala. If that wasn't possible, I would just have to start walking again. I was reluctant to give up my little boat. It had taken me a long way with little effort and less danger.

Cadurcorum finally came into view. It stood on a peninsula, in a wide swing of the river. There was still scaffolding on part of the unfinished wall. A wooden bridge on stone pillars marched across the river. I lurked in a little reed bed upstream, on the southern side, away from the town. I hoped to hide my little boat there and slip out just before dusk to find a way around. Perhaps I could cross the road a few hundred yards down from the bridge. After Torlosa, I didn't want to get too close, in case they questioned and detained me. If I made a loop south overland, I could rejoin the river downstream. But first I would have to get over the road.

I waited until nearer dusk, then left Argo concealed in the reeds. I crept west until I found the road. There were Roman guards on the bridge, at least one manned a gate at the nearest end. I could hear muffled conversation and a laugh. Boats were just visible moored at a dock on the northern bank, next to the town. There was no traffic on the bridge or road. The city gates seemed closed for the night.

I followed the edge of the road further away from the bridge, staying just beyond the ditch. The ground was damp, and I crawled behind some scrubby alder. I chose a spot a few hundred feet south where the ditch was less steep. Then poked my nose over the edge of the road. There was no movement. So, I crept up onto the hard stone, scrambled across and dropped over the other side. Somewhere an owl hooted. I lay still for a moment until there was no other sound.

The river looped around to the north. There were cows lying in a low meadow. A few dwellings stood to my left on higher ground, above the river. I could see their lights behind the shutters. A dog barked, and some geese screeched in return. I made my way through a patch of willow in the dusk. My sandals squelched in soft mud. Beyond, I could see the rising moon shining on the water. It was the river, winding downstream beyond the bridge.

I had never carried the boat this far. The perilous bit would be crossing the road with Argo. I retraced my steps as best I could and made it back in the last of the light. It took me a while to find the boat in the reeds. It was too well hidden. I pulled it out and up onto the bank in the gloom. I packed everything into my bag and put the blanket over my shoulders. Then I crawled underneath, grasped the brace and stood up like an ungainly snail.

I waddled forward a few steps, with Argo on my back. I would have to take it slowly in the dark. It took a long time, but I wanted to make sure I could find the same spot on the road. The pale line of straight stone glowed in the moonlight. The guards on the bridge had a view directly down. I waited for a long time behind a clump of bushes just beyond the ditch. I hadn't heard anything for several minutes. It must have been well after midnight. I began to worry about how much of the dark I had left. I said a silent version of Simon's prayer. Then I started up the ditch and onto the road. I was probably over halfway across when I heard a shout.

'Hey, stop there.'

I kept going with the boat over my head. Someone was running down the road. Down the ditch I scurried and onto the other side. Then I clambered up into the meadow. But it was still a long way from the willows. So, I did the only thing I could think of. I dropped the boat over me and lay still. The paddle rattled. My heart was pounding out of my chest. The bruised alder underneath me stank. I could hear voices nearby, Romans. I guessed they were standing somewhere above me, on the road. One of them sounded a bit like Cato, only younger.

'Did you see it?'

'See what?'

'Something crossed the road, I swear. Like a bear, or a thief, carrying something.'

'I've seen no bears since they stationed us here. They're up in the mountains.'

'I'm sure I saw something. No one crosses the road after midnight who wasn't a thief or a rebel.'

Then I heard the geese start up somewhere. A door slammed. A dog barked in reply.

'Maybe it was a goose that got out and crossed the road.'

'I swear it was bigger than a goose.'

'You fool, at night you can't tell how big anything is. It's a swamp down there and I'm not getting my feet filthy. Get back to your post before someone asks why we're chasing geese in the middle of the night.'

I didn't move for several minutes. Slowly, I lifted the boat and looked out. The trees obscured my view of the bridge. That must be a good thing. I lifted Argo onto my back again and slogged on. My sandals squelched, but I didn't stop until I reached the water. I lifted the boat off and floated it out a short way. Then placed my bag inside before jumping in. I rowed gently toward the middle of the river, then crouched down, allowing myself to drift noiselessly downstream.

The river went north around the city, then drifted west. I waited until I could no longer see the lights of Cadurcorum before I lifted the paddle. Just as dawn broke, I chose a lonely spot where the trees drew down to the bank. I tethered the boat under the branches, ate, then went to sleep.

When I woke, there was a face staring at me.

For a moment, I thought it was Cato. But it was just a curious cow that had come down to graze. That Praetorian was inside my head. His leering face, like a Cyclops, inhabited my dreams. The innocent cow flicked its tail, turned and ambled away. I rowed back onto the water.

The day was getting hot. I splashed myself and my clothes steamed. I was making good progress. The Olt now joined another larger river flowing from the south. I stopped to speak to some fishermen. They told me this was the Garumna, that meant stony river. But that must be a long way upstream, because here it was wide and smooth with banks of mud. It dismayed me to learn it was the same river that came up from

Tolosa. The place where they had jumped me behind the temple of Pallas Athena. I had definitely taken a long way round. My capture by Cato had cost me weeks. But I told myself I was lucky to be free and not in a cold cage, on a ship bound for Capri.

They said there was another river. A few days north overland, called the Duunna, or swift one. It joined the Garumna just beyond Burdigala, to enter an estuary and then the sea. The river here flowed steadily, with no rocks or rapids. The travel was easy, a few strokes of the paddle and the current did the work. Sand martins flitted across the water. The young birds had fledged. It must have been late June. I passed a kingfisher, sitting silent and staring on his stick. Just like the one I had seen the evening before we crossed the Tarn. There were ducklings too, stretched out behind their mother. It was very peaceful.

Then I saw an eruption in the water. A pike leaped and took the little straggler. The other ducklings scattered and made for the bank. Some people talk about a premonition. A sign from the gods, or someone guiding me from the netherworld. Simon might have said it was superstitious nonsense, but I couldn't take the chance. I had been lulled into thinking I was safe before, like the road to Oplontis, where I had been betrayed. That day had changed me forever. An act to punish a person who was dead, to expel their memory. The Lord watches over the way of the righteous, but the way of the wicked leads to destruction. That's what Simon's prayer had said.

I paddled Argo to the southern bank, beneath some trees. I secured it and climbed out onto the bank. There were cattle in a distant field. The river bent sharply here, first north, then south on its westward journey. There was a long ridge overlooking the river, where I could get a better view of the way ahead. As I crept up that slope, the hairs on my neck stood on end. There were three horses standing on that hill. I recognised them immediately, though I was too far away to see their faces. Titus's slouch, Acco's straight posture and the thick menace of Cato.

I froze, praying they would not turn round. Then I crept down the ragged grass and back to the boat. I was not sure how long they had been there. But it was a prime choice for views up and down the river. I could wait until they left and continue down the Olt, but if they were tracking the bank, they would soon see me. Beneath a thick cover of trees, I lay in Argo, waiting until dusk, when I was sure the horsemen would be gone. I had no choice but to abandon my craft and strike north to find this other river, the Duunna. I rowed across to the other side as darkness fell. Rivers were my only guide in this vast place. If I followed them, I would get to Burdigala. But Cato must have guessed that was my destination. He was canny and had been a fugitive himself. I was sure that's why he'd led the vigiles in Rome.

Like Odysseus on his tortuous journey home, nothing was going as I had expected. I would be sad to see it go. But little Argo had taken me as far as it could.

I slept the night in the boat, still reluctant to leave it behind. I'd felt safer on the water than on land. It left no trace for Acco and the others to follow. In the morning, I went for a little scout around. I could not see anyone on either bank. I lifted Argo upside down and hid it beneath some branches. If I had to come back, it would still be there. Then I shouldered my pack and set out north west as best as I could judge.

The country was now open, gently undulating, no mountains like further east. Old tracks were worn into the low hills. Patches of thick forest surrounded by cultivated fields. Scythed hay stood drying in stacks, waiting to be carted away. In the distance were Roman villas, farms and vineyards, a sure sign I was still in the Empire. I didn't dare approach them to buy food. I slept in thickets, hoping not to be disturbed. One morning I came across a square field. Someone had dug a ditch and wall, now overgrown with grass. It must have been the remains of a military encampment. There was no way of telling how long ago a legion had passed this way.

The days were long. It must have just passed the solstice. The sun burned down and streams were running low in the heat. The dust caked my sandals from the dry road. It was the time I remember, when there was a lull at the estate. Just before we would pick olives, figs and grapes. I was starving, so I chewed some lime leaves and kept walking. I found a cache of hazelnuts left from the previous year. Then gorged myself from a cherry tree just off the path and stole some milk from a tethered cow. The wheat was ripening close to harvest. Heavy stems swayed in the warm breeze. The fields here would soon be busy. I thought of Yann and Alban. How much of it was destined for ports like Narbo and then for the plebs in Rome?

On the second day, the road was rough. I came across a despondent trader called Katurix, sitting next to the body of a bloated donkey. His pack animal had died. He sold whet stones to put an edge on scythes and swords. Now he was left with bags he could barely carry. He said he was one of the local Petrocorii who had accepted the Roman rule. I told him my name was Caden.

'Caden, don't sound like you're from around here?'

'My people are the Atrebates, from further north.'

Katurix frowned. 'Atrebates eh, a troublesome lot, but they've seen sense now. Legio Augusta is based up there and keeps an eye on them.'

I told Katurix I was travelling to a farm on the Duunna to work. He told me I was on the right road, but he wasn't going that far. I'm not sure why he took a shine to me, but he liked company and he needed help. He was on his way to a big estate just north. Apparently, a rich Roman called Sertor owned most of the wheat hereabouts. He hoped to sharpen their tools, to sell his stones. If I helped him carry them, he would share his food. I was so hungry it was difficult to refuse. I agreed to carry some of the heavy bags. He shared what food he had left, some stale bread and hard cheese.

Katurix was an admirer of the Empire and knew quite a lot about the legions stationed in Gaul. He knew a little about the Atrebates because he'd travelled through their territory. His whetstones came from a forest, in the northeast of Gaul. One side was blue and the other grey. He used a little water to sharpen my axe and knife to show how good they were.

'No point fighting the Romans. Gets you nowhere. Make yourself useful to them, that's what I say.'

I remembered Simon had said more or less the same. I told him about the old camp and asked him if he had seen any soldiers.

He shook his head. 'I've heard the Fifth is moving up to suppress a revolt amongst the Frisians, but this is a peaceful part of Gaul. On this road, you'll just get farm traffic and the occasional dispatch rider. You're the first person to pass by since that damn donkey died. The busiest time is when the grain wagons go south in the autumn. No trouble here anymore, thank the gods. Traders like me can get on and do what we do best.'

Visiting a Roman estate was a risk, but I was so hungry the thought of food made me reckless. I asked him about the farmstead we were heading to. He said Sertor had been a Prefect in the Twentieth legion, Valeria Victrix. It surprised him I'd never heard of it.

'It was one of the best. Had a symbol of a charging boar. They fought with Tiberius on the Rhine. A great man, our Emperor, don't you think?'

I nodded, but inside my stomach churned. I'd only ever seen that face on a statue in Tusculum. But I was a few feet away from him, twice. The first time he had been shrouded in shade, the second in steam. I was sure he remembered my defiance. Why else would he send his speculatores like Cato to find me? But I was doing everything I could to ensure he never saw me again.

The next day, an imposing villa emerged on a rise, surrounded by trees and wheat fields. Katurix told me that was Sertor's place. The road to the villa was better than the track we'd left. Someone had gone to a lot of trouble to build it. Raised with a ditch on either side, it reminded me of parts of the Via Latina. The wheat on either side was nearly as tall as my head. Here and there thickets of trees had been left unfelled. As we got closer, I could see the villa resembled a larger version of the one I was born on. Laid out the Roman way, the buildings formed a surrounding wall. Gently sloping clay tiles and rows of columns surrounded a garden within. A cover of vines shaded the terrace, just like the one I used to sweep. I was sure there was an atrium open to the sky and an impluvium below to catch the rain. A reminder of my former life and the danger that might lurk there.

I thought of Simon and all he had taught me. I wondered what had my father made of all that happened? He must have realised what Octavia had done. Having me stand by the road with combed hair in fine clothes, on the Ides of March, my birthday. Knowing the Emperor would pass and hoping he would see me. Her triumph on the day I was betrayed. Perhaps it was better my mother died, before she witnessed Octavia's revenge. No doubt she thought me exiled to Capri for years. Or hoped like that Dacian boy, I would end my life myself. The way would be clear for her nephew to inherit. She never expecting me to return so soon. Titus had hinted there had been consequences for my return. Octavia had not escaped the displeasure of the Emperor. That gave me some comfort. Perhaps they thought she had a hand in my evading the pursuit. But the truth was, it was down to Aetos, Simon, and a small twittering bird. I hoped all traces of Simon's complicity had escaped with me in the air. If they had not believed a Praetorian, then perhaps anything Valeria said would be also be worthless.

I was so caught up in my thoughts, I barely noticed someone approaching. Katurix was greeted by a noble Roman, judging by his clothes, and a retired soldier by his bearing. He stared at me briefly, furrowed his brows, but said nothing. We took out the whetstones. He handled one and nodded. His overseer showed us to a shed full of agricultural tools, and we set to work. The scythes needed to be sharp, as the harvest was close. Then we were to do everything else, the axes, hoes, shears, kitchen knives, whatever needed an edge. I did as Katurix showed me and worked fast to make everything razor sharp. By evening, we had finished, and the overseer came back to check our work.

They must have been pleased because they brought us a generous amount of food; cheese, bread, oil, and olives, like a feast at home. It was hard for me to contain my hunger. Katurix finished his meal and left to collect his payment. He tossed me one of the smaller stones. He was happy that he'd sold many of his goods and we had a place to stay the night.

For the first time in weeks, I gorged myself until I could eat no more. I could not bear the bread and cheese going to waste. So, I put the remains in my bag. I need to relieve myself. Katurix had been gone quite a long time. There was a line of trees outside the villa, at the edge of the wheat field. Reluctant to leave my precious bag, I picked it up at the door. The ditch at the edge of the field was thick with ivy snaking up the trees. I stood concealed there and watered the wheat. A flock of sparrows turned and flew over the ripening seed. I could see why Caesar wanted Gaul. This grain could feed entire armies and whole cities. Rome could not exist without vast farms like this. Some of the bread I had eaten in Rome might even have come from here. I was about to return when I heard voices, quite close.

It was Katurix calling me, sounding urgent and angry. Perhaps it was because I finished the food. But something made me suspicious. I crouched down as close to the ground as I could. There was a space where the roots protruded over the ditch, covered in ivy. I crawled in and lay still. Footsteps approached, then I heard someone speak. It was Sertor.

'When did you say you met that boy?'

'Two days ago, on the road south of here,' replied Katurix. 'Said he was on his way to the Duunna, to a farm.'

'Is he a local?'

'Speaks with an accent. I thought he was from the north.'

'There's an escaped slave, a boy of his age, from south of Rome. A dispatch rider came through a few days ago. He's wanted for murder. If he's disappeared now, makes me think it might be him. But he can't have got far.'

I heard someone step through the trees, almost on top of me. Then Katurix spoke.

'Nothing's disturbed the edge of the wheat. He must have gone back down the road.'

'I'll take a horse down there,' replied Sertor. 'Tell my overseer to check the villa, to see if he's hiding somewhere inside. There's an hour of light left, maybe more. If we're quick, we'll catch him.'

I waited until they were gone. It was half-a-mile back to the track we had left. If I tried to run down the road, I was sure they would see me. But if I ventured out in the wheatfield in daylight, I'd leave a trail they could follow. I had no option but to stay where I was. I was a murderer, not just an escapee. The slave who kills a citizen, the worst type of criminal. I knew if it happened in a household, all the slaves would die. Even those who were innocent and played no part. Any slave who committed this act would know they condemned all their fellow slaves to death. Alban was right. The Romans had it all worked out.

I heard an urgent gallop toward the road. There were other voices. I lay there until it was near dark. Then I heard the horse return and a rider dismount. It was Sertor.

'No one's on the road. Either he can run faster than a horse, or he's still around here somewhere.'

'Your slaves say they have combed every room,' replied Katurix. 'They haven't found him. The little wretch. To think I showed him how to sharpen tools.'

'Lucky he didn't cut your throat in your sleep,' snarled Sertor. 'We'll get some torches, come back and comb the entire estate.'

I waited for the footsteps to fade away. Then I crept out from under the ivy and into the field. The moon was large, and the wheat rustled over my head. I tried hard not to tread on the stalks until I was some way in. They might guess where I went, but I hoped they wouldn't risk following me and setting the field on fire. The stars were bright, so I had my bearings. The great bear shone below the north star. It was heavy going in the waning light. I made my way through the wheat, back toward the estate road. When I turned, I could see torches swarming around the trees. Eventually, I stumbled to the edge of the field and reached the track that we had left. I crouched in the ditch beside the road.

There was a horse tethered there. I couldn't see the rider. It must have sensed me and snorted. I stayed still and glimpsed a restless figure walking up and down. It was the overseer. I waited until he had traversed back behind me. Then I made my move, silently over the track and into the trees on the other side. My eyes had become accustomed to moonlight walking. My only thought was to get as far away as I could. I walked until just before dawn. The forest was my friend. It would be hard to find me there. I found a dry spot and broke some branches to hide me in a bed of bracken. My belly was full, and I had a bag of food, but that had been a close call. I slept late and woke in the early afternoon.

I wasn't sure how long it would take to reach the Duunna. The days were long, and I walked hard. There were swallows circling in the sky. Perhaps they had come out of those secret holes only Aristotle could find. I stayed on lonely paths and skirted the edge of woods and habitation. If I kept going north, I knew I must eventually reach the river.

On the second day, I decided to pick up the pace. News of me could reach Cato soon. But I was going so fast I nearly stumbled on a wild sow, crossing the track with her piglets. To avoid being gored, I had to climb a tree. As I sat up there, I fretted about the fate of the slaves on my old estate. And what did it mean for Linus in the villa Jupiter? I had never considered my actions might affect them. It seemed the cruelty of Tiberius had no limits. His rage was following me across the known world. I would only feel safe outside its bounds. But the Romans had killed so many. What was one more insignificant boy?

The angry sow finally left me in peace. I dropped out of the tree and I continued on. That evening, as I lay down, the forest was bathed in tiny lights. Flitting around me like lost souls, the dead warriors of Gaul.

On the third day, I heard the ringing of axes in the distance. It was in front of me, so I slowed and left the path. It was very warm, even in the depths of the tangled wood. The birds were silent now. The bracken was dry and there were deep drifts of leaves. The brittle moss turned to powder beneath my feet.

I got closer, and a distant tree began shaking. Then I heard a crash as it toppled to the ground. As I approached, I could see below a whole patch of forest had been cleared. Raw stumps protruded from the ground. There were gangs of men, Gauls, stripped to the waist, glistening in the heat. Wielding axes, but shackled around the legs. Some were felling trees, others were stripping branches from the fallen trunks. Teams of horses dragged the timber away. A soldier armed with a whip sat on a horse, observing their work.

I skirted carefully around. The trees began to shrink and thin. A thunderstorm broke as I reached a track by the river and the rain poured down. The Duunna lived up to its name. It was swift, larger than both the Olt and Tarn. Too wide to swim easily and attempting it here might draw attention. I stared downstream along the path on the southern bank, looking for any signs of legionaries. I had only walked a short way in the shower when I came to a jetty. It was built out on the river, fed by a road that came up from the south. There were boats, flat bottom barges that towed rafts of lumber. Labourers, boatmen and merchants, standing under trees, waiting for the shower to pass, but there were no soldiers that I could see. Bales of wool were half unloaded from ponies. The patient animals stood unmoving in the rain, waiting to be led back south again.

The rain eased and stopped. The labourers resumed. I asked if the boats were going to Burdigala. A boatman told me they were constructing rafts with logs. They floated their wares downstream to the banks just north of the town. Then broke up the raft and sold the wool and lumber. They had a few more bales to load and then they were leaving. If I could handle a pole or a paddle, they'd take me. I hesitated for a moment. I could choose to walk along the path, but If Cato was searching for me, that's where he'd look. The river was flowing fast, at least walking pace. I saw a swallow skim across the river, then circled round me and back again. Perhaps someone was telling me to take the pole. It was the best chance I had to go beyond Burdigala.

I chose a pole and leaped on a raft of lumber, hitched by a rope behind a barge. The river was wide and deep and the current was strong. The poles were just to push away from banks if we got too close. In the middle of the river there was little to do, other than watch life on the bank pass by. Ducks dived and above an eagle with red wings circled. A warning perhaps that the eyes of the Empire were still searching.

Four days I spent on that river, each night we camped on the bank. The boatmen did not give me payment, but I accepted their food. I had invented so many lies about myself, they just rolled off my tongue. I told them I was a goatherd returning to a farm near Burdigala. That started a debate on which were better, sheep or goats. Of course, it depended on what land you had. Wool was valuable that I could not deny. You wouldn't get much fleece from a goat. But goats were curious creatures, cleverer than sheep. Reckless climbers, who never took the easy option. Why eat grass when you can nibble a spiky shrub? I had even seen them climb trees to chew the leaves. Goats would eat anything and go anywhere. They were troublesome. Perhaps that's why I liked them. It seemed we would never agree. I was clearly a goat amongst sheep. But as long as I handled the pole and kept the raft together, the boatmen were happy.

On the last afternoon, a tributary entered from the south, and the river widened again. It was very warm and swallows chased dragonflies across the water. Then, in the distance, away on the southern side, a large walled Roman town emerged. It must be Burdigala. The boatman ahead told me the Garumna came up from the south and ran by the town. We were heading for a wooden wharf on the wide spit of marshy land between the two rivers, before they flowed together into the estuary beyond.

Wagons were waiting on the higher ground to take the bales of wool. There was lots of activity; carts, horses harnessed to drag out the lumber. I spotted a Roman official counting the bales being unloaded. While the merchants were distracted, I poled the raft to the bank, and climbed off, just upstream of the wharf. I scrambled up the high grassed bank, about to clamber onto the path, when I stopped.

There was the square jawed Acco. At least I thought it was him, conversing with a toll collector. If he was here, then Cato and Titus would not be far away. I tried to blend with the traffic. The ground below the road was marshy, with tall wavering grass. Out of the corner of my eye, I saw him turn and glimpse me. I continued through the press of people and wagons. There were some low shrubs on the left-hand side. I dropped down into the ditch and lay still.

He shouted, 'that boy, did anyone see him, where did he go?'

I could see Acco mounted and forcing his way back along the road, pushing the pedestrians out of his way. Then he galloped off toward Burdigala. Once he realised I wasn't on the road, he'd be back. The willow where I was hiding might be the first place he'd look. To see if I could find a boat, I had to cross the road again. I gathered my gear and made my way back to the road. Then wiggled my way between the wagons and down into the long grass on the other side. I had not gone far when I found I had made a mistake.

I was in a low marsh between the two rivers that ran into the estuary. There were no boats here. The ground was too wet and the water too shallow. There was water on both sides of me now. If they came looking for me here, I was trapped. If I tried to get into Burdigala, they would pick me up at the gates. I couldn't go back to the Duunna either. My only choice was to wait until nightfall. Then make for the Garumna nearer the city, to see if there was anything moored there.

I made my out a little further. Then used my knife to cut some sheaves of long grass. I found a hollow place and lay down and covered myself as best I could. Herons circled above me. I could hear carts rumbling along the road. I had lain there probably less than an hour when I heard the horses. It was getting close to dusk. I should have spent more time concealing myself instead of watching herons.

I could hear Acco's voice. 'The merchants say a boy came up on a raft. He claimed to be from Burdigala, but he didn't sound like he was. The guards at the gate claim they haven't seen him.'

'He could be anywhere,' replied Cato in his distinctive growl. 'Where's that Titus gone now?'

'I left him at the gate, just to make sure,' said Acco. 'I'm just going down this bank to see if there are any tracks'

I could hear the slap of a bridle and the snort of a horse as it trotted past.

'We're wasting our time here Acco,' called Cato. 'Let's get back and start at first light tomorrow.'

The sky was darkening, the sound of the horses faded. The night had saved me. But I waited until it was completely dark before I got up and move toward the lights of Burdigala. The moon lit the river enough to judge where I was, but the marshy ground meant my progress was slow. In places I was up to my knees in rancid mud. As I got closer to Burdigala, I could see the shadows of ships moored up on the near bank and others anchored out in the deeper channel. I wished I had Argo now. I could have easily paddled out to one on a still night like this.

At last, I reached a drier place, where they were building a stone quay. I could see the outline of a broad-bottomed boat that had come up the river on the tide. It had a square sail set on a single yard. A trader, similar to the Salvia, pointing downstream in the direction I needed to go.

I found myself a place under some stacked stone. My mother's coin turned over in my fingers. I had finally reached Burdigala, that place Talos had told me was at the end of the Via Aquitania. My goal from the time I had left Narbo. But my misfortune in Torlosa meant it had taken weeks longer than it should have. I had gone the long way round, in a great triangle from what I could tell. The certainties Simon taught Cadmus were of little use. Caden had kept me travelling toward that dream, the white horse on a green hill. I hadn't realised when I'd taken this coin from my mother's hands, I'd make a promise that would sustain my steps to the edge of the Empire. But now Cato and the others were nearby. As soon as it was light, they would be back. I had a little money left. Tired and filthy from crawling through the marsh. I had come so far, but they must be close to capturing me again.

The voice of Quintus was telling me I had run out of luck.

I awoke in the dawn. The tide had crept up just short of my feet.

'Hey you, boy.'

I froze. Someone was behind me.

'You, with the bag on your back.'

I turned slowly. The master on the ship was staring at me, hands on his hips.

'Are you the swineherd we're taking back north?'

My lying tongue leaped into action. 'Er yes, I am.'

'Well, don't sit around. You're earlier than we were told. I want to sail before the tide falls too far. Get on deck and we can cast off.'

So, I was a swineherd now. I was sure I looked very much like one. A mud-stained youth, in need of a wash, with a stick and a battered leather bag. I probably smelled as bad as Diogenes.

'How far are you going Corbilo or on to Daritorium?'

I took a guess, 'Daritorium.'

'We birth overnight in Corbilo. He recoiled as I walked past. 'If I were you, I'd take a quick dip in the sea once we get there. You smell like you slept with that pig.'

I felt a little sorry for the real swineherd who would find his ship gone. The breeze took us out of the estuary toward open water. The currents were treacherous. I could see why they wanted to catch the tide before it fell too far. It was a warm wind from the southwest and we made good progress. The boat was smaller than the Salvia and the ships my father used. It had a shallow draft, better to track the coast and wide rivers. But the rigging was much the same as I remember. We left the estuary and hugged the coast of Gaul, staying in sight of the shore.

The first port was a town called Corbilo on the northern banks of a river called the Liger, where it flowed into the sea. It was a busy trading port. I heard someone speaking Greek. I was trying to look busy helping unload the cargo when I heard the harbour master approach the captain.

'I can see you've paid the duty on the goods unloaded.'

'All paid.'

He pointed at me. 'Who's the kid you have on board?'

'A swineherd from Daritorium. We were told to pick him up and bring him back. He took a breeding boar to an estate near Burdigala on another boat.'

'If you can vouch for him, then fine. There's an escaped slave, a juvenile we are on the lookout for. But I can't lock up every swineherd and shepherd I see. The cells in the town are overflowing already.'

I spent a nervous night on board. I had a difficult decision; go overland north to Daritorium or stay on board and sail the following day.

But again, the weather made that choice for me.

A storm came in that evening. I took shelter under a canvas they'd rigged up at the back of the boat. I overheard the captain talking to one of his crew.

'Don't like the look of this, not in open water. We'll leave it a couple of days to blow out. Better a delay here than losing the boat. If you need me, I'll be in the rooms across the road.'

When he left, I asked one of the crew. 'How far to walk to Daritorium from here?'

He thought for a moment and scratched his chin. 'Never walked it myself. There are no proper roads, not that carry commerce. It would take at least three or four days, I would think. There's another river further up you have to cross. We're only sitting it out here for a night or two, so find yourself somewhere to sleep in town.'

I would rather trust my instincts on the road than be trapped in the harbour. Waiting here was more time Cato had to follow me. If he found the stranded swineherd waiting at the dock, he might guess I had taken his place. I crept off the rain swept deck. I was drenched, but the mud and stench were flowing off me. If it was winter, I would have frozen, but this was warm rain. The master would assume I had gone to find some shelter.

I made my way through the streets of Corbilo. I found a half-built warehouse with a dry spot and slept inside. At dawn, I bought some bread, and a cured sausage, then merged in the traffic east out of town. Once I was clear of the walls, I went north. I felt far safer in the forest. I trusted myself to find my way to Daritorium overland. Perhaps three days' walk if I kept a fair pace. Far easier, I thought, than the Black mountains.

I couldn't have been more wrong. The walk was at least as difficult, though it was flat. Some of it was wetland and forest, with no roads. Marshy meadows and stretches of stagnant water, surrounded by banks of reeds. Haunted by the cries of strange birds that I never saw. The nights were disturbed by the incessant croaking of frogs. At several points, I sank into the bog waist deep. I was soon mud stained and filthy again. There were isolated cottages in some of the higher clearings. Some of the money I'd saved for my passage to Britannia, I was forced to spend on food. But it was reassuring they were all Gauls here. Alban would have said the land wasn't good enough for the Romans. You couldn't grow the wheat they needed to feed the throngs in Rome.

I reached another river, too large for me to swim across. But I rinsed all the mud off me again. Then got a ride with a fisherman who took me to the other side. He said this river was the Gwilen, and it was now two more days walk to Daritorium. No more big rivers to cross. I would know I was there because there was a large bay with lots of islands.

I kept walking north with the sea on my left, just inland of the dunes. I took off the sandals and walked on my bare hardened feet. The wide beaches were fringed by reed beds. Here and there, streams ran into the sea. Wheeling seagulls cried overhead and wading birds, ran back and forth in the waves. Occasionally, I saw ships moving on the horizon. I collected shellfish from the rocks and I cooked them on a fire. My stomach ached, I was so ravenous, but I had little time to forage. I tried to eke out what food I had.

Then one afternoon, I heard horses behind me. I threw myself flat in a hollow in the dunes behind some marram grass. Three horses rode past me, heading north. I lay still for a while, then in a short while I heard them return, slow to a trot and stop. I recognised Cato's voice.

'You said you saw a fire with charred shells back there? Someone walking alone and hungry. You think it could be him?'

'I thought the tracks walked this way,' answered Acco. 'But they've disappeared in the sand. Must be the wind. Well, he's either tried to swim across and been swept out to sea. Or he's realised his mistake and doubled back toward Daritorium.'

My mistake?

Cato resumed. 'He didn't get back on in Corbilo, and told them he was walking to Daritorium. He must have doubled back, and we missed him. Are there other ports further north?'

'Not for a long way,' replied Acco. 'Daritorium's the principal port, until you get to the north coast.'

'He's trying to get outside the empire,' growled Cato. 'Britannia, that's my guess.' We'll do another sweep east and try to pick up his tracks.'

'I don't have much longer,' said Acco. 'My legion might be moving to the Rhine. Pity we don't have that dog.'

'We don't need a dog, Acco,' laughed Titus. 'We've got you.'

I heard a horse wheel round. 'You'll have to be civil to me, Titus, when I'm a citizen, replied Acco. 'I'll have the same rights as you.'

'The sooner you two stop quarrelling,' Cato grunted, 'the sooner we'll find him. Then we can all go home. You lead the way, Acco. Titus, stay alert and keep up.'

I waited for a long time after the horses had gone. I kept going north for a short way. The trees to my right cleared. Then my mistake became obvious. I was at the southern point of a headland that enclosed a bay of many islands. Beyond them to the east I could glimpse the smoke from a port that must be Daritorium. In front of me, there was a narrow channel and a low headland on the other shore. Between it flowed water connecting the sea to the bay inside. Like the claws of a crab, they came together, but not quite. The distance across the water was perhaps three stadia, a third of a mile, no more. I kicked myself for being so stupid. I'd been told Daritorium was inside a bay. But I'd kept walking without thinking. Now I would have to track back around, and with no idea how long that would take. Not knowing if Cato and the others would be prowling the southern entrance to Daritorium or inside the town. My feet were sore, and I was angry with myself. But I'd stayed in Corbilo waiting for the ship to sail, Cato would have caught me there.

I sat down. I had to think like a Greek. If I came round to Daritorium on the northern side, I might elude them. What would Archimedes have done? Apart from building a machine to throw me across. Or set my pursuers on fire with giant mirrors. But like Odysseus, I had to work with what I had. I watched a stick being dragged out to sea. The tide was rushing out. The water that flowed in the channel would be fast. Like other places, the tide must race in and out twice a day. The tide would turn in a few hours. When that happened, there might be less danger crossing. If anything, I'd be swept inside the bay where the water was calmer. I had to pick that moment when the tide was turning. There might be no current, or a weak one that might help me across. But it was still a long way to swim.

A little curved beach lay next to me, just inside the bay. The last bit of land before the stone that lined the channel. Like a hook, it had trapped a tangle of driftwood. I crept down to have a closer look. A length of thick hemp rope had washed up in the sand. It had snapped at one end and half unravelled. Splayed like the tentacles of a jellyfish I'd seen stranded in the harbour at Oplontis. I pulled it out and rinsed it clean. Then separated the strands and knotted them together to make a longer length of twine.

Odysseus escaped from the isle of Calypso on a raft. I could make one with driftwood. It only had to last a single journey. I trimmed the four largest branches with my axe and dragged everything across the rocks to the channel. Then lashed them all together into a crude platform. I tossed small sticks into the water until I was sure the tide had turned. Then I knelt down using my arms as paddles and started out into the water.

I made slow progress, and it was unstable. An easterly wind started to blow me out to sea. I dug my hands in harder, grunting with effort. I was over halfway across when I felt something snap. The little raft beneath me fell apart. I dropped into the water and went under. The current swirled underneath, dragging me back into the bay. I kept my mouth closed, then came up for air. I grabbed the largest log and kept kicking until I felt my feet hit the shallows. As I struggled out of the water, I pulled off my bag and made it as far as a leaning tree. Then lay down behind it, out of the wind.

Everything was soaked, but my mother's coin was still safe around my neck. I poured the seawater out of the leather bag, then laid out my knife and axe out to dry. All the mud had been washed away. I was the cleanest I'd been for weeks. I ate what remained of my food before it spoiled. Now I needed to find some fresh water to drink. I'm not sure how long I sat there. There was a distant shout, so I turned and glimpsed movement on the other side. A horseman rode up to the edge. The rider dismounted, then descended to the little beach. I watched him come up, stare across the water, then remount and ride away.

I was sure it was Acco, but I don't know why he had come back. Perhaps he'd seen me cross? But it was a long way for a horse to swim. Best to move on before he returned. There was a big river to my right and more reeds, that meant low marshy ground. There was a fresh stream running into it and it filled my skin. I kept on the higher, firmer ground.

I came to a place with hundreds of stones, standing half concealed in the tall grass. There was a field of them, stretching in long lines. Like avenues of giant graves. I walked through them. There were some sheep grazing there and a noisy dog tried to chase me off. I held him off with a stick, then waved to the shepherd who was sitting under a tree. He called his dog back. I trudged over.

'What you doing here?' he asked.

'I've lost my way. I was trying to get to Daritorium.'

He squinted in the strong sun. 'Where are you from?'

'I'm Atrebates, from further east.'

'A long way from home, then? He pointed across the lines of stones. 'You can cross the river further a little further north, then there's a path south east around the bay. Daritorium is half a day's walk from here.'

'Many soldiers there?'

He shook his head. 'Mostly Roman traders, officials on the docks, a small garrison from what I've seen. Occasionally, I drive some sheep to sell. The legions are further east, where the trouble is. This was once all Veneti land. Years ago, Caesar's navy fought their ships in the bay. They were defeated and sold into slavery. It's been quiet here since then.' The shepherd stared up into the wavering tree. 'Mark me, the wind's changing again and there's another storm coming through.'

The sun was shining. I couldn't see it myself. But the shepherd was right, they usually were. I'd not been going long when the wind picked up and rain lashed down. I found shelter through the watery blur, beneath a dolmen on the edge of some trees. Large flat stones formed a roof, supported by others on either side. I thought it unlikely anyone would look for me there. It seemed dry when I crawled inside. My eyes became accustomed to the dim light. Carved swirling shapes covered the walls, like the tattoo on my mother's arm.

The storm brewed outside, so I decided to stay until morning. I wrapped myself up. The wind battered the walls. Angry voices shrieked in the storm. I didn't sleep well. I had strange dreams. Someone was reaching in from outside. A huge hand trying to pluck me out. Perhaps the ghosts from the netherworld didn't like me sharing their space.

In the morning I woke, cold and stiff. For a moment, I wondered where I was. I crawled toward the light somewhere beyond my feet. I reached the entrance of the dolmen and looked out. The worst of the storm had blown through, but everywhere was wet. Great pools of water lay on the sodden ground. I climbed out and followed the edge of a river until I found the bridge. Upstream at a narrow place, planks had been thrown across the bank. I crossed them onto a track. It led east toward a village I skirted around. Beyond I could see the edge of what I thought was Daritorium, on the bay. Masts of ships stood on the water. The key to my escape from the Empire. But I had no money left. The only coin I had left in the world was concealed in the thong around my neck.

And I would never part with that.

Daritorium sat in a spot, sheltered from the wind. There were a few ships in the harbour. Small fishing boats, coastal traders. The town was quiet. I sat behind a tree and observed the gate for a long time before I convinced myself it was safe. I crept in just before nightfall, behind a cart with some straw. It was too quiet. I wished it was busier. It might have been easier to slip around the streets unnoticed. But there was no military presence, or soldiers that I could see. No sign of Cato or the others.

I begged some bread and cheese. Even if I'd had my cloth juggling balls, I wouldn't have used them. I heard from a sailmaker that there was a ship bound for the western tip of Britannia. It was leaving as soon as the weather and tides were right. The destination was somewhere called Ictis, a place where they traded tin. I recalled the little Apollo I cast with Simon had come from there. When my feet finally touch that earth, I thought I would be free. That's what I thought then. But I was just a foolish boy who knew nothing.

I made my way up to the dock. One ship drew my attention, the only one that looked really sea worthy. It had a high prow that I knew made it resistant to storms. It wasn't possible to climb on. There were still people moving on the deck. So, I found a place to spend the night. Under the jetty, as close as I dared. I stared down at the little fish circling the piles sunk into the sand. Staying out of reach of the larger ones in deeper water. Aristotle said there were some fish that could walk on land. The only thing I'd seen do that was the octopus that escaped in our kitchen.

In the morning, the traffic above woke me. It was just after dawn, but I could hear wood creaking under the weight of bodies and voices. I started to climb out, when I heard the tramp of nailed sandals. Just like the ones I heard on the road to Oplontis. I pulled myself back under again. They walked out on the jetty and then back again. Then my blood froze. It was Titus. He had come to look at the ship and now was visiting the inns one by one on the road that led down to the dock.

The others might be somewhere near the gate to spot me if I tried to escape. I waited for a little while. Passengers were assembling above. One of traders spoke Latin with an accent. Others were speaking the language of my mother. I could understand most of what they said. I overheard the fare for a passenger with no cargo. Not that it meant much.

My money was gone. My only chance was to stow away or claim I could crew. In my desperation to get on that ship and out of Gaul, I'd trapped myself. It was too late to slip back into town.

All I could do was hope they left without seeing me. But if the passengers all boarded, I'd be left alone. They'd have me and this time Cato would make good his promise of a chain around my neck. I'd have no hope of escape. If I could get on that ship, I was free. But if they caught me, I was as good as dead. Even if I stayed where I was, they still might find me. I could try leaving Daritorium and going north again, find another harbour, another ship. How long could I keep going? In truth, I was sick of walking. I felt like the frog swimming endlessly in Octavia's impluvium. The cleverness of Archimedes had deserted me. I was not the cunning Odysseus who always found a way. I was Quintus, the cursed. That's when I heard a man praying in language I had heard Simon speak long ago.

'Blessed is the one who does not walk in step with the wicked or stand in the way that sinners take or sit in the company of mockers, but whose delight is in the law of the Lord, and who ponders it, day and night. For he is like a tree planted by streams of water, which yields its fruit in season and whose leaf does not wither, whatever they do prospers. Not so the wicked! They are like chaff that the wind blows away. The wicked will not stand in the judgment, nor sinners in the assembly of the righteous.'

I finished the last line for him. *'For the Lord watches over them, but the way of the wicked leads to destruction.'*

I saw him look over and see me. A bearded man covered in a cloak. 'You speak Aramaic.'

'My tutor was Greek. He taught me a bit.'

'Are you going to Ictis?'

I nodded, and he put his hand down and lifted me up. He had two large heavily bound boxes of wood bound with leather. I climbed next to him into the line of passengers crowding the narrow jetty. The line moved forward and pushed me to the edge of the jetty. It was stationary for a long time. If Cato came now, I'd have no choice but to jump and swim. I looked down, wondering what my chances were. The tide was rising, not far from the peak. We shuffled forward. Someone in front of me lifted his burden and climbed onto the boat.

The captain put up his hand and stared at me. 'I don't remember you paying your fare.'

Then I felt a hand on my shoulder. 'He's my nephew.'

The captain furrowed his brow. 'Are you sure? He's looks like a Gaul.'

'I've paid double for my goods, which are small and light. Have pity, I can't leave him here. He helps me carry my stuff.'

The captain glared. 'Alright, he can come. We have to catch the tide or we'll be stuck here.'

We clambered on. I found a spot where I was out of view behind the mast and sat silent on the deck. The man said nothing. It took a long time for the rest of the passengers to board and stow their gear. After what seemed an eternity, they finally gave the order to cast off. I remember the relief as the boat pulled away from the dock. It started to make its way out through the narrow gap, out into the island-studded bay. It was only then I looked back I could see two horsemen riding back along the harbour. Cato and Acco. Cato was shouting and waving something that glinted in the sun. Perhaps he was trying to signal to the captain with his gladius.

Then a breeze took us between the headlands, and they were gone.

CHAPTER THIRTEEN

The man who had saved me came down and sat opposite. He offered me a dried fig. I hadn't had one of those since I left the estate. I savoured the sweetness. His Greek sounded a lot like Simon's.

'Your Aramaic's a little rusty, but it served its purpose.'

'I don't know much, apart from that prayer my tutor taught me.'

'There is more to you than meets the eye. Two Romans rode onto the dock after we left. I suspect they were not friends of yours.'

'No.'

'Are you an escaped slave?'

I nodded. I didn't see the point of lying. He'd risked a lot to save someone he'd never met before. We were outside the empire now, anyway.

He frowned. 'Our whole people were once enslaved, it is abhorrent to me. In fact, we have a religious duty to free slaves, if it's within our power. So now I have the blessing of god for this voyage, thanks to you. You must be from a wealthy Roman household if you had a tutor.'

'An old Greek, called Simon.'

'You should honour both the old and the wise. One day, with luck, you may become both yourself. Were you living in Gaul?'

'No, south of Rome.'

He rubbed his beard. 'They have chased you a long way. Must have influence from a Senator or a Tribune?'

I shrugged my shoulders. 'I made a promise to my mother to return to her people, where she was born.'

'It is a good to honour your mother. Wait 'till we're safe on dry land. You can tell me your story then. Not that our destination is often dry. My name is Joseph, a merchant from Ramah. Do you know where that is?'

I shook my head.

'A long way away from here, on the other side of the Empire. North of Egypt. It's as warm and dry there as it's wet and cold here. But where we are going, it's even wetter. I presume you've not been to Belerion?'

'No.'

'It is the western tip of Britannia. The journey's not long, but it might be rough. There's a port there called Ictis, the tin town they call it. A place at the very edge of the world. There is an island with a hill, where they keep a fire burning to keep ships off the rocks. They need to. There are plenty round that treacherous coast. I come here to trade what I have for tin. A very useful metal, especially if you blend it with copper to make bronze. It does not corrode like iron. It's still the best for many things; lamps, mirrors, cymbals, and bells. He pointed down at the deck. If you look carefully, this ship's nails are made from it. Copper we can get from nearby Cyprus, but tin, very few places have it. The price increases every time it changed hands, so I buy it in bulk at its source. I trade red saffron, as well as scented resins from desert trees. They are all light and more valuable than gold. But they need to be packed well to keep them dry.' It started to drizzle and Joseph smiled. 'Now if I could work out how to barter sunshine for rain, then I would be a rich man.'

Joseph said there was an island further north and west. The Romans called it Hibernia. He'd never travelled there, but he had been almost everywhere else I'd heard of. He told me about the place he lived. It was hot and dry in summer, with desert in the south. There was an inland sea so thick with salt, it was lifeless and you could not sink. This was not his first trip he had come before, once with his niece's son. He'd sailed from a city called Tyre at the eastern edge of the Mediterranean. A place Simon had told me, Alexander conquered with a causeway. He'd stopped at Syracuse where Archimedes lived and died. Then Carthage, where the elephant armies of Hannibal had come. Through the Pillars of Hercules, to Brigantia on the northern tip of Hispania. He'd survived a storm, and stopped at Daritorium in Gaul, the last port before Ictis. It was a long voyage and not without risk. But it could be quicker than going overland, he said, with fewer tolls and brigands.

I told him my tutor was born in Alexandria. He said he'd seen the big lighthouse there. It was still a place of learning, even though the library had been burned. Poor Simon, the thought of all those precious books in flames had moved him to tears.

Joseph had seen more of the of the world than anyone I met before, or since. More than my father, Simon, or even Cato might have done. He'd travelled on the Nile, the greatest river in the world. He visited Cyprus for copper, where Ariston and Panya had met. It had mountains, he said, with pine forests and snow in winter. He'd even sailed to Crete, once, to trade. But he'd not heard of the Minotaur or Daedalus.

We remained in sight of the coast of Gaul. There were islands, I counted three headlands, then suddenly we were out in the open sea. The wind was from the southwest. We heaved and rolled. The waves crashed over the boat and the saltwater sprayed my face. I remember thinking this water was very different from the sea at Oplontis or even Corsis. Wild and raw with the strong taste of seaweed, colder too.

'You're not frightened?' asked Joseph.

I shook my head. 'I've been in worse, much worse than this. Even spent a day once, floating in the ocean. That prayer, it kept me alive.'

'Then god must be protecting you.'

It was a voyage of three days. Eventually, we saw the coast of Britannia. Lots of high cliffs, but no villas built on them. Just seabirds crying and circling. As we passed a headland, the wind from the west dropped and we sailed serenely into a bay. The gulls followed us in, hovering at the edge of the boat. Joseph scattered bread for them in the water.

'I offer thanks for my safe arrival. There are many treacherous rocks and banks below the water.'

There was a tall island with a port just off the sand and on the mainland a collection of houses. In most of the empire, it would barely be called a town. Joseph held out his hand.

'Well, this is Ictis. Some say it has existed as long as Rome. We have come here as long as I remember, my father and his before him. Back to the time of the Pharaohs in Egypt. A journey from the furthest east to the most distant west. From one of the driest places in the world, to perhaps the wettest. What do you plan to do now?'

'My mother's family is east of here. I am going back to them.'

'There is a local merchant where I stay. His name is Ael. If you have nowhere else to go, you will be welcome to stop with me. You look like you could use a meal. Ael's a curious man who likes to hear news from outside. Though he claims sea sickness and doesn't venture far himself. But I will need to know your name if I am to introduce you.'

I hesitated for a moment. Of course, we had spent three days on the boat and he'd never asked me. Was I Quintus, Cadmus, or Caden?

'Have you forgotten?'

I touched the coin in the thong around my neck. I remembered the promise I had made.

'No.' I said, 'My name here is Caden.'

We tied up at a wooden dock on the western sheltered side of the island. Joseph told me at low tide there was a causeway to the mainland, but it was flooded now. We had to wait. It was a busy place despite its size. There were boats of all types, sea-going vessels like ours, with wide hulls filled with cargo, down to little wicker ones like Argo. I helped Joseph unload his goods. Most of the inhabitants were dressed dourly in grey cloaks, long tunics, trousers and boots.

Joseph pointed to stacks of ingots of bright metal, the precious tin. 'This is what brings people to this cold, wet island.'

I recalled the tin figure that I had made with Simon, the bright Apollo, He must have come from here. The tide was receding. The causeway emerged from the water. Joseph hired a pack pony to take them up into the village. He had many boxes sealed with wax against the air.

'The merchant I know here, Ael. His family has known mine for a long time. He's one of the few here like you, who can speak both Greek and Latin. He claims one of his ancestors came a long time ago from Tyre, but he's a Briton now.' Then it began to drizzle. Joseph held out his hand, and the rain ran through his long fingers. 'Sometimes you think the rain never ceases in Belerion. In my country, it's a cause for rejoicing. But when you see the sun here, that is the blessing from god.'

The loaded pack pony plodded along the causeway, then entered the town. The streets were unpaved. There were no roman tiles or bathhouses. No temples of Jupiter, statues of Tiberius, or Praetorians lurking in doorways. The large house up the hill was comfortable, and they greeted Joseph like an old friend. It looked like the houses in Gaul I'd seen. Inside a central hearth with a pot of bronze. A table and chairs with tallow candles. Chests like the one Simon had and three huge dogs that looked like wolves. They came up and sniffed me before Ael called them away.

We put our cloaks next to the fire to dry. Ael was a big, round man with a dark beard and a hearty laugh. I liked him at once. But he spoke Latin with an accent that was difficult to follow. Joseph unpacked gifts that were gratefully received, then pointed to me.

'This is Caden. He joined me at Daritorium. He's travelling back to his mother's people further east. Don't be deceived by appearance. He can read Latin and Greek and a few other things besides.'

'Welcome,' said Ael. 'You would be useful in Ictis. We get merchants from all over. I've opened another mine since you were here last, Joseph, and found a new seam of ore.'

Ael had never been to Rome. The furthest he had been was Daritorium. But he had an interest in news from the Empire.

'Wars have a habit of increasing prices,' he said. 'Traders cannot ignore what goes on in the world outside.'

Joseph nodded in agreement. 'This trip may be my last. I am not sure who would come next time. I have brought some gifts.'

One was a reading crystal like the one Simon had. It was very precious because Joseph had carried on his person, wrapped in linen.

'I was told it was never to be left in the sun.'

Joseph smiled, 'you have to be careful with them as they are fragile and can break. But don't worry, the sun is rarely hot enough in Belerion to start a fire.'

The other gift was in a small sealed box. Ael unwrapped a dark resin. A familiar odour filled the room. I felt the blood drain from my face and my neck tighten. I was back in Tiberius's chamber. That moment before I ran out onto the terrace. The frantic chase on the cliff and the fall to the sea. That smell had stained my life. It was now the scent of fear. Joseph sensed my disquiet and wrapped it back up.

'Most people like myrrh Caden, in fact, they pay a lot for it. Though it comes from a very unattractive and thorny tree. It has lots of uses, apart from the pleasure of its scent, not least to wash wounds and cure toothache. But for you I can see perhaps, it is different.'

Aels' wife Elowen brought bread and cheese. No one seemed to mind that I ate more than anyone else. The dogs sat under the table and ate any scraps that fell. I sat back and listened. I probably learned more about the Empire in a couple of hours, than all my time with Simon or my father. The Consuls in Rome were Silanus and Nerva. But the real ruler in the city was the praetorian, Sejanus. Joseph said the Emperor was rarely seen. There were troubles in Judea. Their king was a Roman vassal. He was building a town named after Tiberius on an inland sea, but the people were refusing to live there. A revolt was brewing.

Ael shook his head. 'I don't like what I hear about this Tiberius.'

Joseph nodded. 'They say his Praetorian Prefect Sejanus may be worse. An empire ruled by greed and fear will never last. My voyage has been a long one, and the weather was worse than usual. They are building a lighthouse at Brigantia, in Hispania, like the one at Alexandria.'

Ael nodded and agreed it was good for trade. 'Too many ships sink and all our work is wasted. Cargo's no use to anyone sitting at the bottom of the sea. Not to mention the poor souls who never return.'

They shared news of each other's families and put the world to rights. Ael turned to me.

'So, what is a little Greek educated Roman doing this far from home?'

'I'm not Roman' I replied. 'My mother is from the Atrebates tribe. East of here, a place called the Hill of the White Horse.'

Ael raised his eyes. 'Ah, so you are one of us? Were you a slave?'

'Yes. I escaped.'

'You've done well to get this far. There are Roman merchants that come through here, but no soldiers. We have a little silver here, not enough for the Empire to notice yet.'

Joseph nodded. 'The Romans are more interested in grain and gold.'

Ael sat back. 'But for how long? Rome is always greedy for new lands to conquer. Caesar came once further east, I'm told. I think they will come again. Then he pointed at me. 'You could make a good living here, lad. I could do with some younger eyes like yours. My eldest son prefers prospecting tin than reading contracts.'

'That is kind, but I made a promise to return to the Atrebates.'

Ael smiled. 'Well, you can always change your mind.'

They filled the whole wet day with gossip and storytelling. Joseph told me many tales, like Simon recounting Homer. There was a boy who killed a giant and a man who was swallowed by a whale. Ael told me about Lugus, the god of storms, light and travellers.

'The Romans call him Mercury, but he's not the same,' said Ael. 'With three faces, one more than Janus. He killed a giant with a venomous eye using his sling.'

I didn't know which gods to believe in, or all of them? Was it Janus and Poseidon who had helped me? Or perhaps it was Joseph's god or the mind that invented geometry? Now I had reached Britannia, perhaps the three faced Lugus would be my guide? Plato believed in some perfect place, but I wasn't sure where that was. Yet there was something about Ictis. I felt at home and safe there. But then, what did I know? I was just a foolish boy.

Elowen, was preparing a proper feast for the evening. Her youngest child, a son called Mermin, was tottering around her feet. She told me she was descended from the Veneti, who had fled Gaul and settled in Belerion. She was baking bread and boiling duck eggs like the ones I had eaten on the Olt. There was salted herring and salmon fresh caught in the sea. She gave me one of the eggs, and I wolfed it down.

'My husband says you come from near Rome.'

'Further south, a small place, no one's heard of it.'

'Probably not. You look like you haven't had a good meal in weeks.'

Elowen was right. I was half starved. I'd felt all my ribs on the deck of the boat when I lay down to sleep. She opened the cupboard where the food was kept cool. 'Don't worry. We have a good larder here. Even have a few little luxuries from the Empire that might appeal to you.' There it was, an earthenware jar marked with that name, *A. Umbricius Scaurus*. The garum from Pompeii that my mother spooned as I told the tale of Icarus. Next to it, an amphora of oil with an opened wax seal. I felt a tear come to my eye.

I could just make out the horse's head and the broken wings of Pegasus.

They gave me a little space to bed down, adjacent to the hearth. For some strange reason, the dogs lay down around me. I felt like the founders of Rome nurtured by a wolf. I remembered Linus, who was snatched for the Emperor at Lupercalia. I recalled the pack who followed me in the Black Mountains and the dog that savaged Yann and Alban. But these just stared at me and yawned. I scratched one behind the ear. It nuzzled me and licked my face. For the first time in a long while, I slept the whole night. No leering faces, no crows, snakes or eagles disturbed me. It was a deep and dreamless sleep.

The next day, the rain had stopped. It was bright sunshine and warm. The dogs were already up and being fed some scraps of fish. Ael scowled at my footwear.

'You need some decent boots, boy. Those Roman sandals are no good here.'

He found an old pair that fitted me. They came over my ankles and I could lace them tight. Ael took me with Joseph to inspect the mine. It was not much more than a hole in the side of a gorse studded hill. Timber props supported the roof. Ponies pulled out sleds filled with grey stone. The miners emerged covered in dust. There were no armed overseers or shackles, but it must have been hard work all the same. A stone wheel pulled by a pony in a circle crushed the ore. Then they smelted it with charcoal in kilns to yield the precious tin. I watched it cool into ingots, the same size as those stacked on the shore in Ictis. Ael picked one up and handed it to Joseph who nodded, and handed it back.

It evoked that figure I made with Simon. My tin Apollo, the passenger for the many models of Aetos that we made. I wondered what happened to it. Perhaps Simon had kept it, or maybe he had melted it down. Back at the house, they settled on an exchange for Joseph's wares and the tin. Ael had agreed to take me for the first part of my journey east. As far as the place where open moorland started. It was a three-day walk. There was a settlement there where his sister lived. Then he would leave me as he had business on the north coast.

I said goodbye to Joseph. He was leaving to return to Tyre. First catching a ship to take him to Brigantia, then onward down to the pillars of Hercules. Then back east, across the wine dark Mediterranean sea.

'With luck, they'll have finished the lighthouse,' said Ael.

'I hope so,' muttered Joseph. 'We all need a light in the darkness. Goodbye Caden, may the Lord watch over you and remember, the way of the wicked will lead to their destruction.'

Ael had a pony loaded with his goods. A brown, squat mare with a thick coat of hair. Nothing to look at and a bit slow, but tough and sure-footed. He said she had been pulling ore from the pits before he bought her. But she didn't like the darkness of the mine.

'Some beasts take to it, others will never go in. No point wasting good horseflesh. Don't be fooled by her size. She will carry a full load.'

The road was wet, we had to avoid deep puddles. Our boots and the pony's fetlocks were soon stained with mud. Ael said that Belerion was a peninsular that stuck out into the ocean. There were large rivers further south, too big to ford easily. Best to stay in the high country, he said, where they remained streams. Twelve days walking east would take me to a place they called the Henge. A circle of huge stones, three times the height of a man. They stood on a wide plain and could be seen for miles.

An old place of worship where people still gathered at the winter solstice. From there, walking northeast and I would find the Atrebates. But if there was a white horse on a hill, he did not know.

'You've spent too long speaking Latin. You need to practice your mother tongue if you are going to survive here.' So, while we walked, he taught me the local names of all the trees, animals, and birds. It took me a while to understand everything he said. Some of his words were different to the ones I remembered, and he spoke with a drawl. 'I count myself as one of the Cornovii. They speak slower than the Domnonii further east. But don't let that fool you. They're a cunning lot.'

Here and there, we passed small settlements with round houses, grazing cattle and clusters of geese and pigs. There were strange red beaked crows. The first night we stayed in a village. The second night we found a dry camp he'd used before. A shallow cave in the side of a low cliff, surrounded by elms twisted sideways by the wind. We lit a fire, and I scraped off the mud on my boots with a stick. My little axe and knife were tarnished by the sea. I took my whetstone and gave them both an edge. Ael gave me some oil to keep them sharp. He loaded my bag with enough food for several days,

'A mile east of here, you'll come to moorland. Bleak and wet, with columns of stones piled up high. Not many trees there or people either. Earth's too shallow to grow crops and little for cattle to eat. May take you a day or more to walk across. Stick to the higher ground. When you cross that one after a couple of days further east, you'll come to another, even larger. That's another three days walking, at least. Keep asking for the path to the Henge. Most folk know where that is. But it's so old no one knows who built it. They gather there for the shortest day when the druids track the rising sun. When you reach it, travel between the pole star and the dawn. The land of the Atrebates is at least four days beyond that. Of course, if you had a horse, it would be quicker. Some people sail east along the coast. That's not for me. I've only been on a boat once to Daritorium. That was enough. My ancestors from Tyre would be ashamed. I spewed my guts the whole way there and back. I've stayed on land ever since. I'd go down a mine any day, before I'd sail again. People complain about the rain here, but it's no wetter than Gaul. In fact, they looked the same to me. Like the gods split the two lands in half and divided them by sea. The only difference is that there are no Romans here. They came before and then they left. But knowing the Romans, I've no doubt they'll be back again. A stubborn people. They don't give up easily.'

I asked Ael if he heard of Bleydiud, the king who flew.

'An old story we were told as children,' he said. 'I never believed it. Get some rest now. You have an early start tomorrow.'

In the morning, I said goodbye to Ael. He wished me luck and said I was always welcome to return. I headed east across bleak moorland. The ground was sodden, except in the higher places. Rough grass, gorse and bracken were the only plants that grew here. The occasional stunted hawthorn arched over in the relentless wind. No good for cattle or even sheep, but my goats would have thrived. On the summits of small hills, were piles of enormous stones, as if the giant Laestrygones had stacked them, waiting for Odysseus to pass. I camped up amongst them. They were dry and gave some protection from the breeze. One of the red beaked ravens was hopping nearby. I made a little fire of dried gorse. It was just for comfort. I didn't need its warmth.

The following day I got up early with the star they call Orions' dog. The beast that hunts the rabbit Lepus at his feet. A sign of doom for Hector in Homer's tale. Like that dog that had mauled Alban on the Tarn. I knew what it was like to be hunted. They had tracked me across Gaul. I'd escaped by a hare's whisker at Daritorium. Only because I'd learned a prayer by chance. He didn't know it, but it was Simon's most unexpected gift to me.

But I was safe now. I'd left the hunters long behind. Here in Britannia, I was beyond their reach. I was travelling light and fast. Ael had told me it would take two days to cross. By late afternoon, I could see the eastern edge of the moor coming to an end.

That's when I turned to see a white horse galloping behind me.

CHAPTER FOURTEEN

The horse was perhaps less than a mile away, beneath clouds gathering in the west. The rider was wearing a brown cloak, and the hood was up. But it was unable to conceal a familiar barrel figure. It could only be Cato.

No sign of Acco. Perhaps his orders didn't extend beyond Gaul. Or Titus, Cato was alone. It didn't matter. He was on a horse. I couldn't outrun him or hide on the barren landscape. Then I saw it up ahead, a white stone lintel on the side of a small hill, topped with bracken. A barrow with a narrow entrance. I'd spent an uneasy night in one near Daritorium, sheltering from a storm. The hooves were galloping over the turf. I looked back. The hood had fallen back. He may have dressed himself like a native, but I could see his scabbard tucked under his cloak. He'd grown a dark beard, but I knew it was him. As he drew closer his white eye gleamed, and there was a look of triumph on his face.

I raced down, threw my bag in, and squeezed between the narrow stones. Then I crawled as far back as I could into the small space. At the back, it widened a little on one side. I sat down, breathing hard and desperate. Like that octopus I remembered from the kitchen. The one that bit my hand and covered me in ink. I gripped my knife and took my axe out of my belt. Somewhere above me, a small chink of light trickled in. The entrance was tall but narrow. The stone on one side had leaned over. Cato would find it difficult to get inside. I prayed Janus was my guardian.

I heard the horse arrive a few moments later and its rider dismount. Footsteps came to the entrance. I heard him circle around to see if there was any other way in. Then came that growl I hoped I'd never hear again.

'Quintus, I know you're in there. You can't get away. No one ever does from Cato. You have no option now but to surrender and come back with me.'

I certainly wasn't going to come out. I'd rather starve. But he had me trapped like a rat in a hole. I had some food with me and a little water. I could wait a long time. Perhaps Cato knew it.

'You didn't think I would follow you all the way to Britannia, did you? But you underestimated Cato. You wouldn't be the first, nor the last. I look like a local, but I've kept my trusty gladius tucked away. Been with me all over the Empire, cutting throats all the way to Syria and back. I only know a few words here, but gold speaks its own language.'

I stayed silent, worried he might work out how far back I was if I spoke.

He whispered into the entrance. 'Do you think you can stop me, Quintus? Hordes of barbarians have tried, but I never give up. I fought my way out of the forests in the Rhineland. Places so dark it was twilight at midday. Waded my way through rivers of bodies, waist deep. I kept fighting when others cowered around me. Come out now, boy, or it will be worse for you.'

I still didn't move or speak.

'That woman who helped you. Do you want to hear what happened to her?'

He was trying to make me angry, perhaps hoping I would show myself. 'You already told me you hung her upside down in Rome.'

'No, the other one, the woman in the farmhouse north of Narbo. That horse blanket you stole. We knew she was lying. It was Acco's. She must have helped you. He swore he'd go back and have his revenge. He's one for the ladies, that Acco. But he's not gentle, so I've heard.'

I rolled the dice, I could only make this as difficult for him as possible. 'Alive and unblemished, isn't that what Tiberius ordered?'

Cato growled. 'You have a good memory, lad. But I think he would tolerate a few scratches for the pleasure of renewing your company. He wants the minnow who escaped his net.'

I saw his gladius flash in the entrance, but it was too short to reach me. Then he tried poking in a sharpened stick, but I had anticipated that. As soon as I saw it come in, Enora's little axe chopped it in half. I heard Cato curse.

'You little wretch, I'll soon smoke you out.'

I heard him outside, slashing grass and scratching flint and steel. The gods must have smiled because, just as I smelled the smoke, the heavens opened. The rain poured down and filled the entrance to the barrow with water. Joseph was right, this was the wettest place in the world. I could tell Cato was getting more impatient, splashing around.

'You are still worth something dead to me,' he shouted. 'If I can't have you alive, then I'll bring your head back, smiling in a bag of salt. The flesh shrinks, so it looks like they're laughing. A quaint Celtish custom, I understand.'

He knelt down at the entrance and leaned in. I saw his short sword flash again in the space. It didn't quite reach me. I grabbed the severed end of the sharpened stick to fend the blade away. Then Cato did something unexpected. He crawled up on top of the barrow. He pushed his face into an aperture to see where I was. The little glint of sunlight was replaced by an eye glaring down at me.

I struck up with that sharpened stick. Looking back, it was a combination of fright and fortune. I felt the stick pierce deep into his one good eye and I heard a scream. The bloodied stick fell from my quivering hand. I could hear writhing and splashing outside in the rain. It seemed to go on for a long time. Then it stopped.

I sat there listening as the rain lessened and there was a glimpse of sunshine. I could hear a mane shaking off water, then silence. Slowly, I crept toward the entrance. The white horse was tethered and grazing. I could not see Cato. I went a little further. Then I saw his sandal lying still. There was a pebble just inside the entrance. I threw it. It missed, but the foot did not move. I took a deep breath, holding my knife in one hand and my axe in the other as I emerged fully into the sunlight.

Cato was lying there, face up. He must have rolled some way, because his cloak was covered in mud. Blood and gore oozed out of his eye. I could not tell if he was alive, but I tried not to get too close. A little way off, his gladius glinted on the grass. I edged over and picked up his sword. It was short but heavy in my hand. A hated symbol of Rome, everything I was trying to escape. I didn't want him to be marked out as a Roman. So, I threw the blade back into the barrow. The less to say who Cato was, the better. An unfortunate Briton who had had a nasty accident. This part of the moor didn't look well travelled. With luck, he wouldn't be recognisable by the time the next person came past.

Then Cato started groaning. Suddenly, he spluttered and sat up.

'Quintus.'

I didn't answer.

He lifted himself up onto his feet and held his hands out. 'You have my gladius?'

He got no response. Then he fumbled at his waist, pulled out his pugio and waved the stout little blade in front of him.

'I know you're there, Quintus.'

I gathered my bag and circled slowly around the rear of his horse. As I untethered the beast, it whinnied.

'Are you are going to take my horse? Or what passes for one in this wretched place? Leaving a blind man in the middle of nowhere. Come on, you little coward, if you are brave enough, come and kill me.'

I often wondered what I would have done in his place. Diogenes said all men fear the loss of sight, which is why they give money to blind beggars. When I was two dozen yards distant, I felt safe enough to leave the horse hobbled. I moved to one side. Between us there was a fissure in the hill and a drop down onto stone. The tangled roots of a long departed tree writhed at the edge.

'I'm not going to stab you in the back like you did Alban. You have the means to end this yourself.'

Cato edged toward my voice.

'What, take the coward's way out and kill myself, like that fool, Varus? Come on, it's a fair fight, blind man against boy. You'll never get better odds than that.'

There were many reasons to want to kill Cato — too many. His eye socket oozed as I watched him stumble like a raging Cyclops. He must have been in terrible pain. I should have felt cruelty and joy, like Octavia. But I didn't. He'd probably killed countless people in his time, maybe a few were deserving. But Cato was really the instrument of another's evil. If his villa in Tusculum had depended on letting me go, he wouldn't have had a moment's hesitation. He seemed helpless, but I knew that's what the old soldier wanted me to think. Because he was now holding the knife by the blade. I stayed silent and moved quietly to one side. I would make Cato choose his own doom. The way of the wicked would lead to his destruction.

'Quintus, you little coward. You barbarian scum.'

I wasn't going to speak and give myself away. Valeria had called me worse.

Then he threw the knife. It fluttered harmlessly to one side and plunged into the turf. He stopped to listen.

'Goodbye Cato,' I said.

He gave a roar and started running toward where he'd heard my voice.

'I'll crush you with my bare hands, you stupid boy.'

I watched him topple over the edge. He gave a gasp, then he was gone. I heard a thud as his body hit something hard below. I led the horse around and down to see where he'd fallen. He'd come down face first. His feet were tangled in the roots. He was half suspended, hanging there. His head had struck stone. Then he started to shake, his whole body convulsed. The roots gave way, and he fell and rolled onto his back. His lips and beard were foaming with blood. He shook for some time before it stopped. I waited until he was quite still.

Lugus was the three faced god. The one Ael said, killed the giant with one eye. Perhaps it was Lugus who had helped me? At that moment, I didn't really care if it was Lugus, Janus, or the mind who invented geometry. I retrieved the pugio from the grass. As I felt the weight, I noticed my hand was shaking. Titus had once held one against my cheek. I threw it as far as I could. Then I mounted the white horse and turned toward the eastern edge of the moor. The sun was low. I had perhaps two hours of light.

I twisted back for one last look. A red beaked crow had landed on Cato's chest and was pecking at his face. Then I saw it extract his bloodied, mangled eye.

The one I had seen in my dream.

The white mare was small and sturdy. A little taller than Ael's pack pony, but the same breed. It looked like she'd spent all winter outside, grazing on rough grass. Covered with a thick coat and an unclipped mane and tail. Cato had probably paid a pretty sum, but he knew his horseflesh. She was used to being ridden and responsive to my command. Nimble on the rough paths and fearless fording the fastest streams. Her hard black hooves coped with harsh outcrops of stone. And she was swift, perhaps appreciating the lighter load. Or maybe the goddess of horses, Epona, was finally favouring me now.

The moor came to an end. I needed to put distance between me and the barrow. I rode east for the remainder of the light, avoiding any habitation. Best to be as far from the Praetorian's body as I could get. I did not know what friends the Empire might have in Belerion. If Cato had bought a horse, someone might recognise him. The rain started briefly, then stopped, and the sky cleared. I came to a stream and a grove of trees. I tethered the horse near some fresh grass. Then I found some dry wood and lit a fire.

The pony had a saddlebag stacked with Cato's gear. Bread, oats, salted pork, and cheese. I boiled some water in Enora's bronze bowl and made a gruel. There was plenty of money, some Roman gold coins I'd never seen before and local currency he must have got in Belerion. Then I found the letter he had with the Imperial seal. It gave authority to the bearer to be granted assistance from any Roman official and swore them to secrecy. I read it, then I threw it in the fire. There was another letter about a deposit on a property in Tusculum. It said that it was in danger of being sold, unless he paid the rest. I burned that too.

Watching those parchments turn to ash, filled me with profound relief. The face that had haunted me for so long disappeared into the flames. The man who boasted of his escape from the slaughter of Armenius. One of the vile speculatores and commander of the vigiles in Rome. I wondered how many boys he'd sent to the Emperor's bed. He'd chased me for Tiberius halfway across the Empire. Spent his last moments blind on a barren moor in Britannia. Very different from what he imagined for himself. Soaking in the warm water at the baths in Tusculum. Or sharing stories in the forum, beneath the statue of Tiberius. Perhaps Janus had closed the door on his dream. I slept soundly, knowing he was dead.

The next day, I awoke. Packed the bags and set off with the rising sun in my face. Ahead there was a narrow barren peak, scarred with bare rock, the highest place for miles. I encouraged the horse up. Down a valley to the right and a long way off, I thought I could see the sea. To the east, another stretch of moorland beckoned.

I spent two more days riding and found myself at the edge of a town called Keresk, the capital of the Dumnonii tribe, on a river that led south to the sea. The clustered houses were all thatched and round, with no Roman tiles in sight. I stopped only long enough to replenish my supplies. Cato had left me plenty of money to buy bread. I needed to turn north again, but too far, I was told, and I'd find myself in a marsh. I headed out on a path northwest, keeping to the higher ground, with the wind at my back. It led over hills with narrow valleys and twisting rivers. I travelled slowly through forest and farmland with grazing cattle and sheep. There was no trouble finding lonely places to let the horse graze.

I bedded down nightly by a fire. Like the days I travelled in Argo, I slept well and without fear.

Then at last I reached a place of great open hills with sheep grazing. In the distance, I could see a vast circle of stones. This must be the Henge. It was so old, Ael said, no one could remember who built it. As I drew closer, it seemed quiet, deserted. From here, Ael said to go northwest and I would find the hill of the white horse. There was a line of trees marking a river nearby. I rode down to it and let the horse drink. Then I tethered the mare to graze amongst some trees. I cut and sharpened a long ash stave to test the depth of the river. It was too deep. I would need to find a shallower spot upstream to cross. I walked back up the slope to get a better look at the stones. They loomed over me, three times the height of the ones near Daritorium. The wind whistled through them as if they were singing, inhabited by spirits from the distant past. This was the place where my mother had left her old life behind. I walked out onto the wavering grass, fondling the coin that hung around my neck. I recalled the promise I had made the day she died. A few more days and I would keep it.

Then I threw myself to the ground. But if I hadn't, I'd probably be dead.

I'd been too busy staring at the stones, lost in my own thoughts to notice. Until I felt the thudding of hooves on the grass.

The horseman was nearly on top of me, with his sword drawn. I threw myself on the ground and the dun beast leaped over me. A blade whistled past my ear. He kept riding, then wheeled clumsily around in a wide circle. I knew immediately it was Titus. It was the way he lurched in the saddle. He must have come over with Cato. I should have guessed he'd make the trip across, but for some reason, the Praetorian had left him behind. If Titus knew my destination, he could return with support and find me. He had his gladius drawn and was circling me, threatening to charge. I felt the sling on my belt, next to the small axe and a knife. But I'd dropped the stave somewhere back toward the stones. It must be lying in the long wavering grass.

'Quintus,' he shouted. 'I took an oath with Cato to pursue you to the end of the earth. The same one my father swore to never desert the service, or seek to avoid death.'

The sun was scorching over my head. I was already weary. He had a horse and the advantage of open country. The gladius was too short for fighting on horseback. I was lucky he didn't have a spear or Acco's cavalry sword. But the horse could knock me over and easily break my bones. My best chance was to get back to the stones. They were at least an obstacle for the horse. He would have to dismount to fight me there. No real advantage, but better than nothing. I took out the sling. The complacent fool I was, I had only one stone. I wound it around my head. He started to charge, but it was a feint. He then wheeled away, then turned around again.

He was wary, but he knew I couldn't keep this up forever. He'd just wait until I tired myself out. I had no water, and the sun was high. It was nearly as hot as a day in Campania. I needed to say something to get him on the other side of me, away from the Henge.

'My people are coming. They'll be here soon.'

Titus laughed. 'You've forgotten how to lie, Quintus. I passed two shepherds on a distant hill, but there's no one else around for miles. Rome can come anytime they choose and take all this. Remember, we are the best and bravest. It's our destiny to conquer the world.'

'I thought Horatius was your hero. He held off hordes and you're frightened of one boy.'

My taunt must have worked because he turned the horse. 'You son of a whore,' he shouted. 'Let me remind you of your lessons.'

Then he urged his horse into a charge. This was no feint. He kept coming. I wound the sling around and released. He turned, the stone struck the flank of his mount and the animal reared up in pain. Titus hung on, but took a few moments to control the horse and he drifted across and behind me. I seized my chance and started my scramble back toward the stones.

He guessed I was making for them. I heard him galloping behind, getting closer. The Henge was too distant. He'd catch me before I'd reach it. But I didn't even get that far. My foot tripped on the pole I'd left in the grass. I sprawled onto my face. By the time I got to my knees, he was nearly on top of me, leaning over, swinging his sword. I gripped the stave in the grass. As I knelt there, I saw him smile, thinking I'd given up. Then I lifted the point of the ash pole. It took his horse somewhere between chest and neck. The stave was torn from my grasp. I felt something graze my shoulder as he skidded past. Then I turned to see the horse roll and collapse, quivering onto the grass. Titus was thrown clear, but his luck held. He rolled and landed on his feet, still clutching the gladius. Even

Panya might have been impressed. I'd misjudged him, perhaps he could be an Equites after all. Now he had his sword, and I just had a knife and Enora's puny axe. Whatever hope I held abandoned me.

Then I remembered the river. I wasn't sure if Titus could swim, but I knew I could. I ran through the stones, down the hill, until I reached the bank. It was upstream from where I'd tethered the horse. I could hear Titus giving chase. He was too close behind for me to mount and ride away. I dived straight in and was halfway across before I looked back. Titus had reached the bank in a rage, determined to follow me. I kept swimming for the opposite side. There was a splash as he waded in. When I reached the shallows, I turned. He was chest deep, then he struck out. He could swim nearly well as me.

I scrambled up the opposite bank and knelt there, just back from the edge, soaked and breathless. I fumbled at my belt. He grunted as he climbed the bank blindly after me. His right hand, gripping his gladius, appeared over the grassy edge. There was no time to think. I chopped down hard with that little axe. I'd worked on it with my whetstone until it was razor sharp.

It went through his wrist and severed it completely. He screamed and fell back. His bloodied hand lay on the grass, still holding the hilt of the gladius. I heard him slip down and splash into the water. I looked over and saw him on his back, in the shallows. He had a look of horror, holding up the stump of his arm. Blood was gushing out in spurts, like a fountain I'd once seen in Rome. It stained the river bank bright red.

If he'd been a proper soldier, he would have wrapped something tight around his forearm. But he sat there like a fool with his left hand, trying in vain to stem the flow of blood. My horse neighed. He looked over his shoulder and saw it.

'That's Cato's horse,' he hissed. 'I saw a body, days ago, covered in carrion like flies. We should have killed you when we had the chance. I wanted to, so did Acco, but Cato said we had to bring you back, alive. You're nothing but filth, like that traitor Armenius.'

'Where's Acco?'

Tutus grimaced. The blood was gushing between the fingers, gripping his severed wrist. 'Cato sent him back at Daritorium. Had to rejoin his legion. They were leaving for the Rhine.'

I glanced back at the gladius on the grass. That's when I noticed the ring on one finger of the severed hand. It was a gold sealing ring with the winged horse of Pegasus. The moment I knew my father had lied. He'd made Titus his heir, before I'd even left for Capri. I lay back on the damp grass. Valeria was right. I was a fool. I could forgive my father for lying to me, but not to my dying mother.

I prised the dead grip from the hilt. I slid that ring from the cold wet finger and lifted it up to show him. 'This is my father's ring,' I shouted. It seems strange, but I felt angrier about that than the fact he'd tried to kill me.

Titus was rocking backward and forward, grimacing. 'Caecilius adopted me as his heir. After Valeria swore you used to beat and abuse her. He changed his mind, said you were never worthy to be his son.'

'She lied.'

Titus winced. 'Who knows, like the story, you had a pair of wings. The truth never matters, Quintus. You, of all people, should know that. The whole world is built on deceit. The only way to win is to be a bigger lie than everyone else. Like you.'

'What do you mean?'

'No one knows whose child you were. I think he pretended you were his son, because he needed one. But the fool did love you, Quintus, until you showed your true colours.'

So, they had all lied to me. My mother, Caecilius, Simon, all the people I trusted. My whole life was a lie. The only person who hadn't lied was Titus, whose life was ebbing away on the bank. A brutal honesty, like his fists. As I knelt there, I felt tears well up. Then something strange happened. I started to repeat the prayer I had found in Simon's chest. I said it in Latin, perhaps so Titus understood. But I spoke it as if wanted them all to hear it. As if it were my oath.

'Blessed is the one who does not walk in step with the wicked or stand in the way that sinners take or sit in the company of mockers, but whose delight is in the law of the Lord, and who ponders it, day and night. For he is like a tree planted by streams of water, which yields its fruit in season and whose leaf does not wither, whatever they do prospers. Not so the wicked! They are like chaff that the wind blows away. The wicked will not stand in the judgment, nor sinners in the assembly of the righteous. For the Lord watches over them, but the way of the wicked leads to destruction.'

Titus was looking very pale. His breathing was increasingly rapid and shallow. He must have known he was doomed from the strange thing he said next. 'My aunt will never know what happened to me, will she?'

He had imagined himself like Tiberius the avenger. Capturing a little barbarian traitor with a Roman name. He had no intention of bringing me back alive. I wasn't sure why I felt a twinge of compassion. Perhaps I remembered something Simon about virtue, from that book of Aristotle's we'd never finished. I stared at Titus lying below me. His boots were stained with blood, like the wine he'd made me lick from his feet.

'I am sure they will say you died a hero in the service of the Empire.'

All the pain went out of his face and he had the semblance of a smile. Then his eyes rolled back, and he collapsed into the water. I held that wretched ring in my hand. I turned it over in my fingers, not knowing whether to keep it or throw it into the depths of the river. A kingfisher landed on a branch and stared at me. Perhaps it was telling me my mother would have wanted me to save it. A winged horse, the two sides of my mother's coin. Why had I never thought of it that way? I untied the thong around my neck and slipped it on. It ran down the leather until it reached the knot with the silver coin. They sat together now, my father's ring and my mother's coin, around the neck of the bastard child I thought they had created.

I wiped the axe on the grass and replaced it in my belt. I took the gladius and the severed hand and climbed down the bank. The hand that had beaten me black and blue was now limp and cold. I tucked it into Titus' belt. I don't know why, it just felt right. I didn't want his disembodied hand haunting my dreams. I pushed his corpse out into the current. I watched it float downstream, twisting in the slow eddies, until it finally sank from view.

All that was left was the gladius. Something made me keep it. I'd regretted throwing Cato's away. I swam back across the river, holding it in one hand. It was only when I had reached the other side I started to shake. Maybe it was the cool water, fear, relief, or a combination of all three. I wrapped the gladius in cloth and strapped it to the saddlebag. My shoulder was aching. My tunic was sliced where he had swung at me. There was a flesh wound, but the cold must have stopped the bleeding. I had barely enough strength to mount the horse. I stayed close to the river moving west. There were two figures standing close to where the horse had collapsed. Perhaps they thought it was some sort of sacrifice to Epona? I didn't stay to explain.

I wasn't sure who was on that horse, Quintus, Caden, Cadmus, or someone new? Those other deaths had not been deliberate. The praetorian who fell from the cliff, the crushed vigiles and perhaps even Cato. But now I had killed someone consciously, both by action and inaction. Simon would not approve, though perhaps my mother would understand.

Maybe a little bird would tell her.

After three days of slow riding, I came to the vale of the white horse. I saw it emerge one afternoon, from the west. Glinting bright on a green hill.

I stopped. I could hardly believe it. So strange to see that image on the coin. A place I had long imagined and crossed half the empire to find. It was real, but like Aetos, it seemed more like a dream. I was transported back to my mother's knee. She had walked and ridden here. There was a palisade and houses within it. The fields around were covered with corn. Scythes flickered in the fields and stacks of wheat dotted the ground. A trail of smoke rose in the blue clouded sky. For I had come on gathering day, the first day of harvest. Halfway between the solstice and equinox. As I trotted up the road that led to the entrance, skylarks hovered and sang above me. I touched the pale flanks of the mare. I was sure this was how my mother would have wanted me to arrive.

A man came up and asked me who I was. I said the words I always hoped I would say.

'I am Caden, son of Orlagh of the Atrebates.'

He looked at me strangely, then let me pass. I had a deep sense that I was home. I would see out my days as an Atrebates at the hill of the white horse.

At least that's what I thought then.

CHAPTER FIFTEEN

My brother Brolach welcomed me. With deep red hair and a beard, he looked more like my mother than I did. A carpenter who built wheels for carts and chariots, he invited me to stay with him and his new wife. She was seventeen, had a necklace of amber around her neck and was heavy with his child.

I gifted him the horse I had taken from Cato and presented him with Titus's sword. He was pleased with both, but apologised he had no gift to return. I said his welcome was all I wanted. He told me the horse carved in the hill was sacred to Epona, the statue I had first seen in Enora's house. She was Protector of the Atrebates, who gave fertility to their farms and fields.

Their house was smaller than most. The wood posts were starting to rot and wattle and daub were wearing thin. He planned to rebuild it by next summer. He'd been out to the select the trees and coppiced wood to weave the walls. All the houses here were crude circles, no squares, triangles, or straight lines. Euclid had not yet found his way to the hill of the white horse.

I told him our mother had died. That she wanted me to escape slavery and return to her people. She had been taken from Gaul as a captive slave, then lived her life on the estate south of Rome. I told him how she loved the snow and hated the heat. Her life was hard, but she had enough to eat. That her memories of this place made her happy. It was then that I learned the truth. The details my mother had left out of her story. Like Odysseus, I had returned home to find it, not as I expected.

Brolach told me many of the Atrebates had fled from Gaul when Vercingetorix was defeated seventy years before. Their king Commius led his people across the water to Britannia. Our mother had been betrothed at fifteen to his son Eppillus, who already had a wife. Brolach was her first child, six years older than me. But she had run off with a man she'd met at the winter solstice. She did not wait to divorce her husband, as the law allowed. She'd abandoned Brolach as an infant, before he could walk. He had no memories of her, but her act brought shame and recrimination he had borne all his life. She and her lover had gone to Gaul. He had heard nothing from her from the day she left. He was brought up by his father's first wife, after Eppilus died. Then his uncle Verica ruled. Brolach told me Verica had a house here and in a town called Calleva, to the south.

He touched the gladius with one hand. 'They say one of my uncles, Tincomarus, still lives in Rome. We used to trade with Roman merchants along the southern coast. But the druids opposed it. Our real rulers are the Catuvellauni in the east. They did not like our accommodation of the Empire. So, there is no more contact with Rome, they won't allow it.'

I was silent for a moment, not knowing what to say. 'I think my father was her Roman master, a man called Caecilius.'

Then Brolach embraced me. 'It doesn't matter who your father was. Many men think their father is someone other than who it really is. You are my brother. That is all that matters.'

Now I knew she dreamed about coming back to a place that would not have welcomed her. If she had expected forgiveness, then she was wrong. Perhaps she regretted the decisions that she had made and hoped I could atone for them. I could no longer ask her, anyway.

I spent autumn and then winter there as a guest of Brolach and his wife. I worked much as I had done when I lived on the estate. Gathering wood, herding and other menial tasks, but I was happy, and no one compelled me. I amused some of the neighbour's children with juggling. I showed his wife the trick Simon said, Thales discovered. If you rubbed her amber on fur, it would attract a feather. Brolach's cart was like the one I had lain on the Via Aquitania, only better built. It was now pulled by Cato's horse. We used it to haul wood and other goods. There was only one place I was warned by Brolach not to go. A circle of oaks on the high ridge. Next to a Dolmen, like the one I had slept in near Daritorium.

'It is a sacred place,' Brolach told me. 'Only the select are allowed there at certain times. You must never gather any wood from there.'

While I was going about my tasks. I met a girl about my age carrying water. Her name was Mona, a slave owned by Verica. My mother had said nothing about slaves on the hill of the white horse. Mona came from Hibernia, the island Joseph said was at the western end of the world. From a family of weavers, she was their sixth daughter, so they sold her. A long way from home, she reminded me a little of Panya, the way she ran and leaped over hurdles. We bonded over our shared love of goats. Her task was to take a small herd foraging in the woods. I'd missed their mischievous faces and inquisitive bleats as we milked them. I wondered if my goats had forgotten me and who was tending them now.

There was one goat who stood out. A handsome buck with a long curved beard and a huge set of horns. He was moody and prone to sulking, so I called him Achilles. When Mona called, he was always the first to arrive. He always tried to butt me if I went near her or turned my back. Mona told me Achilles liked ivy, so I'd gather it for him. I fed him treats, spoke softly and scratched his head, all the tricks that Simon taught me, to finally win his trust.

One cold morning, I woke to find the first fall of snow. I saw a little wren fluttering around the thatch. It reminded me of the day my mother danced in the kitchen. She had said it was a sacred bird that bested the eagle by riding on its back. I fed it every day until it took crumbs out of my hand. Hoping it would return my message to the netherworld that I had kept my promise.

There was snow on the ground for nearly two months before the thaw. When it first came, I could see why my mother missed it. But when it left, I was glad to see the grass and the blooms on the blackthorn. I helped with the lambing at the festival of Imbolc when the sheep were milked again. Brolach warned me that a druid would come to bless the flock.

'His name is Ruadan, but be wary. Do not say too much to him. He has no love for Rome. When he comes, we welcome him. It is our tradition. He speaks poetry, performs rituals and knows the law of the gods. They say he has an eye in the back of his head that can see behind him and ears that hear all. He carries a basket with the three sacred snakes. The druid has much influence here. I have seen him sacrifice men when the gods demand it. He will be back for the festival of Beltane in early summer, then again at Samhain when the leaves fall.'

I'd met someone with pet snakes before. I thought he wouldn't notice me. But of course, I was wrong.

It was the day after Imbolc the festival of spring. Brolach found me gathering wood.

'Ruadan wishes to speak to you. He has heard about the gladius you brought. I have told him you are my brother and part of our household. Remember, their word is law Caden. Do not do anything to upset him.'

Their word is law. Do not do anything to upset him. I had heard that before. Ruadan came to speak to me. Brolach welcomed him into their house. A stern, thin man, with a long beard and robes that came down below his knees. But in manner, he was the very opposite of Simon. I didn't like him the moment I met him. I am not sure he liked me either. He pointed his staff at me and gave a single command.

'Sit.'

I did as I was told.

'You are Caden?'

'That was the name my mother gave me.'

'I am told your mother defied our laws. She disgraced herself.'

I began to feel very uneasy. 'Yes, Brolach told me. I did not know what she had done here. She is dead now.'

'You lived in Rome?

'No, a long way south of there. My mother was a slave in a Roman household.'

'She wove her own fate. Your father?'

'He was Roman I believe.'

'You are a spy for Rome, then?'

'I am an escaped slave returning to my mother's people.'

He looked sceptical. 'Rome is a long way across the two seas. How did you come here?'

'I hid on a ship. I walked across Gaul. Some people helped me.'

'You must have come for a purpose?'

'It was what my mother asked me to do before she died. She wanted me to return to my people and warn that the Romans may come.'

'I have heard you make things move by false magic.' Then Ruadan frowned. 'What is that ring around your neck?'

'It was my father's ring.'

'Show me.'

I took it off and gave it to him. Ruadan dropped it like a hot coal and hissed.

'A winged horse, an abomination.'

I picked it up and threaded it back on my thong. 'The Greeks call it Pegasus. My father used it to mark his goods and sign documents. He was a merchant, a trader in wine and oil.'

'You have brought accursed things to the white horse hill, first a Roman sword and now this evil ring.'

Ruadan was silent for a while, staring. I disliked this druid as much as any Roman, even though he was supposed to be one of my own.

He pointed his staff at me. 'Your warning is pointless. We know the Romans. Cassivellanus defeated Caesar, their best warrior. They dare not come again. We have war chariots and spears by the thousand in this land.' He touched his head. 'We have secret powers, spells and magic that can defy them. We have the ear of Toranos who makes the thunder, the mightiest of all. More powerful than any Roman god.'

I wanted to say the Romans had conquered the Gauls, who had the same gods, but I kept silent. I could not challenge or argue with Ruadan as I had with Simon. No questions and answers or a gentle discussion leading toward a truth. What Ruadan knew was immutable and true, like geometry. He seemed satisfied for the moment, then he left. I had a feeling it wasn't the last time we would meet.

A few weeks later and the spring was in full bloom. The moon was nearly full. It would have been around the time of my birthday. I reckoned it was a full year since my ordeal began. The calendar here differed from the Roman one. The year divided into half-light and half-dark from the summer day of Beltane to Samhain in the autumn. So, the Ides of March meant nothing to Brolach. For the first time in my life, the day of my birth was not a curse. We celebrated it with a small feast in his house.

Then a few days later, it started. Sickness came to the hill of the white horse. Brolach told me they had never known it before. It began with a fever, then the whole body turned red except for the face and palms. Some recovered, but others died. It took men, women and children. Then the worst calamity of all, the wife of the chieftain Verica, died. I was unaffected. Brolach, his wife and newborn were also spared. Prayers were said over the dead. The druid Ruadan returned for the funeral of Verica's wife. He came carrying a rod of aspen with marks carved on it. Her body was placed with a bowl of coins on his chest in a large grave. He foretold told her spirit would rise again at the feast of Samhain.

Brolach came to me the day after Verica's wife was buried, as I was chopping wood. He seemed fearful, and he whispered to me. 'He wants to speak to you again.'

'Who?'

'Ruadan, of course. You must come now.'

This time I followed him to the middle of the settlement, in front of Verica's large dwelling. The grim chieftain was sitting with a torc around his neck and his cloak fastened with a golden broach. Ruadan was standing next to the chieftain's chair. In one hand, he held a staff and in the other, a wicker basket. Brolach and some of the other elders were gathered round. A log had been placed at the centre of their circle. It moved uneasily beneath me as I sat down.

Verica did not speak, but nodded once. Ruadan walked forward and pointed his staff at me. 'I have consulted the god Lugus on the matter of the sickness here. He sees through the raven and the lynx. I have drunk the elixir of power and stared at the sacred snakes. He came to me in a dream as a raven. I saw you Caden riding the horse with wings. Lugus told me you have come from the netherworld.'

Ruadan paused. I wasn't sure where this was leading. I had a feeling that whatever Lugus had revealed; it was not good for me.

'You are the cause of this sickness, Caden. The gods are angry at your return here. The afflicted have been struck and burned by Toranos. It is a punishment from the god of thunder on the people of the white horse.'

I thought it was strange that Toranos had chosen not to punish me, Brolach, his wife or child with this illness, but I kept silent.

'There is a price for what you have done. I am here to appease the immortal god.'

So Ruadan would decide what happened to me. The log shifted again under my weight.

'What did your father call you?'

'Quintus, that was my Roman name.'

'Your father did not call you Caden?

'No, I had three names. My tutor called me Cadmus.'

This new revelation worked Ruadan into a frenzy. 'Three names. How many tongues do you have?'

I poked it out. 'I've only got one tongue.'

'Do not toy with me, boy. You speak our language, you speak Roman, what else do you speak?'

'I learned a little Greek.'

'Three names and three tongues.' He kept repeating this over and over, waving his basket and walking in a circle around me. 'You have been cast out by Lugus. The one of the three, the god of the sun, of storms, of light and travellers. You are a traveller, are you not?'

I nodded. I could hardly deny that I was.

'He will know what fate has in store for you. You brought this doom upon us, only you can remove it. You must lift the curse you have brought. Great evil has come and all will be destroyed unless this curse is removed. Toranos, the god of thunder, demands a sacrifice.'

I remembered what Simon had told me Posidonius had written. I could not look at Ruadan. Then I looked beyond him at the roof of the chieftan's house. A restless wren was looking for spiders.

Ruadan raised the basket. 'By the serpents of Lugus, I seek a sign.'

The wren flew over and landed on my hand. It stared at me expectantly, bobbed once, then fluttered away.

Ruadan held his staff aloft. 'Lugus has spoken. He sent the sacred bird, a sign from the god himself. In order to remove this curse, you must fly like this bird. At Beltane, you will do this, the feast of Lugus. You will leap off the cliff edge of this hill and fly over Epona's steed, carved in the grass. Only then can the curse will return to the other world. This alone can atone for your wrong. We will appease the god of thunder. Then will this place will have health and peace again. It can rest, knowing no harm can come.'

Then Ruadan stared at Brolach. 'The three named one is not to leave here, or his family will suffer this fate. Your brother Brolach will do the task of Lugus in your stead.' Ruadan glanced back at me. 'Do you understand messenger of the three names?'

I nodded, I understood.

'Ruadan, the druid, has spoken. I will return on the day of Beltane, when it shall be done.' Then he stood up and walked away.

Most who were standing around me were in shock at the task I was set. Verica sat silent and stony faced. Some seemed angry that I was responsible for their sickness. I bowed my head. I had barely four weeks until Beltane. The wren was visible from the corner of my eye. Searching for spiders in the thatch. A small bird, witness again to my suffering and indecision.

I could have sworn it was holding back a laugh.

After Ruadan left, I returned with Brolach to his house. He didn't speak, but he looked at me in despair. He knew I must take up Ruadan's challenge. A druid's word was more powerful than a chieftan. My doom was pronounced and must be delivered.

'You should not have come back, Caden,' muttered Brolach. 'He has asked the impossible.'

'We must build wings like Bleydiud.'

He looked incredulous and shook his head. 'I heard that story as a child. Bleydiud challenged the gods, then fell and died.'

'I must do as he asks. We have no choice. Together, brother, we will build the wings of the eagle. You can use your skill as a wheelwright and carpenter. We will need linen, cloth, twine, glue and leather.'

Brolach helped me, though I wasn't sure he really believed my claim. But family honour was at stake. Shunned by the village, no one would speak to me. I was the source of their misfortune. Muttered curses filled my ears if I wandered past. So Brolach suggested we construct the wings away from the hill. He knew a suitable place, a low clearing where charcoal burners had cleared the alder wood. I made myself an encampment down there. Around it, young birch grew thick on the damp ground. Mona brought me food. But we did not have long. Beltane was only two weeks away.

Brolach told me Ruadan had chosen an auspicious day. 'All fires will be extinguished and lit anew. The women gather hawthorn blossom to decorate the home. Cattle goats, pigs and sheep are then driven through the smoke and out into summer pasture. The magic of the netherworld is strong then.'

My mother had said Beltane was a celebration of spring, as Floralia was in Rome. I thought back to that time with petals strewn on the streets and I saw the elephant. I wondered if Ariston and Panya had ever returned there.

Brolach was a skilled carpenter. 'Birch is the lightest wood,' he told me. 'But it is supple and strong. The tree of renewal, a new beginning. We drink the sap at Beltane. It will please the gods if we use it.'

I tried to recall exactly how we had built Aetos. It seemed so long ago, and Simon was directing it then. We chose a long seasoned spar for the spine and another of green wood which was bent to the shape of a wing. Brolach said both had grown tall in a crowded copse, so there were no knots to weaken the wood. He planed and bent it gently as I remembered, like a giant bow, exactly balanced and strongest in the centre. The linen was from a tent they took to the winter solstice at the Henge. It was weather stained and not as fine as the cloth we had for Aetos, but it was strong and undamaged. Mona was a skilled seamstress who cut bound and sewed it over the front. The glue came from birch bark. It was very sticky and when bound with linen and it set strong. We bent and wove green hazel rods into a triangle. The harness we made from strips of leather. We had no buckle, so I had to tie it on. I worried that Ruadan would return and give some reason why the gods would forbid its use. But he never came.

My new creation did not have the grace of Aetos. Nor would I be able to practice with it. It felt a little clumsier than I remembered, but strong. I called it Iolaire, which was their word for eagle.

When we finished, Brolach stood back to admire the craft. 'You have created a sky chariot, Caden, something beyond all knowledge. Perhaps you are, as Ruadan says, a messenger from Lugus. Now he says you must demonstrate this gift if you are to assuage the guilt of your return. I can only hope Toranos will be appeased and we can live without fear.'

Freedom from fear, peace and the absence of pain. Simon said some Greek called Epicurus claimed these were the key to a happy life. The same fool who said all things are made of tiny particles called atoms and gods play no part in human affairs.

I woke up on the morning of Beltane. I had slept all night next to Iolaire. Mona came down and brought me some breakfast. A meal of honey cake and mead. The last meal before my trial would begin. Her goats were grazing not far off, and she had to go back to them.

She whispered to me. 'There were lots of people weaving wicker yesterday near the place of the sacred trees. That druid is there, directing it. He saw me, so I ran away.'

I was about to ask what they were weaving when I saw someone step out of the birch trees. A figure I'd last glimpsed on the dock at Daritorium. Dressed like a local, but carrying Ruadan's basket. I nearly fell over backwards. It was Acco. He stood there glaring at me. I didn't move or know what to do. He put the wicker basket down.

'Well Quintus, you seem surprised? They call you Caden here, but I know your real name. I have been wandering about making enquiries. I accepted the invitation to come to Beltane. The priest Ruadan has given me an additional task, to see if Lugus favours you.'

'You can go now.' I said to Mona.

She turned to leave, but Acco grabbed Mona and held her in front of him. He drew out his pugio and touched her cheek. 'No, your playmate stays. She may help you remember the truth.'

I pointed back toward the settlement. 'They are all expecting me on the hill. The druid says I have offended the gods. I have been set a task to appease them. If I don't arrive, they will come looking.'

Acco nodded. 'You've made a habit of offending the powerful, Quintus. I know all about this task. Now I've seen this strange rig. Looks like a sail on a boat I once saw from Carthage. I wonder now if that Praetorian's severed tongue was telling the truth. Cursed little Quintus, visited by Apollo, who taught him to fly. It sounds nearly mad enough to be true. But I know these druids, he's planned something special for you.'

I stared at the basket. 'You seem to know a lot about them?'

Acco grinned. 'More than you think. I'm Atrebates from northern Gaul. I lived near a hill fort like this one until I was sixteen. My father had the good sense to cooperate, rather than join their rebellion. I could ride soon after I could walk, so I joined the auxiliary cavalry. Armenius escaped after we defeated him in Germania. They had stationed us back at Narbo for the last few years. Patrolling up and down the Via Aquitania, keeping the peace and hunting brigands. Cato selected me to search for you. You thought you were safe when you left on that boat at Daritorium. You had a lucky escape. Cato sent me back to Narbo. He and Titus planned to take the next ship to Actis. They left their gear with the harbour master. I returned to the Governor and explained they were following you to Britannia. My legion had left, but the Governor ordered me to wait. Cato and Titus never returned. The other Praetorian, Gamo, was called back to Rome to explain their failure. That made the Governor in Narbo nervous. Tiberius doesn't like his orders ignored. Sejanus, the Praetorian prefect in Rome, he's even worse. The Governor vowed to get you back. He ordered me to take the first boat to Britannia in the spring, to find you and the others. It was a horrible journey to Ictis, that filthy rain sodden port. No one remembered you, but Cato and Titus had been there. They had paid ridiculous money for horses and rode east. That was the last anyone heard of them.'

'But you knew to come here?'

'That brigand, we caught sleeping up in the mountains. He told me where you'd be.'

'His name was Yann. He said you were a traitor.'

Acco snorted. 'His sort would. Only fools resist the power of Rome. The term doesn't apply to me. I've chosen my side and stuck to it. By the time we reached the cave and called off the dog, his face was half torn off. But he could still speak and he was cursing you and his brother. Said you had led us to his camp. We roasted his feet against the fire to find out where you'd gone. He kept spluttering something about a horse on a hill. Didn't mean anything to me then. But later I remembered the Atrebates in Britannia lived near a hill with a white horse. So it wasn't that hard to find it, or you.'

I saw him staring at the ring around my neck.

'The winged horse, Pegasus. You took that ring from Titus.'

'It was my father's, his merchant's seal. He marked all his goods with it.'

'You didn't have it when we caught you. I'm sure Titus was wearing it then. He said he'd been adopted by his aunt and someday he'd be heir to a fortune. I never liked him. But I couldn't fault his ambition. Wanted to be a praetorian or a politician, or maybe both.'

'What are you planning to do? Escort me back to Capri?'

'That would be difficult, but perhaps not impossible. I suspect the Emperor has given up wanting you in one piece. I know Sejanus would be happy with your head. But I may let you return alive, if you tell me the truth. Sejanus particularly wants to know what happened to his old comrade, Cato. So, where are they?'

'I don't know.'

Acco snarled. 'Titus always said you were a consummate liar. That ring proves it.'

'I'm expected for the ceremony at Beltane. They're waiting for me.'

Acco put the knife to Mona's neck. 'Then you had best talk quickly. I need to know what happened to Cato and Titus.'

I hesitated.

'Don't push me, Quintus, or I'll cut her throat. If I think for one moment you're lying, she's finished.'

Mona looked terrified but didn't speak. I knew Acco was serious.

'They're dead, both of them.'

He frowned. 'Who helped you?'

'I was alone, but they got separated. No one else was there.'

'I need to know where and how. Remember, no lies.'

'Cato caught up with me on the edge of a moor in Belerion. A few days' walk east of Ictis. He was on his own. He had me trapped in a barrow. I stabbed him in the eye as he tried to come in after me.'

'And Titus?'

'He chased me across a river near the Henge, southwest of here. He had a sword, and I had an axe. It was a fair fight. Not like a spear in the back of a man running away.'

I shouldn't have said that. Acco grimaced and held the knife tighter to Orla's neck.

'Cato always said you were a cheeky wretch. Titus was never up to military service. Proven, if he was bested by a boy. We lost you at least twice because of him. The dog slipped his lead that day you swam the Tarn. He was too lazy to search the jetty, so we missed you by moments at Daritorium. You might have made a soldier, Quintus, if fate had been different. Some actual use to the Empire, other than an Emperor's plaything.'

'I've told you what you wanted. Now let her go.'

Mona was struggling, so he gripped her tighter. His tunic slipped to one side, exposing that blue knot on his right shoulder. The one I had seen on my mother's arm.

'Carmanos,' I whispered.

He hesitated. 'What did you say?'

'Your name is Carmanos, or at least it was once. Orlagh was my mother's name. She had the same tattoo on her left shoulder.'

Acco gave a wry smile. 'I left the name Carmanos behind a long time ago. But I always wondered what happened to the lovely Orlagh. I should have guessed. You're headstrong, Quintus, just like her. There was a rumour that the Atrebates in Gaul were going to revolt. The Governor entrusted me to find out when and how. You see, for every Armenius, there are a thousand like me, loyal to Rome. I could not stop them, but I let the legions know their plans. I was to remain among them, then slip away before the slaughter began. Then I became Acco, servant of the Empire. Orlagh was a loyal fool and would betray me, so I kept her unaware. They sold her and the other women as slaves. But I had no idea where she went.'

'She said you were her husband and you died fighting the Romans. She lost your child at sea.'

'I had met her at midwinter, at the Henge on the day of the wren. She was gifted to some noble with another wife. But she wanted to come back with me to Gaul. A fool to reject what fate had given her.'

Just as my mother had told me, two little birds that rule the world. The robin and the wren. The robin is the beginning of the sun, the wren the death of winter. They battle on that day and the robin prevails. My mother, the wren, the old ways, had gone.

'Titus said your mother was dead,' said Acco.

'My mother died three years ago, from a sudden sickness. She regretted leaving her home and wanted to return.'

'She came freely to Gaul. I did not force her. But she could never see what the Empire could offer. Rome is too powerful to resist. One day the Empire will rule everywhere, the entire world will be Roman. There are those who accept it, the rest will be slaves.'

I think I had heard Simon say something similar. I was confused. Maybe he and Acco were on the same side?

'So, Quintus or Caden or whatever you call yourself now? You're a mongrel pup who doesn't belong here, or anywhere. But you can never escape the Empire, no matter how hard you try. The goddess Roma is all seeing. Once her talons have found you, they won't let go.' Acco glanced down at the basket he had left on the grass. 'I have a little present from your Druid friend. He has lent it to me for the occasion. Seems you are cursed, Quintus, even here. The druid commands you to put your hand inside. It is Ruadan's first test to see if Lugus favours you. Before you walk up that hill.'

I did not know if this was true or not. But I just couldn't bring myself to do it. I knew what was in that basket. Like the frog in the impluvium, I was frozen to the spot. Acco could see my hesitant hand shaking. I saw the pugio tighten on Mona's neck, and she cried out. That blade had cursed the day of my birth. A drop of blood ran down the wicked edge as it pierced her skin.

'Hurry up,' he growled. 'Your playmate here. She needs you to put your hand in. Now.'

Then something came crashing through the trees. I saw Acco half turn, just as the huge horns struck him from behind. It was the raging Achilles. Mona twisted sideways out of his grip and the knife fell from his grasp. Acco was flung forward and landed on the basket. The wicker lid flung open and three angry snakes emerged. Like some strange Medusa, they coiled around his head. Their pink mouths striking at his face and neck. Acco was writhing on the ground, trying to fling them off. The skittish goat disappeared as quickly as he arrived. Acco was gasping as the snakes slithered away in the grass.

Mona seemed unhurt, but breathing almost too fast to cry. Then, she picked up the pugio, ran over and struck out at Acco's leg. It severed his right tendon above the ankle and his boot filled with blood. Acco was crawling. One leg dragged useless. I saw him gasping, his neck swelling, foaming at the mouth.

I pulled Mona away, told her to gather her goats and stay hidden in the forest. Time was running out. Ruadan would be waiting. There was nothing I could do but leave the groaning Acco to his fate.

I touched the thong around my neck. The tiny sliver of silver was still there. As if without it, I had lost the power to fly. Then I picked up Iolaire and walked back toward the hill. Goats may be troublesome creatures. But I knew now the reason I liked them.

I carried Iolaire up the hill, around the edge of the palisade. I could see a crowd on the western side, waiting on the wind rippled grass. There was a murmur from the gathering as they saw me. Ruadan stood in front, holding out his staff, staring. Then he circled me, as if he could not quite believe I had made the journey up.

'This is your sky chariot. Will you become a bird and return to the netherworld, or fail and fall? The power of Lugus will now decide your fate. May Toranos be pleased with our offering.'

Ruadan then said many prayers and incantations over me. But something didn't seem right. He was beaming, like Octavia, as if he'd planned my fate. Brolach had the look of guilt. There was something he knew, that I didn't. He wouldn't meet my eyes. He couldn't tell me.

I positioned myself on the hill outside the palisade. Around me there were hundreds of spectators, watching, waiting to see what would happen. Below was a drop to the horse carved in the chalk. I peered down, like the times I had stared at my mother's coin. I had always thought that this was her refuge, her happy place. She believed I'd return here and be safe. But it was not as I'd expected. I was staring at that horse, not knowing whether I would live or die. Either Iolaire would fly, or sink like a stone.

I had to wait until Ruadan gave the word. He seemed to be waiting for a sign, but I had no idea what it was. My hands were slippery with sweat. I must have checked the leather straps a dozen times. I felt dizzy from standing there so long, suffused with excitement and dread. When

I had flown with Aetos, Simon and a few goats watched me, with no expectation other than skimming the grass. Now I had ample time to think and consider my fate, with a throng to witness my downfall. The white horse glowed in the sunlight. I began to see its legs moving, as if it were running. Perhaps that is where they would retrieve my crumpled corpse. The horse and wings would collide at the moment of my demise. Pegasus fallen to earth.

Then Ruadan gave a gasp. He pointed up. An eagle appeared, circling to the north. Perhaps Lugus smiled on me. A stiff breeze rose from the west. Ruadan held up his hand.

'The messenger from Lugus has arrived. Join him Caden, if you can, then return to receive the blessing of Toranos.'

I touched my leather thong around my neck and prayed those wings would work. I drew a deep breath and lifted Iolaire.

As I ran down across the grass, no one spoke. I could hear only the wind and creaking wood. I was running as fast as I had with Aetos, but my feet were still stubbornly on the ground. Perhaps Iolaire was too heavy? Then a sudden gust of wind hit my face, and I lifted up. Much faster than I expected, almost too quick. I could feel myself slowing in the air. With all my strength I dipped Iolaire and lurched forward. The white horse disappeared behind me. I was gliding faster but still too low, drifting down into the bowl below the hill. In danger of hitting a line of trees. I felt the leaves glance my toes. Then cleared them and passed over the warm, ploughed fields. I turned and twisted, climbing slowly upward. The wind filled the wings, and I went higher. The air was fast here and rough. I glimpsed the eagle somewhere above me.

I had enough height for a wide circle. I had fulfilled the task Ruadan had set. Now I had to think about landing. I turned above the hill. That was when I saw it, in the forbidden grove. Visible from the air, a man of wicker, an offering to Toranos. The realisation came to me in a flash. Like the day I had stood on the road to Oplontis. A sacrifice, then to the Emperor, now to the god of thunder. I had returned all this way to honour my mother's wish to be free. Now I knew what Lugus wanted. I knew why Brolach could not meet my eye. I was to burn as a sacrifice to Toranos. Either I would fall and die or succeed and land. Either way, I would be sent back to the netherworld. Like betting against a coin with the same mark on either side. I was destined to lose.

Ruadan was shaking his staff, shouting. I was too far up, I couldn't hear. I felt something strike at the back of the wing. It was the eagle. The linen flapped and then went taut and held. The sacred bird of Lugus had tried to bring me down and failed. The final sign I could not stay. I didn't turn back. The white horse receded. I was pushed north and east by the wind. The eagle was gone. I flew on over the fields and forests, as far as I dared. Perhaps nearly as far as my first journey with Aetos. I came down near a river. There was a wide soft meadow, with time to slow and run along the grass. I made a better landing than I expected, next to some startled sheep. I tore off the leather harness as a terrified young shepherd ran away.

Was I far enough for Ruadan not to find me? They might try to discover where I'd landed. Like Aetos, Iolaire's task was done. I dragged those wings to the edge of the river. The water was deep here. I turned it over and pushed it in. As it floated away downstream, I made an oath on that silver coin. Like Daedalus, I swore I would never fly again.

I coaxed the boy back. I lied and said I was the son of Lugus from the netherworld. He must tell no one of my arrival and remain with his sheep. He trembled as he gave me his cloak. I took the garb of a shepherd, then walked to the nearest town. It appeared I had landed in the region of the Dobunni tribe, well north of the Atrebates. I kept moving and made some money juggling, milking and herding sheep. Staying away from the white horse hill and avoiding any large settlements, I started my journey back west.

It was a long walk and hard, but I was young then. I knew that place where I wanted to go. Somewhere on the edge of the wild, wet sea. Where if I was careful and quiet, I could live out my life. Free from emperors, praetorians, and druids. The place where my little Apollo had been first coaxed out of the ground.

As Joseph had said, a place at the very edge of the world.

CHAPTER SIXTEEN

I still have a recurring dream, but it has changed. I am flying in the clouds. Someone with wings is flying below me. Perhaps it is Panya or Alban. I cannot fully see their face. Like Icarus, I am high, I cannot help myself. Then an eagle comes out of the sky. Their claws tear at my companion's wings and they tumble into the sea. I stare down to see them floating, helpless on the ocean. I circle, but I cannot save them. Then I wake suddenly, gasping for air.

I am an old man now. Sixty-three on my last birthday. Perhaps older than Simon when he taught me. I am sitting in my house not far from Ictis, in the rainy region of Belerion. I've lived far longer than fate should allow.

On my journey back, I came to the dolmen on the moor. Nearly a year since I had left there. Cato's body was long gone. Not a bone remained. The carrion had seen to that. I retrieved the gladius from the place where it was hidden. It is in an oiled cloth now, in a box of my possessions. I told myself I'd keep it to protect my house from thieves. But really, it is a guard against complacence. True to his word, I worked for Ael. My Greek and Latin, even Aramaic, came in useful. I earned my living in trading tin and Roman luxuries, wine and oil and garum.

A few years later, Ael went for me to the hill of the white horse. He purchased Mona and offered to return her to Hibernia. She chose instead to come to Belerion and be my wife. She told me after I had left, she revealed Acco as a Roman spy. Brolach found him crippled, his neck swelling and writhing in pain. Ruadan placed him in the wicker man that was meant for me. All those years my mother thought him dead, a brave warrior resisting Rome. The husband who had deceived his wife and led her into slavery. Yann had spoken a truth, though Acco never thought himself a traitor. I am told he cursed her and her thrice named child, before the flames engulfed him. I trust Toranos was appeased at last.

So, I came back to the only place I felt truly free. I built a house on a quiet creek where the trees come down to the water. The leaves are starting to turn now, so winter is not far away. I still have most of my teeth, but my knees creak and my hair is grey. I wear a fur hat and cloak to keep out the cold sea mist. Three dogs, like wolves, curl around my feet. We keep a few goats to remind me of Simon. From the outside, I am just another merchant in a foggy, forgotten corner of the world. A leather thong with the coin and the ring of Pegasus still hangs round my neck. I inherited the stone given as a gift to Ael, who is now long dead. I have a seal of my own. A wren riding on the back of an eagle.

I have wealth enough to live well, but not so much as to provoke envy. I can still juggle a few balls to amuse my grandchildren. But I do not endanger them by revealing in my past. Though I have tried to live a life of virtue, I have accepted the mantle of a noble liar. The world is built of artifice and deception. Simon was right, the truth only exists in our mind.

If I close my eyes, I can see my mother, Simon, Panya, Ariston, and Joseph. Even those faces I wish to forget, Cato, Titus, Octavia, Valeria and Ruadan. The only one that has strangely faded is my father, but my vision of him was never strong. I thank Simon for my numeracy and languages. I put my geometry to use in the mines and taught it to my children. The legacy of Simon should live on. They were the lessons I could impart. Those things that will remain forever true.

My only indulgence is the oil I import from Hispania once a year. I specify the amphorae sealed with the winged horse. The one thing I can say my father left me. I feed the birds that come to my window. The little wren reminds me of my mother, the robin of my good fortune. The eagles that circle are different here, with white feathers in their tail. Occasionally I will see them hunting fish and remember Aetos and Iolaire. Though I flew with them long ago, I recall it like yesterday.

Yet news carries even to this edge of the Empire. There was an uprising in his homeland as Joseph had predicted. A Syrian trader told me Joseph's nephew was executed by Tiberius' Governor in Judea. Crucified like Spartacus with two others on a hill. The Emperor killed hundreds, many were Praetorians he thought were plotting against him. The streets of Rome were littered with their bodies, including the feared Sejanus. The tormented minnows were cast from cliffs, back into the sea. I heard that tyrant died in the same room I fled from in Capri. The heir that smothered him in bed, Caligula, was as bad, or worse.

The Atrebates did not heed my mother's warning and Ruadan's boasts proved hollow. Thirteen years after I left, they invited the Romans to Britannia and are now ruled by them. I am told the Emperor Claudius rode on an elephant to meet his subjects. The druids who wanted to burn me as a sacrifice to Toranos, were themselves slaughtered. All the sacred lore they jealously guarded is gone forever.

Rome did at last envelop me. My refuge in Belerion became another remote corner of their Empire. I am thankful there are few Romans here, in the far southwest. They had a few small forts until there was a big rebellion in the east. A woman with my mother's flaming hair took terrible vengeance on them before she died. The Cornovii here are peaceful traders. They need no legions to keep them in check. The nearest Roman town is a long way east, at Keresk on the river Exe. I am still legally a slave, a fugitive. No one has freed me. I suppose I freed myself.

Ael's son, Mermin, had better sea legs than his father and travelled widely for trade. He agreed to visit my old estate. He posed as an olive merchant, enquiring after Caecilius. But I really wanted to find out what had happened to Simon. On return, told me what he had seen. The place he described was run down, a shadow of its former self. The goats ran wild on the mountain. Simon had died long ago in his sleep. Titus, the heir, had never returned. My father was swept off a boat and drowned. Aulus, the garum maker, had bought the shipping business, leaving only the villa and the estate. The new proprietor was carried everywhere on a litter. She told Mermin the elderly Octavia was found face first in the impluvium. My father's wife had tripped and drowned in a few inches of water. Or perhaps she was pushed. For the new mistress was Valeria, my fellow slave from Corsis. Octavia had adopted and freed her. She was granted the dream she was so desperate for me to lose. Now she was a Roman citizen and a landowner. If I ever returned, Valeria would inherit me.

Simon was buried on the hillside where we had watched eagles, not far from where my mother lay. But of my mother's headstone, there was no sign. Simon's grave had a strange inscription that Mermin copied. A triangle inside a circle and Greek letters underneath. *In every myth, there is a grain of truth.* I took it as a message to myself. Mermin also spotted a glint while exploring the ruins of Simon's cottage. Something small and tucked into a crevice in the wall. He picked it up and brought it back. It was my little tin Apollo. I'd like to think my old tutor had placed it there, hoping one day I might return.

Would Simon think I had lived a virtuous life and avoided the path of the wicked? I certainly had fortune, for I didn't drown off Capri or Corsis. I didn't fall to my death like Icarus or Bleydiud. I wasn't murdered by Praetorians, or sacrificed in a burning wicker cage. All this, before I was even half way to my father's false promise. So, I was careful in my later life. I took to heart Achilles lament in Hades, that if he lived his life again, he would be the servant of some humble man. So, for my second chance, I took his advice. Caden, the cautious they called me. I took it as a compliment. If my Telos was to show mortals might fly, then I long ago achieved it. Like Daedalus, I gave up my wings, with no regrets. Perhaps my mother was right in the end. The gods took back what I had borrowed. They never meant me to keep them.

There is one last thing. I was about to put down my reed pen when a ship docked this evening from Gaul. Mermin had returned and came again to my house. He had brought me a copy of something I wanted, but had never read. The last book of Nicomachean Ethics, the tenth, on happiness. The one Simon and I never finished.

He also had news he said, that would interest me. Some weeks ago, the mountain behind my childhood home had erupted. All of Pompeii and everything south to the port of Oplontis was destroyed. The fires raged down to the sea and burned for days. Those fields where I first flew, were now covered in smouldering stone. The estate, the villa, my mother's and Simon's grave, everything was buried under ash for miles. As if it had never existed. In time, people may forget it was there. Now at last, there is no one left to own me.

So here I must finish my story of how I defied an Emperor, twice flew with eagles and survived. I have Aristotle's last book to read before I sleep. Will it reveal if I found happiness? Maybe, like Odysseus, contentment would be a better description. The three-headed dog is at peace with itself. Quintus, Caden, and Cadmus no longer quarrel. But did I achieve wisdom, Sophia, that other gift so few attain? Of that I am less sure, but if I have learned anything, it is this. The things we believe are often lies. Those we think are myth can turn out to be true.

One day soon, my tin Apollo will be interred with me, back in the ground, whence it came. Until then, I will say my prayer. The same one I repeat each night, hoping to wake in the morning to a new day.

FINIS

Printed in Great Britain
by Amazon

19117641R00113